While Sleeping

By
Jennifer Claywood

CRANTHORPE
MILLNER
PUBLISHERS

First published by Cranthorpe Millner Publishers (2021)

ISBN 978-1-912964-69-7 (Paperback)

www.cranthorpemillner.com

Cranthorpe Millner Publishers

To the sparkly man who sits with me in the scary places and still lets me call him husband. To our children, who are already better than we ever were. To my parents, we're still growing.

I love you all.

Fighting Windmills

Monsters aren't real, but demons are
Hiding inside you
Tearing away at you
Made by you,
By people who should be called
Monsters.

If monsters aren't real
Why did you see them
Everywhere?
Can one ever really know reality...
Objective reality
When we are but
Subjective?
We are not robots
Placed here to please without
Knowing what pleasure is.

For some, a demon is a windmill.
And when fighting windmills with words
Is not enough
You find a gun

And no one will really understand
But you knew
You knew
That monsters were real.

Part 1: Sun

"At last, he came to the salon, and when the king beheld Talia, who seemed to be enchanted, he believed that she was asleep; he called her, but she remained unconscious."

    — Sun, Moon, and Talia, Giambattista Basile.

Prologue

June 24th, 1997
New York City

It was the first time she had ever heard it. After five days of silence, she had been starting to think she never would. She had even considered that there might be something wrong with the baby. *Her* baby, she corrected herself. She was a mother now. When she had been pregnant, she had felt so close to her little bean. She had spoken to him in a calm, loving voice, every moment that she could. She had sung to him: not songs like 'Twinkle, Twinkle Little Star' or 'Row, Row, Row Your Boat', but songs like 'Fast Car' and 'I'm Just a Girl'. She had been determined that her baby boy was going to be well-versed in good music. He had already heard every Tracy Chapman album. At least twice. He would get the goody-two-shoes, kiddy shit from school; from her, it would be music exhibiting strong, female voices, both literally and metaphorically.

She had sung to him in public: a young and *very* pregnant teenage white girl, rubbing her belly and singing to him. When she had been given weird glances, she had told herself that people were not staring because they thought her too young to be having a child, but because she was rubbing her belly and singing at the top of her voice. She had smiled sweetly at them and sung even louder; she had thought she knew what loud was. Those people giving her dirty looks had thought they knew what loud was.

It was a heart-wrenching wail that ripped her from her bed in the middle of the night. It paralyzed her at first; she felt like she was stuck in a horrific dream, hiding from an unseen monster, unable to move. It was only a sound, but the reverberation knocked the breath from her lungs, and she was momentarily overwhelmed with panic. Her first instinct was to get rid of whatever was making that awful sound. She must destroy it; bring an end to the sound, no matter the cost. When she realised it was the baby, using his lungs to scream for the first time in his life, she imagined walking up to the dilapidated crib and smothering him with a pillow. That thought accomplished two things: first, it motivated her muscles to finally move; second, it made her realise that, no matter how wrongful the intentions of those dirty-look-givers had been, she *was* too young to have a child.

She put him up for adoption the very next day; told herself it was the right choice; that he would have a better life. Before she left the adoption centre, she handed the cute assistant an envelope with 'Chapman' written across it in a decorative, calligraphic script.

"This is for him," she said.

The cute assistant looked up from the envelope with his dark eyes and asked, "Chapman?"

She smiled back at him. She wondered if he had ever forced himself on a girl. If a girl had ever had to run away from him. If a girl had ever had to give *his* child up for adoption. "I named him after my favourite singer. He'll get to read it one day, right?"

The young man nodded and held the envelope to his heart. "I promise."

She walked out of the brick building and stopped on the front steps. The sun shone full on her face and she closed her eyes, revelling in the sounds of the city: car horns beeping; someone yelling at a taxi driver, as they narrowly escaped a front bumper while sprinting across the street. In the distance, she could just make out the refrain of a street musician, strumming an old blues tune. It reminded her of something she had heard in New Orleans once. She felt good. A great weight had been lifted off her shoulders. She hopped down the stairs, taking them two at a time, humming 'Give Me One Reason'.

A homeless man was selling papers at the bottom of the steps. She reached into her pocket and handed him all the cash she had on her: $24.75. He handed her a paper, and as she looked down, she saw it was a copy of The New York Times. There was something going on in Iraq about an arms ban, and something about young people outnumbering the old in Florida. But the only thing she could have feigned any interest in was a picture of some crash-test dummies and the caption 'Identified Flying Objects'. Apparently, it had something to do with the Air Force releasing a report on the 'Roswell

Incident'. She handed the paper back to the half-toothed guy and told him to have a great day.

Still smiling, she headed back to the hotel room she was currently calling home, sitting herself down at the small desk by the window. She pulled up the blinds: the mechanism was broken, such that the right corner of the blinds lifted all the way to the top, but the bottom left corner barely moved. Still, it was a beautiful day. She started laughing. Beautiful on the outside and broken on the inside. Somehow this felt like a metaphor for her life. Or something. She turned on the radio and the lead singer of Garbage droned on about being 'only happy when it rains'. It wouldn't have been her first choice, but it wasn't so bad. At least it was a strong woman playing on the radio and not some bullshit love song, written by a man to sell music to mindless teenage girls. She reached her hand under the desk and removed what she had hidden there. Staring out at the cloudless, blue sky, she shot herself in the head with the snub-nosed .38 she had stolen from her father.

Chapter 1

January 4th, 2013
Hunter, New York

I have lived in this house, *your* house, for years. You don't even know I'm here. I watch you. I don't mean to, but I can't help it. And when you're gone? Well, what is it they say? 'Tu casa es mi casa'? Not quite right, but close enough.

Do you ever consider how little time you spend in your own home? You are barely here. When you're gone, I choose my activities carefully. I have tried to gather as much intel about your daily movements as possible, so I know how much time I will have. Even though you like to stick to a routine, I know there is always a chance that something will change. I often wait until you're asleep to creep into the main part of the house, searching for the clues that will tell me about your upcoming plans. You have a calendar right by the door, with hastily scribbled notes and Post-its marring the well-organised blocks. They cover so much the month, that I question your sanity. Does this clutter of paper really represent organisation? I always start with the calendar, then check your laptop or phone. You have a Google calendar synced to both devices, so as long as you've left one of them downstairs, I don't have to push my luck.

There have been times when neither device could be found downstairs. I dread, but simultaneously anticipate eagerly, these moments of tempting fate. I quietly walk up the stairs, missing every spot that creaks. Right in the middle of the stairway, between steps fifteen and eighteen, there are two stairs that have not a single place free from singing wood. I have found that I can dash from the far-left side of fifteen and jump over the two stairs to land on the far right of eighteen, catching myself on the banister, and avoid making a single noise. I hold my breath while traversing this tense part of the stairs, only once letting out a gasp when my momentum threatened to take me over the edge. I enjoy the challenge; I have not outgrown my childish desire to become the best American ninja known to man. So good that he is... *un*known.

It is not just silently skulking around the immense house that fills me with a full body tingle; being able to sneak unknown into your room brings the greatest excitement. Standing over you when you are at your most vulnerable, I have never felt more powerful; never felt more like a predator than in those moments. It is stupid, I know. I always stand right outside your door and tell myself, 'just find the laptop or phone, check her calendar, and get the fuck out'. Every time I say it. Every single time. And every single time I know I won't. I can't. There is just something about looking at you. Staring at you. Smelling you. Tucking your hair behind your ear while your mouth hangs open, spit dribbling out of one corner. One time I took the tip of my finger and rubbed it along your bottom lip, capturing a bit of your saliva. I quietly raised it to my mouth...and tasted you...

What was I saying? Oh yes, intel. Your routine. My routine. I stock up on food when I can. Not on my nightly forays, but my daytime ones. I love that you buy canned goods in bulk. If necessary, I will be able to live off canned chili and green beans indefinitely. I have no idea why you buy so much food, but I'm not complaining.

I know that you think of this place as your sanctuary, and I want you to keep feeling safe here. I do everything I can to protect you from the knowledge that someone else is living here. Someone else who is not only watching your every choice but judging you for them. Chocolate ice cream at ten p.m.? Leaving your wet towels on the hardwood floor? Leaving dirty dishes in the sink? I know, I know. I have no room to talk, just look at my place: a smattering of empty food cans, and jugs filled with pee. You probably don't want to know this, but I always bag up my poop in small doggy bags and keep them covered, in a small metal trash can with a lid. When it fills up, I dump it in the neighbour's trash can early on Tuesday mornings, right before pickup.

I try to limit the number of times I leave the house. I know that every time I leave my domain, there is a chance I'll get caught. And I don't want to get caught. I hate having to risk everything just to throw away my trash, so when I can, I try to mix it in with yours. I know there's a chance you might notice extra food cans in your recycling bin, or extra granola bar wrappers amongst your kitchen trash. But, so far, I think we're good. Sometimes, I use one of the six bathrooms in the house, but it always makes me nervous. What if I clog the toilet? What if you come home and I'm paralyzed on the throne, unable to finish?

I do take showers. I don't want you smelling me from inside the walls. I make them quick and I clean up after myself, drying the bathtub and floor on my way out. I have a towel that I keep just for this purpose. I've even used your washer before. It's amazing how exciting normal, everyday activities become when you're trying to do them without anyone else knowing. The question, 'do I use the dryer or not?' feels like I'm debating a life or death situation. Not that you could kill me. But there would definitely be questions. And cops.

This is what I know about you. Your name is Julia Rodriguez. You are an assistant curator for The New York Mountains Foundation; you haven't worked for them very long, and you work hard. You want to make a good impression. You moved here from Michigan, where you worked for The Parker Foundation, helping underprivileged artists. You found a niche there, helping young women who had recently aged out of the foster care system. While your job was to find places for these artists to display and sell their work, your focus was on encouraging them to find healing through their various forms of expression. It was difficult to leave your position, but New York called to you. You plan to use this house as a centre for women. You feel guilty that you have not done anything with it yet. Your birthday is the second of October; and you probably don't know it, but you share that birthday with Annie Leibovitz. Well, maybe you do know that, but you're not as fascinated by photography as I am. You're more of a mixed media kind of girl.

You're single and you don't want kids. You're not sure you want a husband either, but you do occasionally date. Lately, you have been joking about dating women instead. Your favourite ice cream is Rocky Road, and you love staying up late on Friday nights to pore over photographs of artwork. On the occasional Friday morning that you have off, you fill the clawfoot tub with warm soapy water and twist your blonde strands up in a loose bun. Then you put on some classical music, typically comprised of the keening tones of a violin chasing an ever-shifting piano melody. A bath would not be the same without a trashy romance novel, and you're currently reading something with a half-naked Scotsman and a dark-haired buxom beauty on the cover. Seriously?

You like watching movies and no genre is off-limits. You laugh at all the right parts and cry at all the wrong ones. You feel self-conscious about that birthmark on the back of your upper right thigh. You don't realise how beautiful you are. I know that you prefer pads over tampons, and triple-wrap them in toilet paper before disposing of them. I know that you sometimes forget to take your birth control pill; that you meet a therapist once a month, all the way in Manhattan; that your parents are dead. You don't have any brothers or sisters, but you do have a best friend named Isabella, back in Michigan. I know that you sometimes start a fire just to toast marshmallows. But no matter how well I think I know you, you still surprise me sometimes.

I have always been an early riser and I love that you are too. I adore your morning routine. You stumble through the dark, half-awake, perfectly manicured hands rubbing sleep from your eyes. You stifle a yawn, fumbling for consciousness. The back-left burner of the stove roars to life, and as the water begins to heat up, you slowly regain your faculties. You pull down a large white canister filled with your favourite chai and drop a teabag into a proper teacup. The finest of bone china, graced with a large blue flower and dainty gold leaves, the lip and handle further decorated in gold trim. It is beauty and death in the palm of your hand. I wonder if you know why it is called bone china.

Half-n-half is pulled from its honorary place in the refrigerator, and you wait for the familiar whistle of your teakettle. You don't even look towards the kettle as you reach for it with your right hand, but after you've poured steaming water into your cup and replaced it on the stove, you pat its handle as if it were a much-loved pet. The cream is next, and you stare into the swirling depths of your cup as if a hidden life can be found there. You don't start to make breakfast right away, but you always turn on the oven, opening the door to let the heat into the kitchen. Then you sit, a solitary figure perched on a high-backed barstool, as close to the oven as you dare, sipping your brew, legs crossed, and eyes closed. It seems like a religious experience for you. This is your daily prayer, your meditation. After this first cup, there is always another, but with the second cup comes the making of breakfast. Your kitchen is so warm and inviting, and I am happy to share it with you, in my own way.

My stomach clenches during these mornings, but it's not just from physical hunger. I would like to say that there have been mornings I got up early, went into the kitchen, and found family and warmth. That I experienced the joy of hot chocolate heating on the stove; eggs bubbling in butter until the edges are crisp and the yolks still runny; the smell of bacon permeating every corner of the bottom floor. But those were things I only imagined, sitting alone in a cold kitchen, facing a refrigerator complete with two clasps and padlocks. But despite not having the family I wanted, it wasn't all bad. I had my journals. I had my favourite red plastic mug in the shape of the 'Kool-Aid Man', with his goofy smile that sometimes felt like a lie. I would sit at our long table, sipping water from my cup and writing in my journal, alone but dreaming of not being so.

There were times when I came close to experiencing…family. Occasionally, I would be placed in a group home or foster care, but nothing was ever permanent. I was eventually adopted, by my own family as it turned out, but it took me a long time to relax with them; a long time to get to a point where I could just about consider calling us a family. They tried so hard, loved me intensely, but I was so broken. I have often regretted not trying harder with them.

I dream of sharing these mornings with you, as more than an observer. Of pulling up a barstool next to you and enjoying the heat of both a steaming cup and warming stove. What kind of person would I need to be to get such an invitation? I think about who I could have been, and who I could still be. In my few short years I have already left behind so many versions of myself.

Who am I? Who can I be for you? I sigh deeply. It's no use; just like the imaginings of my delusional younger self, longing for a loving family, I know that you will never welcome me into your inner sanctum. I am an outsider. An interloper. So, I take what I can get, and I let my observations of you quell the clenching inside me. I imagine my hunger as a dark sphere within me, and I begin to exert pressure all around it, making it smaller and smaller until it is nothing more than a speck.

Julia poured her second cup of tea, letting it steep as she headed to the refrigerator. She pulled out fresh baby spinach leaves, turkey bacon, provolone, eggs, and tomatoes. She always made time for breakfast; this morning routine helped her to feel focused and grounded.

Plating her omelette, she looked guiltily at the long table in the adjoining dining room. She had yet to use it. She could not believe she had found herself here, in this immense house, alone. The previous owner had left it to her, and she had to sign a very specific contract in order to move here. The contract had stipulated that she was to use the house 'to further the advancement of women, whether through safety, or nourishment of the mind, body, or soul'. She also had access to a generous fund to run this…centre. She took a big bite of her omelette and sighed. What the hell was she doing here?

She had met Kathryn Beaumont on International Women's Day, at the UN Headquarters in 2006. The focus that year had been on including more women in influential roles; enabling women to make big decisions in their companies and agencies. During a quick jaunt to the bathroom, she had literally run into Kathryn in the hall, causing her to awkwardly stumble onto her side. She had looked down at the well-dressed woman, whose long, brown hair fell awkwardly over her face, and immediately panicked. This was not the kind of woman who belonged on floors, accidentally or otherwise.

"Oh my god, I am so sorry!" Julia had been stunned at her own clumsiness, but Kathryn had given her a warm smile and laughed, taking Julia's offered hand

"Hey, no worries. If that's the worst thing that happens today, I think I'll survive. Nice shirt!" she had grinned, gesturing towards Julia's simple grey t-shirt, which read 'Feminist as Fuck'.

Julia had smiled. "Thanks. I'll have to send you one. I've got a few extras."

"Well, I don't want to keep you. It looks like you're in a bit of a hurry."

"Oh! Yes. Right. I'll…see you later then?" Her bladder had taken a backseat to the hallway drama, but once she had been reminded of it, the urge had returned, fiercer than before.

"Sure thing." Kathryn had handed Julia her business card; black, with a gold embossed printing of Lady Justice and a sharp script beside the portrait which read 'Kathryn Beaumont, Women's Advocate & Lawyer, Justice for Her', with contact information on the other side. "Just in case anyone ever sues you for knocking them over."

Julia had laughed. "Thanks, Kathryn. Though, I doubt I'll ever need your services, considering how graceful I am." She had been halfway down the hallway, sprinting towards the bathroom, when she suddenly turned back. "Hey, my name's Julia, by the way!"

Kathryn had waved in acknowledgment before entering the conference room.

Strangers had started casting confused glances her way and Julia had winced, smiling at them, suddenly unsure about the necessity of screaming her name in public.

Neither Julia nor Kathryn had really expected to meet each other again, but they had been seated in close proximity at dinner that night and soon became fast friends. There was an age difference, and since Kathryn had lost a daughter and Julia had lost her parents, each filled a surrogate role for the other. It was more than that, though. They both respected each other, and the roles they each played in creating a better future for women.

They had discussed this house extensively in what had first started as a shared fantasy, long before Kathryn had searched for a suitable location. Julia had never thought it would become a reality. They had discussed all the details over the phone, as Julia had not been living in New York at the time. Kathryn had shared so many plans for this house, and Julia had insisted that she wanted to be a part of it. She would help women by teaching them how to heal through art, and by helping them use art to overcome the obstacles in their lives. Kathryn had loved the idea.

But…this? Even though she had signed the papers, agreeing to Kathryn's stipulations, she felt unsure. Could she really head this whole place by herself? Could she make their shared fantasy a reality? Did she even want to? What had possessed her to make her think she could do this?

Julia wiped away a stray tear and glanced at the picture of Kathryn on the wall. It had been taken right after Kathryn and Alex had bought this place. In it, Kathryn was wearing a long, flowing, white sundress, covered in pink flowers, and a wide-brimmed straw sunhat. Her silver hair, once brown, hung in a loose braid over her right shoulder. You could almost feel how windy it had been that day, her dress billowing to one side of her, her hands clamped down over the top of the hat to keep it from blowing away. She wore a large grin and her eyes looked cheerful, hopeful even. They were here to start a new life. They were here to help give other women the chance to start a new life.

Julia imagined Kathryn shaking her head and clicking her tongue in exasperated disbelief. She imagined her saying 'you know you can do this'. Julia spoke aloud to the picture. "Of course I'll do it. I just need a little help." Then she sighed, placed her dirty dishes in the sink, and headed toward the front door, briefly touching Kathryn's portrait as she walked by.

Chapter 2

January 7th, 2013
Hunter, New York

"If one had to estimate the number of children bought and sold for sex, per year, in the good old U.S. of A, you would be hard-pressed to guess correctly. Indeed, your estimate would probably reflect the type of person you are. If you were to guess one thousand or less, well, I'd wager you were a stay-at-home mom, intent on keeping your kids safe and disbelieving that anyone could..." and here Patrick did his best impersonation of a middle-aged Southern woman, shaking his head and clutching at imaginary pearls, "...do that to a child. You would have warned your children of the predators out there, of course, just to instil some fear into them, to make sure they came home on time and avoided dark alleyways. Such predators are akin to 'bogeymen' in your mind; if they exist at all, they are very, very rare, and only ever found in other neighbourhoods. If you were to guess one hundred thousand, I'd say you were in law enforcement, and a bit closer to the truth. It probably keeps you up at night, from time to time. But if you were to guess two hundred thousand, I would expect that guess to be followed by a smile and a wink, and for you to ask if I was interested in buying some flesh: boy, girl, young, old. Whatever I wanted."

Julia shuddered. She was in the break room at work, seated at one of the round tables that served as a casual meeting place, munching on leftovers brought from home. The break room was surrounded by glass, allowing for a view of the workrooms. Right now, there were ten long tables filled with young girls, ranging in age from ten to seventeen years old. A lot of them were Asian, but there were a few other ethnicities. Julia felt drawn to a young girl with ebony skin and thick eyelashes, her kinky hair a halo around her face. The girl stared off into the distance with her almond-shaped eyes, uninterested in the art project at hand, her cheeks wet and gleaming under the fluorescent lights. Julia made a mental note to discuss a renovation of the work area. Maybe some cosy corners with softer lighting would provide their new artists with a much-needed safe space during activities.

Julia asked, "How did they come to be here, with us, Patrick?"

"Didn't you know? David Washington is on the board of directors." Julia shook her head. "I'm surprised he hasn't met with you; I hear he had a lot to do with you getting this position."

Julia shrugged her shoulders and shook her head. "I've never met him. Never even heard of him."

"Well, he's one of the original members of the foundation. He used to be with the FBI; still has some contacts there. He asked if we could offer some help;

provide a safe space for the girls for a few hours a day. We've also freed up some office space for any social service employees or therapists who might need to meet with the girls."

"That's really nice of him. Them. Us." Julia smiled over the brim of her travel mug which read, 'I'M SO ARTSY I SWEAT GLITTER'.

Patrick smiled. "That's why I love working here. It's the most generous non-profit I've ever worked for. And they haven't pigeon-holed themselves into only offering only one type of help. They're always open to new ideas."

"I miss my previous work, but I love being here. I'm excited to be so close to the city; the art there has a pulse of its own." Julia frowned as she looked out toward the girls again. "God, they're just children."

"What's sad is that some of these girls didn't want to leave the life. Even when they were found living in squalor, with few possessions, forced to have sex multiple times per day with multiple people, they somehow felt they were being cared for."

"I really don't understand who could do that sort of thing." The words were a lie. She did know. She just really wished she didn't.

"You mean, rape children?"

Julia gave a slight nod.

Patrick held a heavy, black coffee mug in his hand, the coffee blacker than the mug. He took a swig as he looked over at Julia, his brows furrowed, his brown eyes looking perplexed. "I read a report once, estimating that many of these children are raped by as many as one thousand men in any given year. So, men. Men are doing it. Usually rich men, but sometimes truck drivers or buyers off the streets. There are so many different stories. It's quick, cheap, easy sex."

Julia looked down at her cold turkey sandwich. It was slathered in jalapeños and Italian dressing, usually her favourite. She put the half-eaten sandwich back in her box and munched on some raw carrots instead. She hated raw carrots, but always forced herself to eat them anyway. Today, the act of chomping and chewing fit her mood quite nicely. It gave her something to do with all the anger bubbling up inside her.

"Do you know how many of these rapists have been put on trial?" Patrick continued.

"How many?" Julia shook her head and raised a hand like a crosswalk guard, but instead of trying to protect children from oncoming traffic, she was trying to protect herself from the truth. Perhaps trying to protect that small, helpless child still lurking within her. "Wait. I probably don't want to know, do I?"

Patrick took a deep sigh. "Not a single one." He shook his head as he set the mug down heavily on the table. He became animated, his voice intensifying, his hands rising into the air, moving in a pattern to enunciate each word, like a composer, conducting the sentences that came from his lips. "NOT A SINGLE ONE. Traffickers have been arrested, sure, but none of the men who paid to have sex with these children have been named or arrested. They not only paid for sex with a minor but also paid for anonymity. They paid to keep their names out of the papers. They paid to treat these girls like…things…less important than their reputations." He had picked up the coffee mug again, his knuckles white as his fingers clenched tightly around it.

Julia smiled warmly at him. "Let's go see if we can help them gain back some semblance of a normal life." She held out her travel mug, green tea still warm inside, and clunked the side of his mug in a toast.

"Hear, hear," he replied in a parody of medieval English, getting up slowly, as if weighed down by a suit of armour. "Let us go forth and aid these young lassies who hath been treated with such ill intent."

Julia laughed. "Nerd." It was good to have co-workers who could make you laugh. She knew that she was not close enough to criminal occurrences to see all the hell in the world; that her position afforded her a safe distance from the worst of it. But it was still hard. Her old boss had once told her 'if you don't see the ills in the world, it's because you're not looking'. She knew it was true, but sometimes you just had to close your eyes. In order to really help people, you had to maintain a balance of empathy and distance. Was that true, or just what she told herself? She had been keeping herself at a safe distance from bad things for years. Bad things? More like emotions. Feelings.

Patrick tapped her on the shoulder and Julia turned towards him.

"You know, sometimes it just takes one person," he said quietly, his hand still resting on her shoulder.

Julia nodded, reaching her hand up to pat his shoulder in return. "Thanks, Patrick. I'm glad we make two."

The words kept spinning in her head… 'it just takes one person'. If she were one of those people who believed in signs, she might have thought Kathryn was hinting at something, through Patrick. Could she turn Kathryn's house into a children's home? Into a home for lost girls such as these? She had always told herself that she didn't want children. Why? Mostly because she thought there were enough unwanted kids in the world. But maybe it was more because children reminded her of her own childhood, and what had happened to her after her parents died.

She had been saved by one person. It had been many years, but she could still remember her pale, friendly face. Her bleached blonde hair that had hung in dreadlocks, months in the making. Krista. Krista had saved her. Was she still alive? She had looked for Krista in every woman she had ever met since; in every child she had helped. In herself. Surely, she was dead? She had to be.

She pushed the idea to the back of her mind and walked out of the break room, moving towards the girl with the ebony skin. She introduced herself and invited the girl back to her office. The girl couldn't have been more than twelve or thirteen years old, and she was hesitant at first. Julia wondered if she would ever trust anyone again.

"It's okay. We don't have to go to my office. You just look like you could use a walk. Maybe we could go over to the café and get a pastry? Or a drink? Are you thirsty? There's a Starbucks across the road."

The girl, named Ava, wiped her face, and gave a slight nod. Julia wanted to offer her a hand up, but she was afraid the proffered physical contact would scare the child. Ava looked back over her shoulder at a friend and waved. Her friend pointed at herself and then motioned toward me and the door behind us, silently asking if she should accompany us. Ava gave a slight shake of her head and kissed her fingers to her lips. Her friend responded in kind. This show of affection and friendship gave Julia hope. Ava was going to make it. She was going to be just fine.

May 26th, 2008
Hunter, New York

Kathryn smiles at the boy as he enters the study.

"Hey there, little man, come in! How are you doing today?" He doesn't quite trust her yet, but he will, one day.

"Fine," he replies sullenly, his voice tired, as he plops himself down on the couch near her desk. He sighs deeply.

"You sound like you didn't sleep very well." She looks at him with concern on her face. He hasn't looked at her yet. He seems to have something on his mind. "What's up?"

After a few minutes of silence, he quietly says, "There's a school project I have to work on. About what I want to be when I grow up."

She wants to say it sounds interesting, but she can sense his lack of excitement. She waits him out.

"I…I just…I don't know! I mean, I love to draw. And take pictures. And I love writing, but I don't think I can make very much money doing those things. And I want to make a lot of money." He looks over at her then, and she is struck by the innocence she finds there. "You make a lot of money. What do you do?"

"Well, I used to be a lawyer. I used to help people in court." Her eyes become moist as she thinks back to her last case.

July 10th, 2006
Courthouse, New York City

"So, the two of you were dating, is that right?" The defence lawyer smiles at the jury, giving them a knowing wink, before turning back to his witness.

"That's right." The witness looks confused, as if he can't possibly understand why he has been brought here today.

"And how was it going?" the lawyer asks, as if he has never asked before. As if this whole charade hasn't been practiced ad nauseam.

"It was going amazingly well. We were perfect for each other. I had met her parents the weekend before. We were spending every spare moment together. I really thought that she might be the one." He looks down at his hands as he wrings them together. "I know we're young, but I loved her. I…" he stammers. "I still love her. Even after all of this." He glances at the table where his victim sits, his face a picture of innocence.

She is crying.

"I love you," he says, his voice filled with passion, and he chokes back a sob.

I am filled with rage. His lawyer looks at me.

"Your witness."

I look at the jury. I feel that I have lost them. One overweight woman, with short, curly, light brown hair, is dabbing at her left eye with a tissue. Another looks pained. I can see it all over their faces…they feel sympathy for this predator. They cannot see him for what he is. Their minds are filled with pretty, fairy-tale stories of strong men loving misguided damsels in distress. Real fairy tales are brutal. It is time to point this out to them. I hope that I have not lost them for good.

I look over at Emily, her hazel eyes downcast, her brown hair in a curled braid on top of her head. She looks shell-shocked. Her hands are held limply in her lap and her eyes are staring at the floor, unseeing. I hope that I have not lost her too. I turn back to the witness.

"You paint a pretty picture. You say you love her. Do you often rape the people you love?"

He looks disgusted at the use of the word. His eyes burn with anger and he stares at me. "I. DID. NOT. RAPE. HER." He dials it back a notch and lowers his gaze. Quietly, he repeats himself. "I did not rape her."

"You walked into a bedroom where she was passed out, face down on a bed. You ripped her underwear and violently removed them from her. You straddled her. You penetrated her. You raped her. And when she mumbled for you to stop, you handled her more roughly. You told her how defenceless and sexy she looked. When she begged for you to stop you pushed her face into a pillow. When she vomited all over the bed, you laughed. You are a rapist. You are a monster!"

"Objection! Does Mrs Beaumont have a question for my client?"

I take a deep breath. "I am sorry, your honour."

The judge looks at me, speaking calmly but sternly. "If you have a question, I suggest you ask it."

I open my mouth to reply but the snake on the witness stand interrupts me.

"Mrs Beaumont, I haven't done anything wrong."

I look at the rapist. How had I lost control of this situation?

"Yes, I found Emily passed out, sleeping in a bedroom. But when I got there, her panties were missing. There was vomit on the bed, and I was filled with nothing but horror and worry. I began trying to wake her up, but when she saw me, she started screaming. I did not realise, at the time, that she thought I had done this to her. I tried to comfort her while I called 911. That's when Kirsten came in and told me to leave the room. I am sorry…"

I watch him choke up as he tries to gain composure but fails.

"I am so sorry that this happened to her." He chokes up again and sobs. He is barely audible when he drops his chin toward his chest, his hands clenching and unclenching in his lap. "To us."

Suddenly there is a collective gasp and a thud in the courtroom. Emily has quickly stood up, knocking her chair over in the process, and has proceeded to run to the doors at the back of the courtroom.

"Your honour, my client and I require a brief recess." The judge nods grimly at me as she strikes her gavel on the desk, and I run after my client, the sound of 'order, order, I will have order in my courtroom' fading away as a chorus of camera flashes and clicks fill my ears.

"Mrs Beaumont, what is going on in there? Is Emily okay? Will your client drop the charges? Are you losing?"

I look at a reporter I am friendly with. "Did you see where she went?" The reporter nods, gesturing towards the corridor leading to the outside garden. There is a guard standing watch by the doorway. I give him a grateful pat on the shoulder as he blocks the door after letting me through.

Emily is huddled on her knees in a corner, hands gripping dark soil, roses in full bloom beside her. She has lost a shoe and her face is covered in tears, mucus, and streaks of dirt. "I know it was him! I know it was him!" She repeats herself over and over again.

That is when I realise I can't do this anymore. I can't watch another woman enter the judicial system, hoping for justice. Regardless of whether we win or lose this case, I know that I can't watch another woman go through this again.

I remove a Kleenex from my pocket and wipe Emily's face, before pulling her close and crushing her in a hug. She clings to me, despite my failings in the courtroom. My eyes water, anger at the injustice of life filling my body. I stare at a statue of Lady Justice in the centre of the courtyard, wishing for once that she was not so blind. Wishing that she would rise up, remove her toga, replace it with armour, and actually use her sword.

May 26th, 2008
Hunter, New York

"Did you like it?" The little boy looks at her earnestly, his blue eyes vulnerable. He has let his black hair grow long, to use as a cover for the large birthmark on his face. She wonders when she will tell him the truth. Will she ever?

"I'm sorry, what did you say?"

"Did you like being a lawyer?" He is not looking at her anymore, and his voice is more unsure this time. She really needs to be careful with him. Not paying attention to him when he is speaking is not going to help her win his trust.

"I did enjoy it, very much. But I decided that I could help people better in other ways. That's why Alexander and I bought this house."

"How will this house help people?"

"Well, you might have noticed that Alexander is redesigning the rooms on the floors upstairs. We are going to turn this place into a women's refuge centre, for families who need help. We will accept applications and help as many women and children as we can. We will give them a place to live; give them free legal advice; provide them with childcare...I would even like to employ a doctor at some point. Maybe one who could come by once a week. I loved being a lawyer, but it is a tough job. It's easy to lose sight of what's important. Easy to focus on winning or losing, and not the people you are representing. I became a lawyer because I wanted to help people. But sometimes, I wasn't able to."

Kathryn speaks wistfully, and the little boy has stopped listening. She realises she has gone off on a bit of a tangent; almost two years later, she is still trying to talk herself into believing that leaving her firm had been the right choice. She stops talking and looks at the child in front of her.

After a moment of silence, he pipes up. "Will we have other kids here?"

"Yes! I mean, I think so. Would you like that?"

The boy shrugs his shoulders and looks down at his lap. His feet are dangling over the side of the couch, moving back and forth, hitting the couch quietly but repetitively. Thud-thud, thud-thud, thud-thud.

"Do you think you might want to be a lawyer?"

The boy shrugs his shoulders again. "I...I think I want to be a detective. Or a policeman." And with that he gets up and heads toward the sliding wood door. Before turning the corner, to head to the kitchen, he looks back over his shoulder and says, "Then I could find my mom."

Kathryn plasters a smile on her face; manages to hold it together...until he has closed the door behind him. Then she drops her head in her hands and weeps. She takes the envelope marked 'Chapman' out from the top desk drawer, her tears smearing the ink. She holds the envelope to her lips and whispers, "Sybil. Oh, how

I miss you. You would love him. He has your eyes, Sybil. He has your eyes."

Chapter 3

January 8th, 2013
Hunter, New York

I have an excellent imagination. Which is why, when your smoke detector went off at three o'clock in the morning, it wasn't the sound that surprised me, but the fact that I had never thought what I would do in the event of a fire. I started wondering about it then. Could I get out of the house without you seeing me? What if you had passed out and didn't wake up? Should I save you? I could say that I was passing by and ran in to save you. But then I would have to explain how I knew you were here...

After a few minutes of panic, walking back and forth in my hidden room, I decided to sit and wait. I couldn't smell smoke. That was a good thing, right? I sat for five minutes. Then ten. The fire alarm continued to ring, and I was beginning to go a little crazy. Was it possible you were out somewhere? Would the neighbours hear? Would someone call the cops? Would I be discovered? I was paralyzed by the fear of being found, but in the end, I had to act. I HAD to act. I could not listen to that damn alarm for ANOTHER. SINGLE.

MINUTE.

I threw my laptop, camera, and current journal into my backpack, grabbed my key, and headed for the air vent that led out into the basement. Before climbing in, I stopped. What if there really was a fire? I turned back and looked at the room I had been calling home for so long. I had journals piled up against the wall; art and photography books scattered here and there; photos pinned to a long piece of string that reached from one side of the room to the other. I wondered how another might view my humble abode.

One wall was covered in newspaper articles and handwritten notes, all about disturbing murders and violent crimes. Pictures of my grandparents poked out from beneath colourful Post-it notes with comments scrawled on them, comments like 'redsurfersnatch mentions a robbery-murder in upstate New York – different date' and 'darksatanlover, more research needed'.

I realised that I might never see this place again. The thought was both terrifying and exhilarating. Just in case, I took a few snapshots of my research board and packed a few photographs, along with my stash of cash. I had no idea how much I had left, but it was surprising how much money you could save by living in a hidden room in someone else's house. I turned to go. This time, I shoved my bag ahead of me, pulled myself into the vent, and didn't look back.

The basement is huge, complete with a brickwork tunnel leading to a wine cellar, with outside access. Kathryn and Alex never used it, but Alex had often talked about it. It had turned into a running joke with them; before almost every evening meal, Alex would say he was going down to the wine cellar to find a good bottle of red. When he then returned to the table empty-handed, he would always say the wine needed to 'age' a little more before they could enjoy it. I had never seen either of them drink a glass of any wine, red or white.

There is a lock on the cellar door, and as far as I know, I am the only one who has a key. I'm always hoping that you won't suddenly decide to change the lock, but if that day ever comes...well...I'll deal with it. After all, I can't live here forever.

In the basement, the chirping of the alarm sounded distant. It was almost tolerable, and I toyed with the idea of making a nest in one of the dark corners and waiting it out. But the thought came again...what if there really was a fire? What if? Isn't the world just full of what-ifs?

Mind made up, I proceeded through the tunnel, my eyes already adjusted to the dark. The cellar opens into the woods behind the house, and has provided me with a great means of coming and going when I need to. I usually head away from the house through the woods, before making my way towards any kind of civilization. But that night, I had an overwhelming desire to walk along the road beside the house, to check for signs of smoke, or life. I could never forgive myself if I had let you die in a fire.

I was wearing a ball cap, and a hoodie cinched

tight around my face. I know I will seem suspect to anyone who gives a fuck, but it makes me feel better anyway. I might look suspicious, but besides a physical description of my clothes, anyone looking at me in the darkness wouldn't recognise me. Hopefully.

I was almost at the front of the house now. Damn, the cellar was far away. I walked quickly and made sure I looked like I had somewhere to be. But as I walked, hands shoved deep in my pockets, I glanced at the house out of the corner of my eye. I didn't see any lights, and there was no sign of smoke. When I reached the corner, I stayed on the sidewalk and took a right, looking first at the driveway. Your red Camry was missing. You never use the garage, so I assumed you were not home.

By the time I passed the house, I had decided there was no fire. I breathed a sigh of relief and continued walking, my gait a little less determined, but still at a quick pace. I was too hyped up to sneak back into the house. I needed something to do.

I decided on the twenty-four-hour diner, at the Lakefront Inn. Alex had taken me here many times in the past, usually before and after our camping trips. I had never admitted to him how much those trips meant to me. I shook my head in self-disgust. Would it have been so hard to show the guy a little love? A little appreciation?

The food was never good in the middle of the night, but they had free Wi-Fi and the milkshakes were delicious. I ordered a thick chocolate malt and a large portion of fries. I hadn't been here in a while, and my stomach rumbled embarrassingly as I placed my order. The waitress was an ancient, heavyset woman who grimaced when she walked, but, man, was she nice. She told me I looked, and *sounded*, hungry, with a nod to my gut; said she would have my order right up, soon as she could.

"I don't have much business right now," she said, as she looked out over the empty dining room. "Do you want a glass of water too, hon?"

I nodded my assent and asked if they had any hot sauce.

"A southern boy, huh? We don't normally carry it, but there's a cook here, Mike, who keeps a hidden supply. I'll see if I can find it."

I hated the idea that I was adding to her workload and began to protest.

"Oh, shush boy. If I can find it, you can have it. In fact, you can have all of it. Whenever he cooks, I can't eat. So, you would be doing me a favour!" She walked away laughing, no doubt imagining Mike coming into work, searching frantically for his hot sauce.

She came back a few minutes later with the shake, fries, a glass of water, three bottles of hot sauce, and a ribeye steak, cooked medium.

"Umm, Ruth, ma'am, I didn't order a steak."

"Well, your mouth might not have ordered it, but your stomach sure did. I hope you're not a vegetarian. It's on the house." She smiled warmly at me and I thanked her as she walked away. "I'll be over here rolling silverware if you need anything."

I picked up a bottle of hot sauce, one with a pen-

and-ink drawing of the Grim Reaper, and poured the entire thing over my fries. It was delicious. Ruth glanced over at me and told me she had never seen a hungry boy eat so slowly.

"I want to savour it," was my response. That was mostly true, but I was also dreading going back to the house. Going back to my solitary confinement. I took the last bite of my steak, closing my eyes while I chewed. It had been too long since I had something this good.

After finishing my meal, I pulled open my laptop and connected to the Wi-Fi. Then I used a VPN to log on to the dark web, traveling to a forum supposedly used by serial killers. This was the first time I had logged in for three months. I was beginning to think that my search would never amount to anything. I had never posted anything, just lurked in the shadows, spending my time reading and researching. Would I ever find what I was looking for?

A couple of hours later, Ruth came over to the table. "Hurry up and put that hot sauce in your bag, boy. Mike will be here soon. I'm serious, now, put it in your bag. Can I get you anything else?"

"No, ma'am, that was delicious. Thank you so much." I reached into my pack to grab some cash and Ruth pushed my hand away.

"You put that away, too. I don't know where you've been, or where you're going. But something tells me you need that money more than we do. Go on, now. Get that hot sauce out of here."

I gave her an awkward hug and thanked her

again, dreading the walk home. As was often the case, a long walk gave my mind time to wander. Gave me time to reflect on my miserable life. And I didn't want to think about it. I wanted to remember instead the taste of steak on my tongue. I wanted to remember the feel of the thick, chocolate malt in my mouth. The coldness had felt so good as it moved down my throat.

I thought back to my brief encounter with the waitress. She had further awakened the longing in me to feel a kinship with others. I had often thought that my strange birthmark was what kept me separate from other people. Funny that…since I was the one who decided to live locked inside a hidden room, away from the world. It struck me then that I had never admitted my role in my own isolationism. Perhaps it was not society that had separated from me…perhaps I was the one responsible…for separating myself from it.

Maybe society could accept me. Perhaps I could find a following on Instagram. I could present my birthmark to the world, a world that only cares about physical beauty. But maybe that was a lie too. Maybe I had been lying to myself this whole time.

From a distance, I could see your car in the driveway, and I must admit I felt a little uneasy. I can be quite indecisive during stressful situations. Should I try to get in, or find some hole in the ground in the woods to nap in? I stopped to deliberate and was immediately covered in a swarm of mosquitoes. After getting bitten several times, the right choice became obvious.

As I stepped into the woods behind the house, I

could see the sun creeping up over the horizon. I unlocked the cellar door, quickly ducked in, and quietly closed the door behind me. I stood silently, letting my eyes adjust to the darkness, willing my heart to slow down. I could hear the muffled sound of the alarm, blaring dully in the distance. As I crept closer to the main part of the basement, I could hear you on a phone call. I stepped over to the hinged vent grate that provided the pathway to my room and quickly pulled myself up, closing it behind me. I had just started crawling when you finally managed to get the alarm turned off. I stopped moving, frozen, and turned my face, dropping it silently to the cold metal. I had no choice but to wait this out, aware that the alarm would no longer block the sounds of my movement.

"Ugh, bloody thing. Thanks for your help. Oh, shit! I've got another call coming in. Talk to you later? Okay. Bye."

I heard a muffled beep as you switched the call.

"Hello? Bella? Hey! Oh my god, I've had the most stressful morning."

I heard you pacing around above me and I waited patiently, listening to your conversation. I knew that if I could hear you, you could probably hear me, at least while I was in the crawlspace.

My domain consists of one main room, but there are three exits to the room. The most accessible exit, or entrance, is through the bookshelf in the front living room. Basically, one of the bookshelves can be used as a door. Pull the door open and you've got instant access to my room. Thankfully, there's a hook on the inside, so unless you know to look for the door, you would never notice it, and you can't accidentally find it.

In the same bookshelf, there is a sliding panel that I can open to look out through. I've often worried that you might discover it, or that I might open it to find someone staring right at me from the other side. Needless to say, I don't use it very often.

You've already heard about my access point to the basement. The other crawl space leads to a decorative grate in the hallway. It's my favourite place to be when you're home. From that vantage point, I can see you both in the kitchen, and in the hallway bathroom.

"I miss you too. Yeah, I mean, I love it, but it gets a little scary sometimes. Being all alone in this big house. Sometimes it feels like there's someone watching me." There was a pause as Isabella spoke. "Paranoid? I'm not the one who walks around with a brick in her purse." Julia laughed. "A taser gun? That might not be such a bad idea. Are they legal here?"

You switched the phone to speaker, and I could hear Bella swearing that she was going to visit soon, and that she was either going to bring you a taser, or a German Shepherd. Your laughter was pure magic.

I heard you walk up the stairs, your voice fading off into the distance, and slowly finished the trek to my room. Crawling across the floor, I climbed into my 'bed', a mattress covered with old Justice League sheets, and a comforter that had not been washed in months.

I picked up The Valley of the Dolls, some book I salvaged from your trash can, and tried to read. After a few minutes of staring at words, and supposedly reading them, I realised that I was ten pages into the novel and couldn't remember a single thing. I closed the book and threw it across the room, picturing you reading the novel to me instead. I imagined your warm, throaty voice filling my ears, until I eventually drifted off to sleep.

August 12th, 1992
Ephratah, New York

"Tell me a story before bed, mamma?" the little boy asked in almost a whisper. He was always scared to approach her, her moods being what they were. He was too young to realise that there were good mothers out there. Too young to do anything but love this woman, who insisted on being called Mamma. Although he had tried to sound and appear submissive and respectful, he had once again misinterpreted her mood and what was expected of him. He knew not to run from her. Running always made it worse.

The woman had been sitting at her desk, clothed in a silk negligee and matching pink robe, her long black hair hanging in mats down her back. She exuded a smell of depression, of weeks without a shower and days without food. She seemed older than her age and was surrounded by an air of having grown up too fast.

She did not appear to be busy. Or dangerous. She sat staring at a photo in front of her. The photo showed a young couple lying in a hammock, the woman on her side, her arms tucked underneath her head in the crook of the man's arm. Their eyes were closed, and the man wore a handsome grin. She had once told the boy that these were his grandparents. It had been bedtime, and the photo had been on a little nightstand by his bed. Before falling into a crying fit, clutching the boy to her chest, she had apologised. 'I'm sorry you'll never meet them' had been her words. She had held him for what seemed like hours after that, tears and snot falling onto his hair and face. When she had finally settled and fallen into a fitful sleep in his bed, the boy had placed the photo back in its place and walked to the kitchen to scavenge for food.

Suddenly the woman sprang to her feet and reached forward to slap the boy in the face. "What did you say? Speak up, boy!"

The slap left a red mark on the boy's face, but he didn't cry. With his hands clasped behind him, he straightened his back and looked her in the eyes. "I would very much like a story, if it pleases you, mamma."

The woman huffed and looked like she might slap the boy again. Instead, she asked, "And what story would that be?"

He responded, "Sleeping Beauty," then quickly added, "if it pleases you, mamma."

"Alright then, have a seat on the rug."

The boy hurried to the rug but did not run. Running would quickly result in a real whooping, but dawdling was just as bad. He found his spot at the foot of the large leather chair and waited for her to settle in, wrapping the blue and gold throw over her legs.

She never read books to the child, but told stories, her voice filled with emotion. She played each character distinctly, easily switching between deep, scary voices and light, happy ones. The boy would often imagine her as the nice characters she portrayed.

"Once upon a time, there was a king, who had a beautiful young daughter," the woman began. She told the story that we are all familiar with, except that her version was much closer to the original. In the original Sleeping Beauty, the sleeping girl is not only kissed, but is raped in her sleep by a married king. In the end, the king's wife is killed, and the king marries the girl instead.

The woman had always had a fascination with the origins of modern-day fairy tales and was determined to pass down that love to her son. She had once told a teacher that she would like to go to school and learn about stories from the past.

Mrs Robinson had said, "Well, that sounds like you should study literature and English!"

Literature. Lit-er-a-ture. Over the years, she had whispered it into her pillow at night. She liked to imagine herself as a professor, telling students that everything they had ever been taught in life was wrong. That history was really just a long line of lies, told by powerful people.

She looked down at the boy. She was determined that he should learn the truth about life…that everyone was always trying to sell you something. "What's their motive? What's in it for them? That's what you should always ask yourself. They dress up the 'truth' in pretty bows and hand it to you on a silver platter. But you won't buy it, you hear me? You'll know better."

His eyes were wide and enthralled by her words. He really was a good boy. In a rare display of affection, she tousled his hair and told him it was time for bed.

"I'll have to show you the Disney version of Sleeping Beauty sometime, then you'll understand what I mean. The *real* story is rarely pleasant."

"Was it the king that made you pregnant, mamma?" She rubs her swollen belly for a long time before answering in a dreamy tone. "Yes. While I was sleeping. That's right."

When his brother Lucas was born, his life took a turn for the better. His mamma was always busy, which meant that he was left to his own devices.

She was fond of telling him, "If you're going to make it through this life, you need to learn to entertain yourself."

They lived in a large house in the woods, and had few visitors. It was a solitary life. His father came by the house once a month, and he always brought gifts and food. Sometimes, he would also bring a doctor. There was also a foreign maid who stopped by once a week, and although she couldn't speak any English, she was nice to the boys, and often brought them baked cookies and other treats.

The boy had mixed feelings about these visits. He loved seeing his father, but his parents would inevitably end up yelling at each other. And when they weren't screaming in front of their kids, they were behind closed doors, making other weird sounds. The boy would often collect his little brother and carry him to the attic on the other side of the house, taking the baby as far away from their parents as he could. Parts of the house were locked away to him, but even without access to those spaces, the house was immense.

The attic had become their hideout, and so far, his mother hadn't discovered it. In a dusty corner, the boy had discovered a large trunk full of leatherworking and wood carving books and supplies. It had taken him weeks to get the trunk open, the lid too heavy for his tiny arms, and the hinges too rusty. He had brought countless tools with which to wedge the lid up, and they still lay scattered about…butter knives, a saw, scissors, a pickaxe, and two shovels.

Countless times he had tried to talk himself out of the task. He had told himself that what he would find in the chest would be boring and not worth his time. But he couldn't let it go. He had looked back on his decision to open the trunk many times in his life, wondering how different things would have been if he had never found it.

He was a patient child. Slow to speak and even slower to act. His fear of beatings had taught him a lot. He had not rushed through the contents of the trunk when he finally got it open. He had taken things out, one at a time, puzzling over their use. He often did this with his eyes closed, standing or kneeling beside the trunk and reaching in, heart beating with excitement, eyes only opening after he had touched the prized object and felt every nook and cranny of its structure.

At the very bottom of the chest he had found a Polaroid camera and a slew of Polaroids, all featuring young women in various stages of undress. While the Polaroid pictures were of little interest to him at first, the camera became his pride and joy. He treasured it above all else and would only use it when his mother was asleep. He was frightened that such a fabulous toy would be confiscated, or purposely broken in a vicious rage. He had taught himself how to use the camera, taking pictures of useless things. The old furniture in the attic, the window frame, the tall tree outside, his foot. He would quickly learn that there was a limit to the number of pictures he could create. When he ran out of film, he frantically searched for more. After learning how to insert the new film, he used it much more sparingly, only taking pictures of the most important things. One photo, a picture of his sleeping mother, would become a mainstay in his life for years to come.

He had never been anywhere besides this house, nor had he met anyone outside of his family, the maid, and the doctor. At the age of six, he did not know how to read or write, and could not have answered the simplest of mathematics problems. But he could draw. He could whittle fantastical sculptures out of wood. And he could work and tool leather.

Eventually, the father had him put in school. He had obviously been behind, but he caught up quickly. While his mother showed little interest in him anymore, she would occasionally show appreciation for his grades, or the art pieces he brought home. Though the art he produced at school was far different to the art he would make at home.

He did not get along well with the other children; he had very little in the way of social skills. He learnt not to discuss his real home life with other classmates. Instead, he would listen intently to the things the other children said and would often use them to weave imaginary parts of his life into casual conversation. It was a troubled time in the boy's life, but things would get better. He would soon realise that although he was different from other kids, it wasn't a bad thing. There was no one in this world he needed approval from. No one, except himself.

Chapter 4

Julia sat on a padded, beige couch in the office of her therapist, a stunning black woman named Nia. The psychologist kept her head bald and her eyes intricately accentuated and maintained. Today, her eyelids were painted with a warm, gold gradient, eyelashes thick, with winged eyeliner. A diamond nose ring sparkled, a silver chain connecting it to a stud in her left ear. She was slightly older than Julia, but not by much.

While she was a trained clinical psychologist and could have been referred to as Dr Nia Dixon, she preferred for clients to call her by her first name. She had a large mahogany desk that remained mostly empty, except for the pictures of her wife and two children, one boy and one girl. There were two photographs of her wife: one was a shot of a kiss on their wedding day, both brides in white dresses; the other was a pregnancy photo, both of them looking equally pregnant, hands held between their swollen bellies. The photographs were turned towards the window, away from visitors, but if anyone asked to see them, she always shared them openly. Nia knew many psychologists who would balk at the idea of sharing such personal information, but she always found that her relationship with clients improved if she shared a bit of herself with them.

They had been sitting quietly for several minutes now, Julia lost in thought. Nia took in her appearance: Julia's thick, blonde hair looked unwashed; there were dark circles under her eyes, and despite her petite stature, she had well-defined muscles in both her arms and legs. To the untrained eye, she must have looked like any other young professional working in the city, with her black business skirt, low cut blazer, and white silk blouse. There was also a personal touch to her outfit: a stunning silk scarf, tied at her throat, featuring Van Gogh's Almond Blossoms.

Finally, Julia began. "I feel guilty."

Nia had only met Julia four times before this; she did not know her well, but had already learnt not to push things. If pushed, Julia would often retreat from the dark thoughts that troubled her and present her well-rehearsed persona of happiness. Whilst Nia acknowledged that it was important to have coping mechanisms in place, she had tried to steer Julia towards being able to express her vulnerability. She knew that Julia often kept people at a safe distance; she feared losing them. After losing both of her parents, it was certainly a valid fear, but if Julia did not learn to open herself up, her life would continue to suffer the consequences. If she did not overcome her fear of losing loved ones, she would end up alone.

Julia continued. "People often assume that I'm

married, because I present as white, but my last name is Rodriguez. People assume I can't be a Latina, so they often think I got my last name by marrying a Hispanic." She smiled. "It almost makes me want to marry a white man and keep my last name, just to confuse people even further."

She looked over at Nia for reassurance, and the older woman smiled warmly, silently encouraging her to continue.

Julia cleared her throat and rushed on. "I've been working with some high-school kids on a project for a new art show. I'm hoping to find a gallery in the city that will accept their pieces. One of them asked me why I do what I do. She asked why I spend my time helping them. I told her that I knew what it was like, growing up poor and afraid, and that I had found an outlet through art and wanted to share that with others." Julia looked away uncomfortably. "She laughed at me. She laughed. She said that I had no idea what she and the others had been through, because I had white skin. I realised that she was right. I have definitely had an easier time of it."

Julia stood and started to pace, trying to release the pent-up anxiety bubbling up inside of her. "But she doesn't quite know what it's like to be me. Race was always a weird thing for me. My father was Cuban, and my mother was Russian. I looked white but I never fit in with the white kids. Then again, I never fit in with the Hispanic kids either." Julia was talking very quickly, afraid that if she stopped talking, she wouldn't get it all out. She felt stupid for getting emotional over the words of a teenager. "Saying that aloud makes me feel so foolish. White Latinas aren't getting gunned down in the streets. It's not the same thing. And I just feel guilty. I feel guilty for feeling that my past and my suffering are somehow equivalent to the systemic racism facing the black individuals in our society." She took a deep breath, then sat down again, closing her eyes, and sinking into the couch. "I know, it's stupid."

Nia shut her notebook and looked over at Julia. "What did we say about these personal insults?"

"They're not productive."

"That's right." Nia moved to the front of her desk and took a seat on its clean surface. "Julia, you're entitled to your feelings. It's good of you to acknowledge your privilege, but it doesn't make the trials and tribulations you have suffered any less real or less painful. How well do you know this girl?"

"I've only known her for a couple of weeks. So, not very well, I guess."

"My suggestion is to get to know her. Find out if there are some common threads between the two of you. Be honest with her. Be vulnerable. Share your art and your story with her."

Julia rolled her eyes. *Be vulnerable.* Easier said than done.

Nia laughed. "Out of all my patients, you're the one I get the most eye rolls from."

Julia bit her lip and stood up. "Sorry, Doc."

Nia raised her eyebrows and cocked her head to the side. "Doc?"

"Oh, right. Sorry! Nia. Thanks, Nia."

Nia nodded and waved off Julia's slip of the tongue. "No harm in it. Before you go, is there anything else that's bothering you?"

Reflexively, Julia started to shake her head, then remembered that she was trying to be honest with this therapist. She switched her head movement to a nod. "Well, yeah, there is. But I don't want to get into it right now. Next time?"

Nia rose from the desk and walked Julia to the door. "Next time it is," Nia smiled, opening the door. "One more thing. Last time we met, I suggested it might be a good idea for you to take a trip back to Michigan, to see Isabella and your old co-workers. Have you given any more thought to that?"

"Yes! Isabella called the other day; she's planning on coming here for a week. Her brother, Daniel, is coming along too, it's going to be great! It's not for three months or so but that gives us time to plan. Daniel and I are organising a little bachelorette party for her."

Nia smiled warmly at her. "Wonderful! When is she getting married?"

"Well, she's not. It was supposed to happen last year, but...well, her fiancé turned out to be a crazy, lying, cheating asshole. So, we're going to celebrate that he's out of her life and she's moved on."

"Okay, I can definitely get behind that. Any big plans?"

"Actually, yeah. Have you heard of the K-pop Kings?"

"Yes! The Times had an article about it in the Arts section a few Sundays ago. They're Korean caterers with a dance show or something, right?"

"Exactly. I'm not quite sure what to expect, but I'm glad we were able to book them."

"Well, I hope it's a success. See you next month?"

"Sure thing. Have a great day…Nia."

After leaving Nia's office, Julia decided to visit a nearby art gallery, portraying local and emerging artists. One piece in particular captured her attention. In it, a couple were standing under a subway stop sign, labelled 'Times Square', wearing their wedding clothes. The woman stood in white, staring down at the ground, clutching a bundle of red roses. The man, clad in a black tuxedo, held her outstretched hand, his lips pressed on her knuckles. There was a subway train in motion behind the couple, and on the ground in front of them was a murder scene. The victims were two young males, each stabbed in the chest multiple times. The murdered men and the couple shared the same space in the image, but the murder scene was in black and white, whilst the couple were in colour.

After a few minutes of quiet contemplation, Julia noticed a man standing to her left. She smiled at him and started to walk away.

"Do you like the piece?" he asked, his voice just above a whisper, almost in reverence.

She turned back towards the piece in question. "I do. Although, I'm not sure exactly why. It makes me think of Eve, for some reason."

The man laughed a little. "Eve, of biblical fame?"

"Yeah. It's like the woman is heading towards death, and the husband is trying to stop her. She's heading towards the knowledge of tragic things, but she doesn't realise it. And the world is speeding by them, not caring that this woman is all that stands between them and paradise. Adam knows. He tries to hold her back. But he still loves her, no matter her decision."

"Interesting interpretation. Allow me to introduce myself, my name is Charles Ivanov. But my friends call me CJ, or Charlie. My brother is fond of calling me Xavier."

"Xavier?"

"Yeah, you know, Charles Xavier? The bald dude in the wheelchair, head of the X-men?"

"Oh! Yes, right, sure. Nice to meet you." They shook hands and Julia asked, "What do *you* think of the piece?"

"Oh, I bet it was made as a cash grab, some desperate artist trying to make a buck. Figured he could get some New York art critics to take a liking to his work."

Julia winced and smiled.

He took in her profile and continued, "Or maybe it's just a plea for help. Maybe the artist is a cynic who thinks that marriage leads to obvious death." He winked at her.

"Ouch. I hope you aren't a published art critic." She looked for the title of the piece and noticed that it was called 'Saying Goodbye', by the artist…Charles Ivanov.

"Oh! Wow. I didn't realise…"

"We are our own worst critics, aren't we?"

"I guess so…anyway, it was very nice meeting you, but I've got to get back home. I have a half-gallon of Rocky Road waiting for me." She pulled out her business card and handed it to him. "I work for a foundation upstate in Hunter. I'm an assistant curator there. We typically show work from artists around the northeast, but they also do musical productions and concerts with local talent. The proceeds often go towards scholarships for local youth in need. Maybe you might be interested in volunteering some of your time, or showing some of your work? We're always looking for artists to draw in customers from the city."

"Interesting. I will definitely consider it." He looked down at the business card. "I didn't realise people still used business cards. How quaint." She looked slightly offended. "No offense…Julia."

Julia laughed, feeling rather uncomfortable. She took a silent breath to calm herself. "None taken. I am probably the last person left in the world who still uses business cards whilst simultaneously hating smartphones."

"You don't own a smartphone? Oh, you poor thing! Well, welcome, Julia, to something we like to call…civilization."

She laughed. "The only thing I need from civilization is a good cup of hot tea in a fancy teacup."

"Oh, well, we'll send the toilets right back!"

She offered her hand, laughing. "Goodbye again, Xavier."

Charles shook her hand. "Is this your work

address listed, or home?"

"My work address."

"Would you mind giving your home address to the receptionist up front? I'd love to include you on the mailing list."

"Umm...sure."

"Great! Thanks for stopping by. Enjoy your ice cream." Charles watched her walk to the front desk and speak with Lori, then leave the gallery. He approached the desk.

"Hey, Lori. The woman you were just talking to, Julia, did she provide you with her home address?"

"She sure did. She said something about being added to your mailing list. I didn't know you had one." Her aqua-green eyes looked up at him.

Charlie leant casually on the counter. "Would you have 'Saying Goodbye' shipped to her address, please?"

"I'm sorry, sir, but she didn't provide me with a form of payment."

"I'll be paying for it, actually."

Lori was taken aback. "Oh, okay. Well, that's highly irregular. I'm not sure if..."

Charlie interrupted her. "Lori."

"Yes?"

"Just ship it. As soon as possible. If there's any fallout, just send Dorothy my way. I can handle her."

"Yes, sir." She moved out from behind the desk and walked towards the piece, intent on fulfilling his request.

A voice came from his left. "Damn, she's got a

nice ass."

"Yes, she does." Charles' gaze did not follow the woman walking away, however. Instead, he turned towards the man seated by the door; dressed in a dark suit, a white, button-down dress shirt, and mirrored sunglasses. Any onlooker might have assumed he was asleep, or even dead, sitting there so unmoving. He could just as easily have been an art installation rather than a living, breathing human being.

"How are you doing, Ronald?"

"Pretty good, boss. Happy to be in the city, but bored of sitting, doing nothing. Do you have anything pressing you need me to do today, or can I take off a bit early?"

"You don't like hanging out at the gallery all day?"

Ronald, Charles' personal assistant, driver, and sometime bodyguard, did not answer.

Charles laughed. "Go on, man. Get out of here. Don't get into any trouble."

"Are you going to be staying in town?"

"Yeah. I'll let you know if I need anything."

Charlie left the gallery and headed home: an apartment in the Upper West Side, which he shared with his brother. He was hoping to have a few beers with him tonight, to celebrate a large sale he had scored earlier that day. A single buyer had purchased four of his most expensive prints, all from the 'Criminal Lives' series.

It had been some time since the series had been introduced to the public, but it was still his most popular.

He sighed deeply. While he appreciated the money, he had grown tired of the series and longed to start selling something fresh. He had a few ideas bouncing around in his head, but he had not committed to anything yet. The gallery he was currently showing in, Future^2, or Future Squared, was owned by two brothers, and they had been generous about giving Charlie time to come up with his next big thing. Dorothy, the director of the art gallery, was not so gentle.

Dorothy had asked him to come into the gallery earlier that day to meet with a potential buyer, and he had given the gentleman a tour of his pieces on display, feeding him the usual bullshit; discussing how he used his art to exorcise his inner demons and blah, blah, blah. The tour had resulted in the sale of four of his pieces, with talks of procuring more. He had been quite proud of the sale and had expected Dorothy to appreciate his efforts. Instead, she had only mentioned that there were now four blank spaces on her walls.

"When are you going to show me something new, Charlie? What are you working on?"

Ugh. Fucking bitch, he had thought. Aloud, he had been more polite. "Right now, I'm doing some collecting."

"Collecting what?"

"I've been collecting newspaper articles about violent crimes against women. I'm thinking about doing some mixed media pieces with the articles, maybe getting some models who look like the victims, and...I don't know...maybe shooting the models at the cemeteries of the deceased?"

"That's sick, Charlie. I love it. Any other ideas?"

"Well, I also have something in mind similar to my 'Criminal Lives' series."

"Go on."

"I call it 'Sleeping Beauties.' I'm imagining female models, dressed in nightclothes. Very expensive ones. Surrounding them with wealth and luxury items but having them in impoverished conditions. Juxtaposing their luxury against an environment of poverty."

"Can you give me an example?"

"Okay. How about this? Homeless man, middle of winter. He's lying on a flattened cardboard box in the park, under a bench. Is he asleep? Is he dead? To the woman clothed in an expensive nighty, lying on furs spread out on top of the bench, it just doesn't matter."

"I like that better. Think you can have it together for a spring exhibition? At least thirty riveting pieces. Maybe donate a couple of them before the show, get the word out."

Charlie had shrugged his shoulders and hesitantly said, "Yes?"

"Charlie, come on. That's plenty of time. If you can't give me something by then, I'm going to suggest we drop you."

The phone was ringing as Charlie walked into his apartment, and he ran over to pick up before it hit voicemail. As he silently listened to the voice on the other end, a huge grin formed on his face and he answered, "This is him. I'd love to hear about it."

For the next twenty minutes, he listened to some kid in a call centre, telling him that he had 'won' an in-home carpet cleaning for 'free'; informing him that a brand-new vacuum cleaner had just come on the market, made in the good old US of A, and how after the carpet cleaning demonstration, he would surely agree that this new model would make the perfect addition to his home.

"Well, I have to tell you…what was your name again?"

"Jeffery, sir."

"Well, Jeffery, I'm super excited to see this vacuum cleaner. I hope it's as good as you say. And I'll be able to sign up for payments if I like it?"

"Yes, sir."

"Well, that just sounds dandy. Will you be the one doing the demonstration?"

"No, sir."

"Well dang, that's a shame. Let me check my schedule." Charlie looked over at the calendar, making a note of his brother's shifts for the upcoming weeks. "Could you send someone around eight a.m. on Saturday morning?" Charlie waited on the line while the young man confirmed the appointment. "That's right. And they will need a code to get into the building, it's one, one, zero, four. Can you read that back to me?"

Charlie hung up the phone in good spirits, chuckling hysterically to himself. He had just signed his brother up for an early-morning wake-up call with a vacuum cleaner salesman, and he didn't feel in the least bit guilty. He still owed his brother for the last prank, from the year before. A funeral director, Mr Whitmore, had shown up at their door to discuss his funeral arrangements.

"Your brother told me all about it. I am sincerely sorry. I lost my aunt to cancer, dreadful illness. I'm here to make sure you get exactly what you want."

The man had seemed so sincere and caring that Charlie could not bear to explain that the whole thing was a practical joke. So, he had spent the next hour sitting with Mr Whitmore in the living room, picking out a casket and flowers, deciding on colours and times for the viewings. After the funeral director had left, he had called up his brother.

"Guess whose funeral I just planned?"

Charlie was still laughing. He was not sure if the vacuum salesman's visit would quite make up for having to plan his own funeral, but he hoped it would come close.

March 19th, 1993
St. Johnsville, New York

The school had sent home letters, asking for conferences. Calls always went to voicemail and there had never been a response. Every teacher, every student, every person on the administrative team agreed: the boy needed therapy. They knew there was trouble at home, they just did not know what the trouble was. The school counsellor did what she could. It was strange to see someone so young exhibit such problems. He was an intelligent lad; she sometimes thought perhaps he was *too* intelligent. He had no friends, but he wasn't a bully. He was just…there was something not right about him. The word she wanted to use was scary, but she could not even say it to herself.

Currently, his class was at recess. He felt alone on the playground, crouched beside the broken tyre swing. The other children were off playing tag or using the new plastic play structures. They usually left him alone. When he had first arrived at the school, half-way into the school year, they had started off by picking on him. But they didn't do that anymore. For the most part, people pretended he didn't exist, children and adults alike. That was the way he preferred things. He, in turn, pretended that *they* didn't exist. It was a good balance. He had, long ago, decided not to care.

Right now, he was mesmerized by the bird. He had never seen anything so beautiful. At first glance, the feathers appeared to be black. But when he looked closely, and caught the light just so, he could see the feathers shimmer like a dark opal, with hidden colours trapped in its depths. One feather had come loose and lay alone in the long blades of grass, beckoning. He picked it up delicately and with reverence. He closed his eyes and drew the feather across his face, a holy ritual of anointment.

"Hey, it's time to go back in. Ms. Shelley asked me to come tell you."

The girl's voice did not startle him, it merely annoyed him. He did not turn in her direction.

She started walking closer to him and he heard her ask, "What are you doing?"

What in the world was he looking at? He seemed transfixed by something on the ground below him. She didn't want to get any closer to him, but she was a curious child. Instead of stepping closer, she started walking around him, to get a wider view of what held his attention. She was almost close enough to see when he turned to face her. She gasped. His face was covered in a red goop that looked an awful lot like blood. Flies swarmed around him, and by his bent knees, a dead bird lay open. It could not have been dead long, as blood pulsated from its open wound, bubbling up and dripping down to the hungry ground.

The girl turned and ran as fast as she could back to the school, her lungs fighting to provide the air necessary both to breathe and to fuel the shriek of terror that surged from within her. As she ran, she looked back over her shoulder, sure that the crazed boy who kneeled, a grin upon his face, would suddenly arise and chase her down, rip her open, and rub her own blood on his lips.

She never returned to the school and would forever split her childhood into two parts: the innocent time before the incident, and the hellish time after. She would eventually recover from the trauma, find her voice again, and get accepted to New York University to study sociology. She would learn to trust again, make friends, and start dating. But even years after the incident, she often awoke in the middle of the night, her skin soaked in sweat, with the taste of blood in her mouth.

The boy was moved to a private boarding school and put into daily behavioural therapy. It was there that he learnt how to blend in. He became a chameleon, able to match the social cues of others; to become popular and well-loved. But no matter how accepted, he never truly fit in. He was a predator, hungry but patient. And he never forgot the little girl who had run from him on the playground, her long, brown braid whipping her face as she turned back to stare at him, a scream on her lips. It had been then that he had experienced his first hard-on. He would keep the feather for years, often using it to trace along his naked body while whispering her name, "Emily".

Chapter 5

January 6th, 2014
London, Ohio

Jakob was sitting at a small oak desk, wedged into a dark corner of the Ohio BCI, Bureau of Criminal Investigation. The desk was ornamented with a single lamp, the lampshade askew and too big, its trailing power cord dangling onto the floor. There was no outlet in sight. It was his first day on the job here in Ohio. He had jumped through quite a few hoops to get here, but his record as a soldier and as a trooper had helped. Coming here had felt like a crazy decision, and he still wasn't sure he had made the right choice. So far, he had spent twelve hours going through the case files Cindy had piled onto his desk, and he had come up empty. It looked like Sagan had covered every possible angle with the investigation. Jeez, this might end up being harder than he had thought it would be.

Jakob had spent a great deal of his youth in Kentucky before he and his mother had moved to Georgia. He used to dream of living in California, swearing every day that he would be living the good life out west. But here he was, an adult, now living in Ohio.

He had spent many years feeling out the racism in each place of residence. Thinking about it, tasting it, living it. He knew that a lot of people had said, and would continue to say, that racism was dead in this country. But he could not recall a black person ever saying it.

Now, he knew, he *knew,* that things were not nearly as bad as they used to be. No one could claim he was owned, could say that he was an item of property. But at the heart of racism was fear. And people were still afraid. Sometimes you could smell the fear coming off a white person. What was it, exactly, that they were afraid of? Sometimes, they acted as if black people were from another country; foreigners in this blessed country of theirs. Jakob expected some white person to come up to him sometime and ask him if he thought in English or Ebonics. He wondered if white people truly thought he had less of a stake in the US than they did just because his ancestors came from Africa rather than from some other place?

Being in law enforcement had not made it any easier for him. He had spent time in Atlanta, Athens, and then some small country town he couldn't even remember the name of, where he'd been called 'house nigger', and 'Uncle Tom'. But he had never taken it personally. He understood where the anger came from. When he was younger, the police had been the bad guys. The ones to keep away from. The ones killing black boys in the streets, hiding guns on dead kids, talking about how they 'feared for their lives' when their adversaries were a bunch of skinny twelve-year-olds with afros.

He never thought he would become a cop. His

dream had been generic, a dime a dozen in the projects: he had wanted to play ball. Basketball, football, baseball; he'd had a talent for all three, so it had varied day to day and season to season. But that was before the accident. Before the violence that crept around the edges of his life had seeped in, destroying his world.

For as long as he could remember, it had been him and his mama. He asked after a father every now and again. But it rarely came up because his mama took such good care of him; he didn't have room in his life for contemplating what he was missing. Mama taught him how to grow up in a world without a father. The world would teach him how to live without his mother.

In the spring of 1995, on a Friday night, they drove out to Covington Missionary Baptist, just like they always did. His mama organised a teen night there once a week; they would have Bible study, music practice, and sometimes they would work on a drama production, depending on the time of year. But everybody knew it wasn't Jesus who put those kids in that church. It was Renita May Collier's cooking.

She and Jakob would always get to the church a couple of hours before teen night was due to start, and she would work her magic, turning simple, inexpensive ingredients into food fit for kings. There would be fried chicken, mashed potatoes, and brown gravy (she didn't have no kind of patience for white gravy), collard greens with bacon and ham, simmered for hours at home and finished off at the church, black-eyed peas with plenty of juice for soaking cornbread, sweet tea and lemonade, and some kind of cobbler or pie for dessert.

On that spring night, there was a huge turnout, with twenty-six kids from the surrounding area showing up. The teens all pitched in and helped clean up, so they were out by eight thirty, earlier than usual. Renita and Jakob walked slowly to their 1974 Buick Estate Wagon, waving at the last kids as they got picked up or drove off in their own cars.

Renita sat down heavily in the car and put the key in the ignition, turning it to the first position. The oil indicator lit up and the radio came on: Dr Dre and Snoop Dogg singing 'Ain't Nuthin but a G Thang'. She moved to turn the radio off, but Jakob started begging from outside the car, popping his face through the open passenger side window.

"Please, mom. Please, leave it on!"

She looked over at his soulful eyes and continued moving her hand over to the radio dial. His face fell as he opened the door, but instead of turning the radio off, Renita turned the radio up, dropping her hand back in her lap and shaking her head.

Jakob became animated, dancing in the parking lot, enjoying his mother's laughter, even as she shouted over the music, "Alright, boy, but you need to start listening to some real music!"

Jakob rolled his eyes and started rapping along with the radio as he dropped to the ground, spun around, and came up to throw his body forward on his left foot, raising his right leg behind him. As the music faded into an advertisement, Jakob climbed into the car.

"Thanks, mom."

"I love you, boy. And I must admit, you got some funky dance moves." She stroked his face and he pulled away in mock horror.

"Come on, mom."

"Uh-huh. Okay, let's get out of here. Buckle up, now."

As they were fastening their seatbelts, Renita suddenly exclaimed, "Oh shoot! I left my purse in the darn church. Jakob, be a good boy and run get it, would you? I think it's on the counter by the stove. Here's the keys." She looked down at the car dial and realised the oil light was still on; they had been having problems with the oil for a few weeks. "I'm just gonna top the oil off while you run in."

Jakob sprinted across the blacktop, the side door of the church illuminated by a single yellow lamp. He hopped up the stairs and found the key for the door, looking back to see his mama popping the hood. He laughed to himself. There she was, wearing a white dress with black polka dots, in high heels, bent over their car and holding onto an oil can. He felt guilty for laughing, then felt guilty that she was putting the oil in. It didn't sit right that she should be the one doing it. He was the man of the house and there she was, probably going to stain her dress, when he should be doing it instead.

He shouted back to her, "Mama! I can do that when I get back, just hold on a minute!" He ran into the church, kicking the door closed behind him, sure his mom would be proud of him. She was always reminding him that 'he wasn't born in no barn'. He didn't bother with the lights on the way to the kitchen. He was still a little scared of the dark, sure, but this was a church. God wouldn't let anything bad happen to him.

He threaded his way through the main chapel, zigzagging in and out of the lanes between the pews, making a game of it. Proving to God that he wasn't scared. He heard the hood of the car thud shut and cursed under his breath. He had been so busy playing, his mom had put the oil in herself. "Goddammit!"

He quickly apologised to God for the curse before running into the kitchen, slamming on the light with the whole palm of his hand. Her purse was right where she said it would be, some ugly leather-looking green and black thing, folded over on itself. He grabbed the purse and headed back towards the side door. As he cut off the light, he heard an engine revving up, out in the parking lot. It didn't sound like their car, it sounded more like a truck. Halfway through the chapel, he heard his mother screaming, and two tinny pings outside, followed by the sound of a vehicle screeching away, burning rubber on the asphalt. He knew what those sounds were.

Dropping the purse, he bolted out of the door, praying to God that she was okay, that it had just been some stupid kids trying to scare her. He ran down the steps, searching frantically for his mother. Where was she? The air was still filled with diesel fumes, and clouds of smoke from the burnt rubber. He choked on regret, telling himself that he should have been the one outside. He should have been the one putting oil in the car.

He circled around their car and dropped to the ground, his heart a crazed bird in his chest, rivers falling from his eyes, lungs drowning in grief, unable to suck in oxygen. He heard someone wailing, someone repeating "No, no, no, no. Please, God, no." He never realised that the words were coming from himself.

Renita was face down on the pavement with a gunshot to the head and right shoulder, her eyes and mouth open; her breath coming in choked bursts; her mouth pulsating like an ugly guppy out of water.

Her voice entered his head. "Stop that crying now, you hear? You get me up, boy. You put me in that car, and you drive like hell. You drive like hell and get me to a hospital. You can do it. You can save my life."

Jakob dragged his mother up into the backseat of the car, her body light and feeble. "I got you, mama, I got you, I got you." These words would be his mantra for the next several minutes. Jakob was fourteen years old and he had never driven a car before, not unless you counted sitting on his mama's lap and poking around a parking lot at five miles an hour as driving. He didn't have to pull the seat up, since he was taller than his mom.

The keys were still dangling in the ignition and the Buick roared to life as he turned her over. He quickly strapped on his seatbelt and tore off through the parking lot, the car jerking to a standstill as he figured out the difference between the gas and brake pedals. Soon enough, he was on his way, driving in the darkness, gaining speed whilst simultaneously trying to find the switch for the lights. He accidentally flipped on the windscreen wipers, the worn-down rubber squeaking against the dry glass, and he continued his search, screaming out for God to help him. He hollered, a triumphant call tearing from his lips as he found the lights. The scene before him suddenly became clear, and he had only the briefest moment to acknowledge that he was heading straight for a copse of trees. He slammed on the brakes with both feet, and the car skidded and spun, the back end hitting a tree at forty-five miles per hour. The car was not equipped with an airbag, and Jakob was almost instantly knocked unconscious, his head hitting both the driver's side door and the steering wheel.

When he came to, he was being dragged out of the vehicle by strangers, intent on strapping him onto a gurney.

"No! Get off me. Mom! Where's my mom? Mom!"

The EMTs were struggling to hold the boy down and one called for a tranquilizer. But when Jakob's mom came into focus, the struggle left his body. His mother was on the ground; a Georgia State Trooper was giving her chest compressions; EMTs were rushing over with an AED. As he fell back against the gurney, the EMTs strapped down his arms and he was given an intramuscular injection on the side of his upper right thigh. He didn't wake again until the next day.

Jakob blinked and opened his eyes, sunlight painfully streaming into the room. There was a middle-aged white man sitting in the chair to the left of his hospital bed. The man was leaning back in the chair, his eyes closed, and his legs stretched out. He was huge, bulky with muscle, and he made the chair look as if it had been made for a child. Jakob studied the man while he snored, taking in his plain jeans, white t-shirt, and lame sneakers. This guy was someone he didn't know...why the hell was he in Jakob's room?

The man let out a loud snore and came to, his eyes filling with kindness as he looked over at the hospital bed. "Hey there, son."

Jakob was about to tell the white man that he was not his son, when he suddenly recognised him. He was the cop. The one he had seen breathing into his mother's mouth. The one he had seen straddled over his mother's still body. "Mom...my...mom...?"

"Your mom is alive."

Jakob visibly relaxed and a smile started to form on his lips as he leaned back against the cheap pillow.

"But I have to be honest with you, son..."

Jakob's heart tightened in his chest. He closed his eyes and tried to mentally prepare himself for what was coming next.

"She's not okay. I don't think she's ever going to be like she used to be. She has just come out of surgery; they were able to remove the bullets, but she's in a coma, and they're not sure if she will regain consciousness. If she does, well, she's got a long, hard road ahead of her. She might never walk again. She might never talk again."

Jakob had begun to sob and was struggling to rise to a sitting position, trying to catch his breath. The man stepped over towards the bed and started helping the boy up, but Jakob struggled against the help, choking out a tortured wail.

"Yo, get off me, man!" he yelled. "I don't need your help. I don't need your help!"

The cop helped anyway, pulling Jakob up and turning him into a sitting position, with his legs thrown over the side of the bed. While tears ran down Jakob's face, he attempted to fend off the well-meaning man, his hands curled into fists.

"Jakob, my name is Roger. I'm going to do everything I can to help you." Roger held onto the boy as he fought against him, the kid's skinny body wracked with sobs. He whispered to Jakob, told him that everything was going to be okay, told him that he would find the people who did this. Eventually, the boy grew quiet against him.

"Thank you."

Roger took a step back from the boy and looked him in the eyes, one hand on each of his shoulders. "I promise you. I will do everything I can."

There was a war building inside of Jakob, a splintering of the mind. Here was a white man, a cop no less, who had not looked at him as an enemy. Who had instead, looked at him with dignity and kindness, and who had promised to somehow make things right. He had spent the better part of his childhood holding on to a hatred for men like this, nameless individuals safe behind a badge and the colour of their skin. Part of him clung to that hatred and that anger, but deep inside him there was a shift towards diplomacy. A shift towards respect. His future lay in darkness and he had no reason to trust this man, but he could not trust God right now.

So, he took his hope, he took his faith, he took

everything that made him who he was up to this moment in his life, and he hit the pause button. He was going to let this play out. He was going to trust this cop. And if it didn't work out? Well, he would come right back here, to this place in time. He would come right back to this moment, where he had trusted the wrong man, and he would undo it. He would never trust again.

Turned out, if you lost your faith in God, well, Georgia State Trooper Roger Barnes made a pretty safe replacement. Officer Barnes took Jakob into his home while the boy's mom recovered in the hospital. He made sure that Jakob was able to go home with his mom when she healed. He made sure that they had a nurse come by every day, and he himself visited at least once a week. And when the kid's mother died, four years after the shooting, Roger was there to help Jakob keep it together. It was no surprise to anyone when Jakob decided to become a state trooper.

The path to his current position had been a varied one. He had joined the Reserve Officers Training Corps in high school, enlisted in the army as soon as he got out, spent four years in active service, and then went to Georgia's State Patrol Trooper school, while still in the reserves. While he was serving his first year as a trooper, he had gotten a call from Roger.

"Hey, son."

"Hey! How's it hanging, old man?" The familiar jibe did not elicit its usual good-natured laughter. Instead, silence filled up the space between them. "Roger, what's wrong?"

"Well," Roger let out an intense breath of air before continuing. "The gun involved in your mom's shooting. It's turned up. They got the perp. Some agent with the Ohio Bureau of Investigation...a Cindy Griffin...well, she's the one who got him. I don't have any details, but I wanted to be the first one to tell you. You want me to give her a call?"

Jakob was speechless.

"Son? You there?"

"Yeah, yeah. I'm here. After all this time, they finally got him?"

"Yeah. God, I'm sorry. I'm sorry I wasn't the one. I wanted to...to...be the one. You know?"

Jakob could tell that Roger was having a hard time holding back tears. "Roger, man, come on. You did everything you could. And then some. You saved my mom. You saved me. There is nothing, you hear me? NOTHING that you could have done any differently. You did right by me and my mama. You didn't have to do none of it. I will forever be grateful. I love you, Roger. I don't want you having regrets on my behalf. You got no reason for it. You hear me?"

Roger sighed heavily into the phone. "Thank you, son. That means a lot." He sighed again and Jakob could still hear the regret there. "I got her number here. I can call."

Jakob closed his eyes. "I think I'd like to call instead. That okay?"

Roger read out the number over the phone and Jakob copied it onto the corner of a used Burger King napkin. It took him a few months to get to it, but on a cold Sunday morning in November, Jakob had headed out to his mom's gravesite, bottle of Jack Daniel's Tennessee Honey in hand. He had rested his back against her tombstone, unscrewed the bottle, taken the crumpled-up Burger King napkin out of his front pocket, and placed a call to Ohio.

That call had resulted in his move to Ohio from Georgia. It had resulted in him becoming part of a task-force intent on finding a serial killer, joining forces with people he had never worked with before. But after talking and meeting with the spit-fire force that was Cindy Griffin, well, it had just felt right somehow. He hadn't been sure about John Sagan at first, but he had eventually warmed to the guy. It wasn't easy being the newest member of the team, but Cindy hadn't been there too long either, at least, not officially.

They had met a few months before, in Atlanta. When Jakob had called her, Cindy had been on her way to check out a murder scene for Sagan, in the good old Peach State. On a whim, she had asked if he wanted to meet for a drink. They had met in the bar of her hotel, and she had told him all about the sting operation that had resulted in the capture of his mom's killer. The discussion had then turned to the reason for her visit.

"John is a colleague, and a family friend, really. My dad and him go back a little ways. I don't usually work with him too much, but he's a little short-staffed at the moment. There hasn't been much movement in the case he's working on, and people don't usually stay too long. Either they can't stand the violence, they feel like they're wasting their time, or they just can't handle working with Sagan."

Their conversation and drinking had lasted until the early hours of the morning, and they had eventually found themselves in a shared bed. When Jakob had woken up alone in her hotel room, he had found a hastily scribbled note written on a pad on the dresser. 'Had to head out early. The bill is paid and there's breakfast available until ten thirty. Just make sure you're gone before noon. Nice meeting you'. The note hadn't been signed.

He looked over at her now. She was curled up in a rocking chair, feet tucked under her bottom, afghan around her shoulders. They were the only occupants of the 'relaxation' room. Cindy had told him that the room had started off as a great idea, a place where agents could wind down between tasks. But, just like the personal lives some people tried to have, the work had slowly inched its way in. Unmarked boxes were piled beside the rocker, and even the windowsill had been used for storage. Jakob moved some boxes off the sofa and stretched out as much as the short couch would allow, sure that the rocker was the more comfortable choice. Nothing like sleeping at work during your first day on the job, he thought.

October 24th, 1999
New York City

She was seated in an old rocking chair, in one of the playrooms of the orphanage. A large black woman, she didn't take no shit from those damn kids. They feared her, but, boy, did she adore them.

Right now, she was holding a young, white boy. She looked down at the child in her arms, almost two years old now. He was so cute, with his pale skin and dark, curly hair. She couldn't believe the boy had yet to find a home. He had arrived early in his life, and white, male new-borns were typically placed in a permanent home very quickly. In all her years of working at this place, she had never seen a white boy quite like this one. He must have been born under a very unlucky moon.

He was asleep, his startling blue eyes hidden behind closed eyelids. He did not sleep peacefully, and his eyes twitched back and forth beneath his skin. Every couple of minutes a stifled cry escaped his lips. The boy wore a strange birthmark on his skin, a dark, star-shaped splotch that covered most of the left side of his face. While the birthmark had most certainly lessened his chances of being chosen by eager, would-be parents, that wasn't the main reason he was still here.

In his short life, he had already been fostered by three different families. It was always the same story.

"The boy won't stop crying, not even while we feed him…he literally fights the bottle!"

"He even cries in his sleep."

"I'm sorry, but we just can't."

The longest time he had ever spent away from the orphanage had been five days. Abbie shook her head, disgusted. She raged inside her mind. She couldn't believe these damn people, acting like babies was animals. Bringing back a child, bah!

This boy tugged at her heartstrings. Ever since he had arrived, they had developed a special bond. Every time the baby would start that crying up, everyone would say 'take him to Abbie, she'll calm him down'. Yep, she and this boy had some kind of special bond. Her Willis had died the night little Chapman had come to the orphanage. She had done a lot of crying in those first days and her little Chapman had been there crying right along with her. How she had clung to that boy. How he had made her feel needed.

With her Willis gone, she had been telling herself that God didn't have no use for her no more. But when she had come back to work a week later, she'd met her Chapman. She started hanging out at the orphanage even when it wasn't her shift. If she hadn't been so old, she would have tried to adopt the boy herself. But God knew no one could raise a child on what these here folks were paying her. So, she promised the boy she would be with him until God didn't need her here no more. She was a bright spot in the boy's life until he reached the ripe old age of eight. God must have thought he was spoiling the boy, letting her stay for so long.

Abbie and Willis had never had any children. They had never had the money to find out why, but it suited them just fine. Willis had been a door-to-door insurance salesman and Abbie had worked in the orphanage most of her life. Anyone looking in on their lives might have felt sympathy, or even sadness, for their situation. But they had loved each other, and most days that had been enough.

What little money they had left at her death, Abbie had willed to the orphanage, to go into a fund for Chapman. She had figured that would get him some nice Christmas gifts until he was eighteen. She had said in her will not to tell him the gifts were from her, but to say they were from Santa. The boy had been gifted with such an imagination and had once written her a Christmas story about Santa moving to Florida. In it, Santa had ended up burning his fat belly in the sun and Mrs Claus had shown up and dragged him back to the North Pole by one ear. The elves had spread marshmallow cream on his sunburn, and it had magically disappeared.

While the orphanage hadn't paid Abbie a large wage, they had shown their appreciation for her in other ways. After her husband had died, they had given her a retirement party every year, even though she had never retired.

Every year, some random employee would say, "Abbie, you retired?"

"Nah," she would say, shaking her head. "Ain't never gonna happen."

As much as Abbie had been feared by those children who had tried to shirk their chores, she had been even more so loved. On the day of her funeral, paid for by the orphanage, most of the children were walked down to the church to pay their respects and say goodbye. When they returned, they had been treated to one last retirement party and had enjoyed her favourite treat: German Chocolate Cake. She had discovered the cake at a bakery expo she occasionally attended with a women's group from her church. It was such a rich confection that she and 'the girls' had joked that it must have been created by the devil himself. Abbie had not known if the devil was fond of baking, but she had known she never wanted to find out. With every bite of the rich confection, she had crossed herself. Just in case.

Chapter 6

July 8th, 2010
Seattle, Washington

John Sagan was seated on a stage, his white Stetson, black cowboy boots, and silver metallic belt buckle setting him apart from the other speakers. He was restless and excited, the heels of his boots tapping wildly against the wooden flooring. On the ground between his feet lay a manila folder. His hands were itching to open it again. Instead, he made them busy by holding onto his hat, spinning it slowly as he moved his hands along the rim.

They were in a crowded conference hall, people milling about, finding their seats, ready to get started. He was in Seattle attending Criminal Con, a convention more for crime enthusiasts than professionals, but he had always found the experience enlightening in the past. Used to be that he would refer to some of the people here as 'vultures', picking at the carcasses of the world's ills. He had also compared them to rubberneckers, unable to look away from the everyday accidents that claimed people's lives. But he had come to realise that there were good people in these crowds, some interested because of mere curiosity, but others ready to lend a keen eye and thoughtful detective work to help law enforcement. With all the crime in the country, there was no way that every law enforcement agency was aware of connections across state and county lines, and crime enthusiasts could sometimes provide overlooked information crucial to solving a case.

The din was loud, creating a torrent of sound that seemed to come from one entity. Why were people so oblivious to the strength of their own voices? Sagan looked out over the crowd. Did they realise the difference they could make in the world if they all just got together and…well, he supposed that was why they were all here, wasn't it? Sure, they were here to be entertained; to scratch that itch, that burning curiosity, that fascination with human degradation. But despite all the horror he had seen in the world, Sagan still believed that, at the end of the day, most people truly wanted to be heroes. They were here because they wanted to be part of the team. They wanted to be one of the good guys.

Sagan shook his head. Was that what he was? A good guy? Did he really believe in such childish notions anymore? He had learnt a long time ago that the world was not divided into good and bad people. He knew that everyone, no matter how much they loved their child, or their spouse, or their dog…everyone could do bad things.

As the MC headed to the stage, the din died down to silence.

"Welcome to this year's Criminal Con!"

The excitement was thick in the air, the crowd

erupting into hollers and applause. The MC went on to introduce the speakers, and the events that would be held at the convention. Sagan was there to hold a lecture on basic forensics and crime scene processing. He enjoyed sharing his knowledge with others if it was in a lecture format but did not do well with questions. He chalked this up to his lack of team spirit. Fortunately, the people who usually signed up for these lectures were newbies to the scene, and rarely had the guts to ask questions.

He was personally interested in the Cold Case workshop, a new class at the convention. Attendees who had paid for the workshop would be assigned a cold case randomly, have the opportunity to look into the case for the duration of the four-day event, and then would be asked to turn it back in, with any notes or insights they had come up with. A fresh pair of eyes on a dead case sometimes helped.

Sagan was taking part in this workshop himself and had been assigned a case from California, a case that seemed eerily familiar to one he had recently been asked to consult on. Before taking to the stage, Sagan had taken a moment to peruse the contents of the file; he had read a small part of the summary, discussing the sexual molestation and murder of a young white girl, found with carvings upon her body and a Polaroid picture, featuring another assumed victim, this one with black skin and bearing a carving of a werewolf.

February 6th, 2010
Athens, Ohio

"Hey, John. Thanks for coming out. I appreciate having some fresh eyes on this one. We've got nothing."

Sagan reached out his right hand. "Good to see you again, Joe. Wish it could be under better circumstances. You wanna walk me through the scene?"

Joe Collins, a homicide detective with the Athens Police Department, lifted the yellow police tape as they ducked underneath it. They were both wearing gloves and shoe coverings, as the scene hadn't been cleared yet.

"We were called to the scene by the mother of the victim, born as Robert Smith, known at the time of death as Sadie Smith. The mother, Geneva, had come by with a pie. She hadn't talked to her son...sorry...daughter...in several months. The last time they spoke, there had been a big argument. Apparently, they used to argue a lot, and always about Rob's...umm, sorry...Sadie's decision to...become a woman. Mrs Smith blamed Sadie for breaking up her marriage."

"Do you like the mom as a suspect?"

"Well, we have considered it, of course, but it really doesn't make any sense. And we have her voice on a recording at the approximate time of death. She had been making a call to a suicide hotline. She and a counsellor had spoken for over two hours. Two days later, she showed up at her child's place to make amends. Says that she made peace with God and wanted to apologise to her daughter. She wanted to let her know that she was loved and accepted."

"A little late for that, I guess."

They had come to the front door of the dilapidated wooden house and Joe began rummaging through his pockets for the key. "Yeah. She's been having a hard time. Apparently, she and her ex-husband are working on getting back together." Joe finally located the skeleton key and turned the lock.

As Sagan followed the other detective into the house, he asked, "And the father?"

"He was in Alabama at a family reunion. Tons of pictures, credit card purchases, and more. Iron tight alibi. With this one, it just don't sit right that it was someone in the family."

"Friends?"

"Well, there was this one girl, Mary. She showed up at the funeral; there were very few people there, so we were interested. She was crying and carrying on. I interviewed her, investigated her. Turned out she had a lot of hate posts against trans people on her Facebook page. Me and Jimmy, we questioned her hard. Gave her the whole 'good cop, bad cop' bullshit. Turns out, she had been coming out of a club downtown one night, ended up on the side of the building throwing up. A couple of guys grabbed her and dragged her down behind the dumpster. Started ripping off her clothes. And Sadie, well, Sadie rescued her. Took off her high heels and started using them as tools to beat the men. Scared them off. Saved Mary from rape. Or worse."

"Wow."

"Sadie wanted her to go to the police, but Mary

was so drunk she said she wouldn't be able to identify the perps."

"Didn't Sadie see them?"

"Well, Mary didn't think the police would listen to a black trans woman."

"Hmm. Maybe I could talk to her? Surely she knows some locals who might have taken it upon themselves to get rid of…" Joe was shaking his head. "What?"

"Well, the girl killed herself. She was pretty fucked up with guilt after the murder. Blamed herself for feeding into the whole anti-trans rhetoric. And there's a lot of people here who think she done it. A lot of people thanking her for it."

"But there's no actual evidence pointing that way."

"That's right. Chief wants to make sure we've done everything we can before he closes the case. The last thing we need is some national coverage saying we didn't do our jobs because the victim was black and trans. You know how it is these days."

The officers walked through the kitchen and out into the hall. The wall was covered in an old green floral wallpaper, with several large areas that had peeled away to reveal ugly concrete beneath. A large mirror covered the wall to the right, and it looked as if the mirror had been punched. Cracks travelled out in multiple directions from a single place of impact, and pieces of the glass were missing.

"Indication of a struggle?"

"No. According to the mom, that's been there a

while. Sadie punched it a few months back during one of their quarrels. His...I mean...her body was found in the bedroom upstairs."

"From what I've heard, the scene was brutal, but I haven't seen any photos yet."

"I brought the file with me. I've got the pictures here, and a video recording back at the station if you want to take a look." They were standing in front of the bedroom. Someone had closed the door.

"Was the door closed when the mother arrived?"

"Yep. It was locked. A skeleton key can be used on any of the doors in the house."

"The mother had a key?"

"Yeah. She had insisted that she needed a key, especially since she provided the down payment on the house for...Sadie."

Sagan opened the door and stepped into the room. The linen had been taken off the bed, but the mattress remained. It was soaked through with blood. There was no obvious blood anywhere else in the room. Sagan walked around the bed, noting a broken lamp on the floor.

"When we arrived, the mother was hysterical, standing outside the house. She said she couldn't walk into the room, and I believe her. There wasn't a trace of blood on her. There was a single drinking glass with an unknown substance on the nightstand beside the bed. I'm still waiting on the lab for a full analysis, but it should come back soon."

"You said you have the file?"

Joe handed him a folder and Sagan spread it open

carefully on a nearby dresser.

"As you can see, the penis was removed from the body. Severed with a serrated blade. Full autopsy hasn't come back yet, but it's likely blood loss was the cause of death."

"What am I looking at here?" Sagan was holding a glossy photo, turning it in multiple directions, trying to figure out how it should be viewed.

"That's his chest area, around his left nipple, and then down his...damn...I mean, her side. Sorry, I'm a little new to this whole gender-changing business, but my ma always told me to respect the dead."

"I understand, Joe. You're doing just fine for an old geezer." Sagan gave him a wink and then looked back down at the image. "Is that a...werewolf?" A carving had been made on the woman's chest, the nipple cut away, the exposed flesh forming the snout of the creature. The wolf-like creature was standing on two legs, and a giant penis hung between its legs.

"There's another carving on her back. It's of a sheep. We're assuming it's some kind of hate crime, or maybe a jilted lover? Man, I don't know. We've questioned just about everybody in the damn town. Nothing is turning up on this one."

"Where was the penis found?"

"It wasn't."

Chapter 7

May 15th, 2011
London, Ohio

"You didn't?! Right between his legs?"

Cindy was laughing. "Yep, kicked him square in the dick. Even gave him fair warning."

Cindy was sitting with Brittany, the local bartender at Jim's Bar, a hangout for local cops.

"I heard some of the guys talking about it, but I didn't know it had been you! Wow. You know, he hasn't hit on me since then." Brittany took a swig of her beer and added, "Well, nothing physical anyway. He's still asked for my phone number a couple of times."

Cindy leaned over the bar and whispered, "You should get a cattle prod." The two women burst out laughing.

"Damn, I can dream, honey. You know, I've heard them talking to that new guy, Steve. They were warning him off you."

Cindy drained her glass of whiskey. "Yeah?"

"They weren't telling him about the bruising you gave Jamie, they were telling him to treat you like a little sister."

"Hmm, well isn't that something. Can't be because I'm a respected co-worker, huh?" The women both shook their heads. "I don't know how you do it, Britt. I would not survive in a place like this."

"Most of 'em mean well. They just ain't got no sense, especially when they're filled up with beer. I don't know how you handle 'em sober."

"Well, they have a little more sense when they haven't been drinking."

"No, I mean, I don't know how you can stand them when *you're* sober." This triggered another laughing fit. A group of men were staring over at them anxiously.

"They're probably thinking nothing good can come of two women laughing hysterically." Cindy laid a twenty on the bar and got up from her stool. "Catch ya later, woman. Make a shit ton of money tonight!"

She walked out the door and headed to the liquor store across the street. She felt like picking up something fancy. And the cashier just happened to be a young blond guy with blue eyes. Perfect.

He greeted her as she walked in. "Something I can help you find?"

"You got something for a single lady who likes whiskey and who has the next couple days off work?"

"Have you ever tried Sheep Dip?"

She raised her right eyebrow, put a hand on her hip, and asked, "Is that a euphemism or something?"

The young man, whose name tag said Angus, laughed. "No, ma'am, it's a brand of whiskey from Scotland. We just got it in, and it's been selling really well. All we have left is the gift pack which comes with a fifth of the whiskey and two shot glasses."

"Hmm. Angus, huh? Did Scotland send you over here to sell whiskey?"

"Yes, ma'am. I mean…no…ma'am." He looked confused. "Should I ring you up?"

"Well, abso–fucking–lutely! Let's give it a try. Just promise me you'll stop calling me ma'am. At least for now."

While Angus headed towards the cash register, Cindy ripped out a blank page from her notepad and scribbled down her phone number. After paying for her purchase, she handed the slip of paper to the young man in front of her.

"There's two shot glasses in that box, Angus. And I'm hoping that one of them has your name on it." She was delighted to see him blush. "Give me a call when you get off. Hopefully, I won't be too drunk to know who you are."

As she turned to walk out, her phone started ringing. It was an unknown number. She picked up after the third ring. "Goddammit. This better not be Sagan."

"Hey, Cin."

"This can't be Sagan, because Sagan told me that I wouldn't hear his pretty little Texas drawl all weekend. Sagan told me that I would have the WHOLE weekend off. Weekends. You ever heard of those?"

"Please tell me you're not drunk yet."

"I am not drunk. Yet."

"Great!" The joke was lost on him.

"I said yet. As in, I am in the process. Of getting

drunk."

"Well, I'm glad I caught you in time."

"Okay, boss. What's up?" She turned back towards the cash register, certain that her weekend plans were ruined. She looked directly at Angus, noticing for the first time that his long hair covered a scar down the right side of his face. Why were scars so damn sexy? She imagined running her finger down that scar and tracing a line to his lips, getting her finger, and other things, wet. She heaved a deep sigh. She knew she didn't have time for a relationship. She wasn't asking for one. All she wanted was a night…just one goddamn night.

"I'm not even on your payroll, you know, Sagan."

She could imagine the death grip Sagan had on his phone when he said, "We got one. It's him."

"I'm going to have to ask for a rain check on that glass of whiskey, Angus. Don't lose that number now, you hear?" He waved at her as she left the store, bell jingling as it opened.

"Angus?"

"Don't worry about it, boss. See you in ten." She took one last look inside the store, at the handsome young man, as she walked away. He had gotten out the broom and was twirling it around as if it were a dance partner.

"Cindy?"

"Yeah?"

"You might not be on my payroll, but you still call me boss." Sagan erupted into laughter and then hung up on Cindy spewing obscenities down the dead phone line.

March 23rd, 1993
Ephratah, New York

Arthur Blakemore was not what you would call a handsome white man. In fact, he almost looked like a genetic experiment gone wrong. He was bald and overweight, his face pudgy and uneven, his eyes slack, with one drooping lower than the other. You might be drawn in by his appearance and immediately want to look away. But you would have to keep looking. The hairs on the back of your neck would stand up straight; your hypothalamus would signal your pituitary gland to release a chemical signal into the bloodstream, while simultaneously transmitting a nerve signal down the spinal cord, both signals heading to the adrenal glands. Why? To tell you to wake the fuck up. To tell you that you should either put on your running shoes or strap on your boxing gloves. Arthur Blakemore might be one ugly son of a bitch, but he was rich. And he exuded power.

He had never married, and rarely had female company, but he had a soft spot for little girls. And they had a soft spot for him. His ugliness gave him an advantage when it came to young girls. They felt sorry for him. They always felt like they alone could love him, could save him. He had never meant to keep one. But after seeking her out night after night for a month, he had made arrangements for one of the girls to come live with him permanently.

Legal papers had been drawn up, showing a distant relationship between them, and a sad story of dead parents that painted him as a generous benefactor who would now care for the girl. He had placed her in a country home, and for a time, had stayed with her. Eventually, she had become pregnant and he had come by to see her less and less. While the girl had been loving and kind to him, he could see that she was slowly becoming despondent. He had thought of abortion but decided against it, hoping the child might bring her some joy. He was no monster; he had wanted her to be happy.

His infatuation had ultimately left the poor girl, and her two children, in a rather sad state. Eventually, he had decided the kids should be schooled and had more papers drawn up: more distant relatives shown to be now in his care. While the oldest child had been told that he was his father, he had told both boys to call him 'Uncle Art', and had never responded to 'father' or 'daddy'. He had often told the girl not to refer to him as such.

"I am no good as a father," he had told her.

She had then cried and run from him, her hopes and dreams dripping warm down her face. Like always, she had tugged at his heart. He had wondered how long he could keep this creature locked away from the world, a thing bought, a thing paid for, a thing owned.

When he had learnt about the incident at school, he had taken a special trip out to visit the large house in the middle of nowhere, the kind of nowhere that consisted of two hundred and fifty-six acres worth of estate. It had been evening when he had finished reading the article in the paper about the school incident. He had just taken a bite of his ribeye when he had realised the strange boy described in the article, from the school where his two illegitimate sons attended, might be his. He had thrown the paper away from himself and at the same time, pushed off from the table, the chair legs shrieking as they had bitten into the wood floor. He had spit the steak from his mouth in disgust and exploded out of his chair, calling for his driver.

When he had arrived at the house, the girl, who had once stirred his passion like no other, was passed out on the couch, empty wine bottles surrounding her. He had looked down at her snoring form, languidly taking in the short jean shorts and the tight, white tank top that exposed her midriff. He had always loved her dark, exotic skin. He had reached out and squeezed her breast through the cotton, toying with her nipple until it was taut between his fingers, before moving on to the next one. He had known that he would have to handle this situation; do something for the two boys this miserable creature had brought into the world. But not just then. Just then, there had been more important matters at hand.

The girl had roused and smiled up at him, asking, "Am I dreaming?"

He had taken her dainty hand, not much bigger than a child's, and moved it to the crotch of his pants. She had immediately unbuttoned him and pulled down his zipper as he removed his own shirt. She had moved clumsily, still full of alcohol and sleep, and the man had reached out to flip her face down onto the couch. He had entered the girl roughly. Knowing this would be the last time he imbibed of this particular vintage had made this encounter almost as good as the first time. He had dug his nails into her back while thrusting himself inside her, rivulets of blood forming at the base of her neck. He had bent down to lick the red streaks, some animal instinct causing him to bite into her flesh. God, he would miss her.

She had turned her face away from the couch and he had taken the opportunity to press his hand against her skull, to better gain traction for his thrusting. He had seen her eyes widen in surprise and she had tried to make some form of protest, but he had quieted her with a gentle shushing and wrapped her hair around his fist. He had thought she was responding to his power over her, but her surprise had been directed at the eyes, staring out at them from the dark corner by the chair.

The father had been unaware that his eldest son sat watching while his mother was yanked up by her hair into a kneeling position. Unaware that the child had seen him invite his driver over to partake of the naked flesh he held in his grip. Unaware that little ears had heard him say to the girl, "I really let this go on too long. I'm sorry". He had been oblivious to the wide eyes taking in his every move, as he had walked over to his leather satchel and removed a syringe. Oblivious to the boy noticing the flash of jealousy which had crossed his features, as he took in the scene before him: another man fucking his prized possession.

His driver had been on his back, skin pushed into the rug on the floor, the girl sitting in his lap, held up by the driver's hand around her throat. He had held her in place while he pumped his hips, his other hand gripping her ass. He had moaned and whispered up to her, "You like that, huh? You like that big cock?"

Frank was not only a driver for Arthur Blakemore, he was also a 'fixer', and he had the customary look of hired muscle. He was tall and well-built, with slicked-back dark hair, wearing an expensively fitted suit and dark shades. He was well-paid but counted Arthur as a friend, not just an employer. Not the kind of friend who would invite you to eat at their table, of course, but a friend you could count on to get you out of a tough spot. He would never call Arthur a friend to his face though. Arthur was his boss first and foremost. He respected the man, loved him even, and he would do anything for him. He was surprised when Arthur invited him over to share the girl, but it didn't set off any alarm bells. He took it as a boon, a reward, for a job well done.

They had come to make the girl disappear, but that didn't mean they couldn't have a little fun with her first. God, she was cute, even with the stench of alcohol exuding from her pores. Her brown hair surrounded her face, but he could still see that her eyes were closed. She appeared drugged and out of it. He moved his hand up to her throat, tightening his grip enough to get a response from her. She opened her pale green eyes, and suddenly looked sick.

He had just enough time to say, "Don't...don't do it..." before he climaxed into her while she vomited all over his chest, the top half of her body falling to the ground beside him as she did so. There was nothing like having warm, putrid vomit spewed out onto your chest while reaching nirvana. Frank was stunned by the event and quickly moved to push the girl off his lap and stand up. Thinking to himself that his day couldn't get any worse, Frank was ill-prepared when Arthur grabbed him from behind and stabbed him in the eye with the syringe. As the syringe was depressed and the fentanyl-laced concoction entered his brain tissue, Frank barely had time to register that his day had, in fact, just gotten worse.

Arthur let the rancid man slip to the ground and stepped over him to reach Frank's clothes. Arthur was still naked, and he was looking forward to a hot shower. After a couple of minutes of searching, he found what he was looking for, in a leather sheath placed carefully in a shoe. He looked at the Persian rug below his feet, admiring the washed-out blues and golds that lay in a pattern he had been fond of for years. It was a shame, but he would have to sacrifice it. He felt no remorse for the fact that he regretted the loss of the silk rug, but not the loss of the man at his feet. He had long ago come to terms with the type of man he was, and he didn't lose any sleep over it.

He walked over to the girl, slumped on her side, vomit sticky in her hair. Arthur tenderly moved the hair away from her face and wiped her skin clean with Frank's discarded white button-down. He ran his thumb across her bottom lip, then drew the serrated blade across her throat, warm blood drenching him and the rug below. He stayed with her until she was gone. It didn't take long. He gently laid her lifeless body face down on the carpet, then turned to deal with Frank's body. He rolled the man up in the Persian rug and tossed it onto his shoulder, making such a feat appear effortless. He buried the body in the woods, the hole already prepared by Frank, hours before. He knew he still had a body to bury, but he went to take a shower anyway.

After Arthur had left the living room, the little boy crawled out from behind his hiding spot and stared down at the woman who had been his mother. Her blood had made two jagged streams on either side of her shoulders, joining into one and stopping just below her shoulder blades.

"Mamma?" His voice was unsure and barely audible. The house was so quiet he was not sure that he had spoken at all. This world seemed incapable of containing sound. It seemed as if he were in a vacuum, unable to even think. "Mamma!"

Her eyes were open, but they did not see him.

He crouched down and touched her face, blood squishing between his toes. The boy was naked except for his tighty-whities. "Mamma, please wake up." In his hands, he gripped a round piece of leather, heart-like shapes carved out around the edges. They were far from perfect, but he was proud of them, and he had been driven to share the leatherwork with his mother. The boy snuggled up beside her and stuck his thumb in his mouth, a habit that he had broken two years before.

When Arthur walked back into the living room, clothed

in a red tracksuit already dripping with sweat, he found the boy sleeping against a corpse long cold. He roused him awake, the boy reaching up to cling to his broad neck, quiet. They sat on the couch and Arthur reached up to unhook the boy's hands and face him forward in his lap.

"What did I tell you about thumb-sucking?" Arthur had meant it as a rhetorical question, sure the boy would be too shaken to answer. He was surprised when the boy, his son, answered in a crisp and steady voice.

"That it's only for babies," the boy had said, removing his thumb from his mouth, his eyes transfixed on his mother below him. The leatherwork lay on her outstretched right arm, blood peeking out through the heart-like cutaways.

"I'm really sorry, son." It was the first time he had ever called the boy that. "Your mother wasn't doing a very good job of keeping us together. She wasn't doing a good job raising you. Or your brother. I've made some arrangements for both of you." The boy did not react, sitting stoically in Arthur's lap.

"I've put a couple of bags by the front door. Do you think you could go pack up some of your things?"

The boy nodded.

"Just the most important things. One bag is for you and one is for your brother. Can you pick out some things for your brother as well?"

Another nod.

"Alright, run along now. I have to take care of your mother, okay?"

The boy looked up at him and his voice was

steady when he said, "Okay, Uncle Art. Just the most important things." He hopped off the couch and ran in the direction of the front door.

Arthur had already procured new surnames for the boys, hoping their pasts would not follow them. He knew of a prestigious boarding school that would take the boys with no questions asked, as long as the right palms were greased, and their bills paid for. Money was never an object, and he would make sure they were cared for. His eldest, well, he would need some extra care. Behavioural therapy should do the trick, Arthur would spare no expense. No matter his insistence that the boys were not to call him father, he had an uncharacteristic liking for the eldest.

The next few minutes were easy for the boy. He packed away his camera and a single Polaroid of his mother, the black feather he had kept from the bird, his leatherworking and whittling tools, a few clothes, and even fewer toys. Then he packed his brother's clothes, his Superman night light, a few toys, and a blue satin baby blanket. After putting the filled bags next to the front door, he went to fetch his brother, who was untroubled in sleep, a peaceful visage of a dreaming child.

The eldest boy began to cry softly and crawled into the bed beside his brother.

"Bubba? Was wrong? Bubba?"

"Shh. It's okay, Lucas. Go back to sleep, now."

"I'm thirsty."

"Okay. Okay, I'll go get you some water."

"I get it. I'm a big boy."

"Alright, come on. Follow me."

The two boys made their way to the kitchen, Lucas trailing a soft blanket behind him. Lucas used the stepladder to reach the sink and poured himself some water into a plastic tumbler.

"See? Told you," he grinned, walking to the table and sitting down with his brother, a look of pride and accomplishment on his face.

"Good job, Lucas. You're such a big boy."

"Is mommy sleeping?"

"Listen, Lucas. I must tell you something important, okay? It's a little bit scary, but I don't want you to cry."

"O...kay. Okay, bubba."

"Mommy went on a trip, but we're going to be with her soon, okay? Uncle Art's going to take us on a trip. And it's going to be scary, but we're going to be together. I'll always be your big brother, and I'll always take care of you, okay?"

It would be almost fifteen years before either one of them returned to the house.

April 19th, 2013
Hunter, New York

I heard the doorbell ringing from the comfort of my warm room and jumped up from my laptop, running over to my spy panel. It was risky, but I opened it up anyway. Surely, curiosity doesn't always kill the cat? I could hear you running down the stairs, your voice giddy as you yelled excitedly.

"Coming, girl!"

I was about to see the infamous Bella, your most trusted confidant. I don't know why my heart fluttered manically in my chest at the thought of finally seeing her. Perhaps your excitement was just contagious.

You opened the door and were instantly embraced by an Asian beauty with long black hair, tips frosted. The female squealing and hugging lasted for about ten minutes, and was finally broken up by a skinny, gangly Asian guy with a dark black moustache and expertly tousled hair. He wedged an arm between the two of you and demanded a hug of his own.

"Daniel!"

You hugged him warmly while Bella made her way into the house.

"Damn, Jewels, this place is fucking CRAZY!"

Bella ran into the front living room and dove onto the giant sofa, throwing her purse in my general direction and kicking off her heels.

"Damn, that drive was long. Can we just chill here tonight? I don't feel up to a night on the town."

"I figured you wouldn't."

You and Daniel joined her on the couch, one on each side of her long body. You were all so comfortable with each other, as if this were an everyday occurrence, the three of you inseparable. Isabella put her head in your lap.

"Jewels?"

"Yeah?"

"Please tell me you have ice cream."

"Oh, I've got ice cream, but we've gotta eat first."

You said it with a mischievous glint in your eye and Bella was clearly intrigued.

"Ooh, what do you have?"

As you stood up from the couch you said, "Well, I don't have it yet."

And that was when the doorbell rang again. I had overheard you talking about your plans for a 'bachelorette' or 'over-the-bastard' party with Daniel, but I wasn't quite prepared for what was about to follow.

You opened the door to an older Asian gentleman, who briefly bowed his head before stepping inside. He headed to the kitchen, followed by six other men, all of them younger and wearing considerably fewer clothes. Each one of them was pushing a tall, covered cart. While most of the men appeared Asian, two had a much darker complexion than expected.

You looked towards the couch to find two mouths agape.

Bella said, "Okay. Please tell me you have alcohol."

Daniel stood up. "No alcohol for me, but I will go have another look at those fine ass men."

The three of you headed towards the kitchen and I quickly moved to my favourite viewing spot, the grate above the hallway. From there I could see that the men had started cooking. Most were chopping fresh ingredients. Only the oldest man seemed to be allowed to do the actual cooking, and he was enveloped in a halo of steam at the stove. The younger gentlemen shuffle the three of you into your seats at the long table and bring over wine glasses. One opens a bottle of Pinot Noir and pours each of you a glass, Daniel apparently forgetting that he turned down alcohol only moments before.

Julia looked over as the half-naked man filled Isabella's glass. Her best friend's mouth was still open, and she was in complete shock.

She kept looking over at Julia and mouthing, "What the absolute fuck?" over and over again.

Daniel grinned. "This is even better than I thought it would be."

"What?! You knew about this, Daniel?"

Daniel did not answer immediately, too busy watching the men move around the kitchen.

"What? Oh yes. I knew. This is all for you, honey. Just for...you," he said, never taking his eyes from the kitchen scene. "I've never been one to go in for all that K-pop nonsense, but girls...girls...this may just be a turning point."

"K-pop?" Isabella asked, puzzled. "What do you mean?"

At that moment, one of the men pulled a boombox from the bottom of a catering cart and carried it into the middle of the room. The other men joined him in a v-formation, and he leant over to push a button. Suddenly, the kitchen became a dance floor, with the caterers dancing to the recently popular song 'Gangnam Style'.

Bella erupted into laughter, dancing in her seat, an almost empty glass of wine in her hand.

"Jewels, I fucking love you, girl!" She moved to sit closer to Julia, hugging her as she passed by.

As the song progressed, each man broke away from the dance group and delivered a food item. The table quickly filled up with dishes: strips of beef marinated in soy sauce, sesame oil, garlic, and sugar; bowls of rice and noodles; kimchi; other vegetables; some kind of chicken soup, and a multitude of dumplings, some steamed and others fried.

While the friends ate, the men went about cleaning up the kitchen and preparing dessert. The three of them had finished three bottles of wine and demolished most of the food by the time the desserts were ready to be served: two serving dishes piled high with what looked like pancakes on one, and baklava on the other.

With the desserts laid out on the table, the men again took their places on the 'dance floor', the older man joining them this time. Then the music started playing: a recent release by PSY, entitled 'Gentlemen'.

The men engaged in a slapstick K-pop dance, the older man, seemingly so innocent, playing pranks on the other dancers until they all ended up on the floor while he stood above them, laughing. Julia looked over at Bella, entranced by the woman's mirth, and reached out an arm to envelope her friend in a hug.

"Love you, Bella."

The dancers finished cleaning the kitchen and packed up their things, leaving the desserts behind.

"Still want ice cream?"

Isabella laughed. "I never want to eat again. Thanks, guys." She hugged both of them tightly. "April twentieth, two thousand twelve. That was supposed to be the happiest day of my life. But this...this tops every expectation I ever had for my wedding!" They all fell into fits of laughter, Daniel ending up on the floor, his nose on a tile.

"God, I can still smell them. Jewels, make them come back?"

Julia slapped him on the ass and beckoned him toward the stairs. "Come on stud, come on Bella, let me show you guys your rooms."

Isabella came stumbling behind her, slurring her words. "I used to ha...hate...all that...K-pop sh...shtuff."

Julia wrapped her arm around Bella's waist. "I know."

Isabella continued. "Asians aren't just some...some...fetish...or something. Some fat...fet...fetish...for white people."

Daniel chirped up behind them. "Well, they can be a fetish for this Asian anytime."

They may have been drunk, but they were not drunk enough to handle the searing look Bella threw her brother's way over her shoulder. Daniel caught himself on the wall as he went into full-body laughter. He was gasping for breath.

"Was that? Was that supposed to be scary?"

The girls left him at the bottom of the stairs, each shaking their heads, Julia pushing Bella from behind all the way up to the second floor.

"I should change, Jewels."

"Don't worry about it. We can bring your luggage up tomorrow. One night without PJs won't kill you."

There were no further objections. Bella fell onto the bed, face down and diagonal, making it near impossible to get her under the comforter. Eventually, Julia gave up, spreading a baby-blue throw with pink flowers over her friend instead. Before Julia had even reached the door, Bella was snoring. Blowing her sleeping friend a goodnight kiss, she turned off the lights, closing the door behind her.

The next week went by in a blur. Daniel and Bella spent most of their time at the foundation while Julia worked; there were plenty of things to keep them occupied, and they made fast friends with 'the Starbucks girls', so named because of the young women's newfound obsession with the coffee shop.

When Julia had first met with Ava, they had walked across the street to Starbucks. Ava had picked out a vanilla bean Frappuccino, venti of course, with a ton of whipped cream. When she had returned with the tasty beverage in hand, it had not taken long before every girl was clamouring for a sip and a drink of their own. Julia had walked them all over to the store and used the foundation's credit card to order them whatever they wanted.

Upon hearing their story, the manager of the Starbucks provided each of the children with a reusable tumbler and told them they were welcome to come and fill it up with a drink once a day, on the house. The girls were never without their tumblers after that.

Bella had enjoyed drawing in the past but had not picked up her passion since high school; it wasn't a talent her parents had wanted her to pursue. But being at the foundation gave her an opportunity to start working on a piece, and she had picked up a variety of pencils and started on a self-portrait. She hadn't meant for it to be much of anything, but by the end of the week, it was, and she had managed to capture her own face in a photorealistic style that impressed the daily viewers of her progress.

She had started off drawing in the main workroom, supplies laid out in front of her on a long cafeteria-style table. By the start of her third day, Patrick had met her in the workroom and brought her to a small studio, her portrait arranged on a drawing board attached to an easel.

"Thanks, Patrick. Can you let the girls know where I am if they ask?"

"Sure thing! There's a stereo here, if you'd like some music. And there are chairs in the closet if anyone wants to join you."

Patrick looked over at the easel and shook his head. "That's amazing. Do you show anywhere?"

Isabella laughed at him. "No. My parents don't raise artists. They raise doctors."

"And are you a doctor?"

Isabella laughed again. "No, I guess I'm not. My brother and I are the black sheep of the family. I'm a speech therapist…"

Patrick let out a shocked gasp and clutched his chest with his right hand, as if her career choice were the most scandalous thing he had ever heard.

Bella laughed. "I know, right? How dare I do that to my parents?"

"And what does Daniel do?"

"Well, I don't think you will be surprised to hear that he works at a beauty salon. His main thing is hair, but he's quite fond of doing nails as well."

"You don't say?"

Daniel had been spending his days doing free haircuts and makeovers for the staff, as well as the children and adult patrons coming and going for art workshops. He had brought his supplies, under the assumption that the victims of a sex ring might enjoy a reimagining of themselves.

On his way out of the door, Patrick said, "I'll see you later, Bella. Good luck with your work!"

Bella spent several hours working on the portrait, even skipping lunch with Julia and Daniel. She had been taken over by an insane urge to finish. It was no longer just a thing to do to kill time. It was an exorcism. A way to sanitize the corners of her mind. A way to bleach her ex out of her life.

In the portrait, Isabella's head was thrown back in pain, her mouth open, teeth missing, with blood, dripping out of the corner of her mouth. In her hair were tangles of fingers and hands, twisting and gripping her strands and pulling them away from her skull. Her eyes were clenched shut, but miniature arms could be seen among her eyelashes and eyebrows, each struggling to open her eyelids. On her left eye, a few had succeeded, and in the visible part of the iris, you could see a reflection of the bottom half of a man and woman, engaged in the act of sex.

On either side of her face, growing from each cheek and protruding outward from the jawline, was a thick tusk. Carved into one tusk was the word 'fetish', the letters formed out of rolled-up hundred-dollar bills. The other tusk was adorned with carved images of some of the girls Bella had met that week: Ava, Cadence, Honey, and Asia.

She wasn't exactly sure what it was all about, and she was the one who had created it. How strange. There was definitely something in there about moving on from William, but it wasn't just that. It was about the expectations her parents had for her. Expectations from society. It was about getting used. And stereotypes. As she sat there staring at the piece, she had an overwhelming desire to set fire to it. To watch the flames curl up the paper and burn away the woman in pain.

"That's amazing, Bella. Are you done?"

Isabella was startled. She hadn't heard the girl come in. She looked up at Honey, a young girl originally from the Philippines. She gave the girl a smile, and was overjoyed to get one in return.

"I think so. I haven't done anything to it for the past hour; I've just been sitting here staring at it and thinking."

"What are you going to do with it?" Honey

pulled a chair up to the easel and sat down next to Bella.

"I was just thinking of burning it, but I don't know."

Julia came into the small studio, carrying a stack of artwork. "Don't know what?"

Bella turned around and smiled. "Hey, Jewels! Honey was just asking me what I was planning on doing with my self-portrait here."

"Perfect timing, then. Here, Bella, have a look at these." Julia spread out the art pieces on the floor in front of them. Each was a self-portrait of a girl. "Seems you've been quite the motivator. The girls have been working on their own pieces, and they've asked if they can have a show. An exhibition. I think it's an awesome idea. Why don't we include yours, too?"

Bella appeared to think it over. "Sure. I guess I'm not going to give it to my parents as a gift or anything."

Julia laughed. "If you're thinking of giving them a drawing as a gift, may I suggest one of their gay son, doing hair?"

"Shit, Julia. You are a badass."

"Just don't tell them I was the one who suggested it!"

The rest of the week went by in a blur of bars and museums; late nights with the three of them sitting in one big bed eating ice cream from the carton, and laughter.

"Thank you so much for coming, you guys." Julia stood on the front porch, each arm wrapped around a friend. There were smiles and tears and promises to visit again soon as she walked them down the front stairway and helped to put their bags in the SUV. After more hugging and more tears, Julia watched them drive away, waving until they were no longer in sight.

She turned and looked up at the house, laughing over the memories of the past week, walking slowly to the front door, afraid that the place would feel more empty than it ever had before. Instead, a warmth enveloped her as she stepped over the threshold. She had missed Bella, more than she had realised, but she was starting to feel as if she had made the right choice in coming here. Closing the door, she turned the latch, put on some classical violin music, and stripped on her way to the bathroom. She plugged the tub, added some bubbles, and turned on the water. While she filled the bath, she went to the kitchen and grabbed a Woodchuck hard apple cider. It was going to be a good day.

Part 2: Moon

"Crying aloud, he beheld her charms and felt his blood course hotly through his veins. He lifted her in his arms and carried her to a bed, where he gathered the first fruits of love. Leaving her on the bed, he returned to his own kingdom, where, in the pressing business of his realm, he for a time thought no more about this incident."

— Sun, Moon, and Talia, Giambattista Basile

Chapter 1

January 23rd, 2014
North Jackson, Ohio

It's the skin that does it for me. Well, at first, anyway. I trace every inch of skin with my fingers. My tongue. Caress every hollow, squeeze every piece of flesh in my hands. It is my canvas. For many men, I suppose, it's the breasts. They want to find their way back to their mother's bosom; suckle youth and lack of responsibility from a nurturer. Let her take care of them. But I want the back of her. I want that great expanse of skin laid out before me, hair pulled to the side, neck exposed. I want to see her helpless, wrists clasped together in my grip at the dimple above her ass, face crushed against the sheets, legs spread wide. I do not need mothering. I do not need the fake gasping of pleasure from a thing evolved to serve others. I just need skin.

I smile at the thought. Who am I kidding? I need more than that. I have never been turned on by the touch of another, and to hide my disgust, I do what pleases me instead. Paramours have always felt lucky to have such a generous and giving lover; lucky to have the attention of my body upon theirs. Those who were never exposed to my inner desires do not appreciate that they are right to feel lucky.

I look down at my latest conquest, so peaceful in her sleep. She has been drifting in and out of consciousness, crying a little when she comes to, and her eye makeup is smeared. I climb off the bed and reach for my camera. I zoom in on her face, capturing a smudge of black trailing down towards her lips, parted and wet. I make sure to get the broken earring in the shot: a green, crystal droplet hanging loosely from a strand of smaller, clear crystals, the missing pieces strewn across the bed and floor. I envision her several hours ago, picking out jewellery for her foray into the nightlife, nervous that her earrings might be too much. Too formal for a casual night of debauchery. I imagine her saying, 'fuck it, you only live once'. The thought makes me laugh and I put my mouth against her ear as I whisper, "You only *die* once too."

She had been divorced for ten months, and in that time, she had not sought any solace in the dating scene. Friends had begged and pleaded with her to 'find someone else, even if it's just for one night!'. She did not relish the idea of trying to 'score' in front of her friends; she didn't want the experience marred by their expectations. But they were right. She did need to 'get out there', and she was going to try tonight. She knew it was a stupid idea. In this day and age, you didn't go out by yourself if you were a woman. But she didn't care.

She looked at herself in the mirror, fluffing her

red hair with her hands. She couldn't tell if she looked sophisticated or trashy, in her green wrap dress with white pinstripes, a deep V in the front, and a push-up bra, which made her breasts easily visible, even if you weren't seeking them out. The dress was cinched, closed with a belt that tied into a gaudy bow. She shook her head in disgust. She looked good, yes, but she also looked like she was 'asking for it'. Her mom would not have approved. And neither would Alan, her ex-husband. That thought steadied her resolve.

She picked out some black heels that she hadn't worn in two years and grabbed her clutch from the large armoire. She caught sight of the last gift Alan had given her…a pair of dangling, teardrop, emerald earrings. They were gorgeous. She had not been able to bring herself to get rid of all the jewellery he had given her over the years; as much as she had come to despise him, she could not deny his taste in beautiful things. She sniggered. Yes, his secretary had been one such beautiful thing.

Mind made up, she delicately put on the earrings, having to pierce through skin that had not seen an earring in over half a year. Immediately, she felt better. Calmer. She loved jewellery and had not realised how much joy she had been denying herself these past months. Her legs had been shaved earlier; it had taken three razor blades to get the job done. She had forgotten how important self-care was. The reflection she saw in the small mirror of the armoire looked stunning. Her makeup was flawless, and the earrings sparkled. She tried a smile and found that it looked genuine. She was going to do this. Any man would be lucky to have her.

Speaking aloud, she made a pact with her reflection. "From now on, you shave at least once a week. And you wear as much jewellery as you want, whenever you want." She nodded at herself and then headed to the garage.

She was going to be visiting an upscale wine bar called Gallery. It was a posh place with rich clientele, and not only had a full bar of rare and expensive wines, but also showcased artwork from local artists. She wasn't sure that she would meet the right kind of guy there, but she was confident that she wouldn't meet anyone she knew, and that was the important thing.

She found a parking space that wasn't too far away; she had barely walked in the heels and they were already killing her. No wonder she hadn't worn them in so long. She made a mental note to burn them as soon as she got home. Well, assuming she didn't get 'lucky'. She wasn't even inside and already she wanted to run back home, hide under her covers, and cry herself to sleep.

"Goddammit! You are going to do this. You deserve this." Cursing to herself, she grabbed her clutch bag from the passenger seat and exited the car. As she locked the Mercedes, she heard the familiar beep that meant it was secure. The familiarity made her feel stable. Placing the keys in her purse, she patted the small can of mace she had hidden in there. She would be fine. Tonight, she was not a young divorcee. No, she was going to be someone else, someone who liked fancy bars and expensive wine. She took a deep breath at the door, composed herself, and stepped inside.

Ten minutes later, she was seated alone at the bar, a glass of port in her hand. She had told the bartender, "Give me something sweet and expensive, and keep them coming."

He had looked her over like a piece of meat, hanging in a butcher's window, and asked, "How expensive?"

Good call, Mr Bartender. She had floundered at the question, but Mr Bartender had come to her rescue.

"Tell you what, hon. If you're paying, I'll give you the twelve-dollar port. If someone starts picking up your tab like you're hoping…" he directed a pointed look towards her exposed cleavage and gestured to her with a twirl of his hand "…I'll give you the thirty-dollars-a-glass port."

Some women might have been offended by the bartender's demeanour, but Candace found it refreshing. She had a soft spot for flamboyantly gay men, and people who were frank. This creature was both. She glanced down at his nametag and asked, "Jerome, what if he's wearing a Rolex?"

"Ooh, honey! Then you will be drinking from the top shelf, baby. You don't even want to know the price." They both erupted into shared laughter, and she was briefly disappointed that he batted for the other side.

"Have a seat…?" he looked at her expectantly.

"Oh! Candace. My name is Candace."

"Girl, you need some alcohol, pronto. First time?"

"Oh, you can tell?"

He just shook his head back and forth, his beaded dreadlocks swinging from side to side as he poured her a drink. He leaned over and whispered conspiratorially in her proffered ear, "Don't you worry about it. It won't be long before someone comes up here and starts buying you drinks. You're going to be just fine." He patted her hand as he said it, putting her at ease.

She thanked him and smiled. She would think back on this moment later; she would think back on it and wish that he had been right.

The man helped Candace to her car, an arm around her waist. She leaned into him as they walked, inhaling deeply. He smelled earthy and dark, like black coffee brewing over a campfire. She was attracted to him instinctively, on an animal level, her reptilian brain having spoken for her repeatedly throughout the course of the evening. She felt embarrassed thinking about how brazen she had been. Well, she had decided to be someone else this evening, right? And it had worked. A really hot guy was taking her home.

What name had she given him? She couldn't remember. Fuck. What was his name? They stepped up to her car and he slipped the key out of her purse. She hadn't remembered telling him which car belonged to her. Had she? She must have. God, she had never been this drunk before.

"I...I can't...can't...driiiveee."

A dark chortle came from the man beside her. "I'm aware, dear. This is definitely not my first rodeo. You are not driving anywhere. Just have a seat in the back here."

The man opened the back door and helped her inside. She patted his left wrist, noticing for the first time that he wore a Rolex. "Th...thanks...so...nii..." She slipped down into the seat, and the last thing she noticed before she lost consciousness was that he was wearing black, leather gloves.

He spoke to her unconscious form on the way to the house, telling her that he had been watching her for a long time, waiting for the perfect moment.

"When I saw you in that green dress, I knew it had to be tonight. Green is my favourite colour. You might assume it's red, but you'd be wrong." This brought delirious laughter from his lips. His mom had always said 'if you want to make it through this life, you have to be able to entertain yourself'. Man, oh man, how right she had been.

He heard Candace murmuring in the back seat. She had given him some bullshit name like Sally or Sandra, but it didn't matter. He knew who she was. He had seen her on campus earlier in January, and assumed she was a teacher or someone's mom. He had been there, hiding behind a camera, and he had discreetly followed her, watching her red hair poking out from beneath a pom-pom-topped, white-as-snow cap. She had never noticed him, but he had been close enough to overhear a phone conversation with a friend about her divorce. She hadn't accepted any blame for the situation herself, of course. Most whores didn't.

He couldn't exactly say what drew him to Candace, or any of the others. They just had something that called to him. He didn't *always* kill them. Sometimes, he just watched them. It was their accessibility that decided their fate. If they were surrounded by people and lived in close-knit communities, with houses built mere inches apart, they would more than likely be safe. He liked privacy. He liked to spend time with his girls. And socialites or suburbanites didn't usually allow him that kind of time.

He slowly manoeuvred the Mercedes down the long, tree-lined driveway. He wasn't sure of the variety, but he liked the pink blooms. They reminded him of roses. His mom had always liked roses.

The house was dark except for a single light by the side door. He pulled the visor down and pushed the button to open the garage door.

Candace stirred in the back and murmured, "Where are we?"

"I brought you home, love."

Candace was confused. She didn't remember telling this man where she lived. What was his name? God, she was never drinking again. Where was she? Oh, right, in the backseat of her car. She really needed to get her shit together. She was definitely blowing it with this guy. She tried to focus and remember more of the evening. How had she gotten so drunk? She fumbled for consciousness, but all she could feel was tiredness and hunger. She was so damn hungry. When was the last time she had eaten? The gnawing sensation growing in the pit of her stomach felt like it was slithering up the inside of her body, until it reached the base of her brain, causing a million neurons to fire all at once. The hunger brought focus and suddenly she could remember every piece of chocolate cake she had eaten, every medium-rare steak. She didn't just remember them, she could taste them; could feel warm peach cobbler sticking to her teeth, vanilla ice cream melting against her tongue. She heard the man open her door and she smiled up at him. "So hungry...so, so hungry..."

"I bet you've got something to eat in there. Leftover chicken and dumplings or something?" Her smile faltered and she suddenly felt a chill travel up her spine. She had made chicken and dumplings the night before. She suddenly felt the need to flee her own house, to run out of the garage and...run to where? The closest neighbours were miles away. She and Alan had wanted something out in the country. Something private. She told herself he had just made a lucky guess, chicken and dumplings was a common enough meal choice after all.

He was walking her into the house now, and the hand that had felt so supportive just seconds ago felt like a vice. Even if she did decide to run, there was no way she would be able to escape his grasp. He helped her to the table and she instantly felt better as she left his hold, falling into a chair. She watched him move around her kitchen as if he had been there before, pulling open a cabinet to grab two plates, opening another to find two glasses. While the leftovers warmed up in the microwave, she watched him set the table. He hummed a little tune while he did so, taking every opportunity to smile at her. She thought that she should feel calmed by that smile, reassured by this man taking care of her.

Instead, she felt scared and vulnerable, and every nerve in her body felt tense, as if her muscles were preparing to run.

He laid the steaming plates on the table and sat across from her. "The last time I had this, it was cold. I'm sure it's much better warm." He brought the first bite to his lips and blew on it. Before putting it into his mouth, he said, "You're an excellent cook."

January 26th, 2014
Cleveland, Ohio

Police looking for answers.

CLEVELAND (AP) – Ohio authorities have released very few details about the case of a deceased woman, found in her home in North Jackson, right outside of Youngstown. While they have labelled the death as homicide, sources close to the investigation have declined to comment, insisting that doing so could harm their search.

The nature of the homicide has not been revealed, but friends of the victim point the blame towards the woman's ex-husband, who is currently being held by authorities. When asked to confirm the ex-husband as a suspect, John Sagan, an agent assigned to the case, said that multiple leads were being followed.

The killer may be still at large, and residents in neighbouring cities remain scared and paranoid, leaving late-night businesses barren. Women have been cautioned against traveling alone and police have set up a tip line, asking for help from the public.

Chapter 2

January 26th, 2014
Youngstown, Ohio

It was after midnight and Sagan was alone at 'his' desk. Normally, when he wasn't in the field, he was stationed at the main BCI office in London, just outside of Columbus. The Ohio Bureau of Investigation had seven locations in total, and he had been to every single one of them. Currently, he was stationed at the one in Youngstown.

For the past few years, Sagan had been working on an ever-evolving serial killer case, and as far as he knew, no one outside of his small circle was even aware of its existence. He and his team assumed that the victims had been raped prior to murder. Though there had never been any semen found, there were other signs of rape, and spermicide was often present, alongside vaginal tearing and bruising in many cases.

The bodies were each mutilated to varying degrees; in many cases, victims' breasts had been removed, and sometimes the clitoris. But what they all had in common was some type of carving on their skin, and at least one Polaroid picture left at the scene. The

Polaroid pictures always featured the faces of sleeping girls, or rather, women, presumed dead. So far, ten of these women had been identified as victims, but there were twenty more unassigned. Sagan hoped that the other pictures did not include women who were still alive, and in need of rescue.

He sighed deeply and rubbed his eyes, taking a swig of coffee from his mug. He grimaced. Not only was it ice cold, but the cream had created a film that stuck to his lips as he drank.

The victims had been found all over the U.S., and a victim profile had been almost impossible to create. Some were White, some were Black, some were Hispanic. Their ages ranged from sixteen to fifty-one years old. There had even been a transgender woman. A few had been associated with schools or colleges, but most of them appeared to have lived solitary lives, away from the bustle of a city, in places of seclusion. Apparently, the sicko liked to spend time with them.

Sagan had been assigned to the Special Investigations Unit of the BCI four years before. Previously, he had been part of the Crime Scene Unit, a position that had required him to be more of a team player. He had not been well suited to it. But spending endless days alone, compulsively following up clues that would lead nowhere...now, that was more his style. When he had accepted this position, his old boss had described him as a 'tenacious, masochistic bulldog'. He had told her that he would take that as a compliment, and had stuck his hand out for a final handshake goodbye. She had stared at his outstretched hand and walked around the desk, giving him a warm hug instead.

She had said, "This is going to be a tough one, John. If anybody can crack it, you can. But don't beat yourself up over it if you can't find the guy. Don't let him kill off what life you've got left, okay? Promise me."

He had been unable to accept her request. He had been a little crazed back then, riding on an exhilarating high. He had caught the scent of this psycho, and he was willing to do anything to get to him. He knew he would never stop until he found him.

"I promise I won't die until I've found the guy. Happy now?"

Janice had just shaken her head. "Good luck, John. You'll always have a place here. Even if you get too old to go out into the field."

"Shit, Janice. You know I'll never get that old!"

God, that had been almost four years ago. Four years and he was no closer to catching the guy. Four years and the only thing that had moved in this case was the number of victims. He looked over at the map on the wall, murders pinned in red, and knocked the coffee mug off his desk in disgust.

His task force had become a joke, agents arriving then leaving again, as fast as they could, before their careers died. He was lucky to have Cindy on his team now, and the new member she had secured, but Sagan still felt as if they were headed nowhere fast.

"Goddammit!" He exploded out of his chair and started pacing, raking his fingers through his hair, trailing spilt coffee from one end of the room to the other.

"What am I missing?" he yelled at the empty room.

He looked at the photos of the dead women again. The women's backs had been expertly carved, reddened negative space creating ghastly, intricate scenes. In one, forbidding trees surrounded a short, quaint house. Two lone figures stood to the side, hand in hand. In another, a side view of a wolf's snout and face could be seen, and in another, a sleeping woman was laid out on a table, encircled by roses. How much time had these things taken and what was the killer trying to say?

Next to the images was an index card with 'fairy tales?', written in Sagan's usual chicken scratch; 'scarification?' was written underneath. He had cross-referenced fairy tales with the colleges associated with some of the victims. While he had met various literature professors, a few of whom had made it onto his list of suspects, he still felt like none of his associations were anywhere close to hitting home.

Suddenly, the overhead lights came on in the main room, startling him back to reality. A chorus of voices followed the lights.

"Hey, Sagan! You made it here before us?"

Cindy was a morning person. Did she fucking wake up like this?

She took a closer look at him, his button-up shirt wrinkled and stained, and said, "I guess not. You've been here all night haven't you?"

Over-exaggerating his slow, Texas drawl, he asked, "Damn, agent, what gave it away?" He laughed good-naturedly while Jakob surveyed the broken coffee mug on the ground. Sagan looked over at him. Jakob was wearing a navy suit and white shirt as usual, but today a matching navy vest peeked out from under his jacket. His dark blue tie was covered in a diamond pattern, created by thin, white lines, and tied up in some complicated knot. Sagan had once asked him why he dressed so nicely.

Jakob had responded, "No offense, but I guess I would rather the first thought a white person has of me is that I think I'm better than them, instead of them automatically assuming they are better than me."

Sagan had been taken aback by his honesty, and things had been a little shaky between them for a while after that conversation. While Sagan had never thought of himself, or most others around him, as racists, he had come to see the way other white law enforcement officers talked about Jakob; the way they often excluded him.

He smiled over at Jakob. "What in the hell is that knot around your neck?"

"This little old knot right here? This right here is the Linwood Taurus knot. You like it?"

"It looks like you got an elephant head tied around your throat."

"I'll take that as a yes. You want me to show you how to do it?"

Sagan laughed. "I'll save it for retirement."

Cindy looked at the mess on the floor. "He might not need to know how to put on a tie, but someone definitely needs to show him how to use a broom." She looked over at Jakob.

Jakob rolled his eyes. "Oh, and since I'm the black guy, I gotta be the one to do it? Yes, massa, I'll get right on that, massa, sir." Jakob made a loud show of going to collect the broom and dustpan, dramatically cleaning up the shattered pieces of Sagan's broken mug.

Cindy took all this in and said, "Hey, Jakob, when do you think we're going to get sick of cleaning up this cowboy's messes?"

While dumping the broken pieces into the trash can, he responded, "I guess when he gives us a thank you?"

Sagan responded, "Well, there you go. The number one reason to never thank you."

They shared laughter as if they had been childhood friends, instead of co-workers for just a few weeks. Sagan's eyes grew serious. "Thank you, though. I don't know what I would do without either of you."

Sagan looked back up at the board and said, "I'm going to go catch a few hours on the couch."

Cindy shooed him out of the room. "Sweet dreams, boss."

It didn't take long for him to fall asleep, but while he was drifting, his mind caught between awake and asleep, a Polaroid from the murder board came into focus. At that moment, he thought to himself, "The guy's a photographer."

Three hours and forty-five minutes later, Sagan sat straight up on the couch from a dead sleep and shook his head, like a dog shaking water from its fur. He always woke up like this, shaking the sleep from his mind and body, as if it were some dirty secret that he was ashamed of. To him, the need for sleep was a weakness. He would have plenty of time to sleep when he was dead.

He came out of the small room and winced at the overhead lights. Cindy and Jakob were both on the phone, fielding calls from the tip line, no doubt.

They had a new victim, and as much as he hated calling it so, a new lead. Maybe they would catch a break this time. He went over to the huge whiteboard next to his murder map and started assigning tasks. The first thing that needed to happen was to get some different people on the phone line. He needed Cindy and Jakob out in the field. He assigned some locals to that task and then started a list:

Check the status of the autopsy: see if any fingerprints or DNA has been found – Cindy

Interview ALL her friends & find out where she was the night of the murder/where she's been in the past week. Bring a photo of the carving on her back and see if anyone recognises it – Jakob

Consider the photography angle, figure out how to dig in – Sagan

It was a good start. He knew he could trust Cindy and Jakob to do their jobs.

Cindy had gotten up from the phone and walked towards him, her full hips swinging naturally. As she approached him, she asked, "The photography angle?"

Sagan looked over at her. She had that

combination every girl seemed to dream of: an hourglass figure and the ability to run in high heels. She had fiery spirals of red hair encircling her face, and every day she would style it as if she were a member of an '80s rock band. No one took her seriously. Until they knew her. And no one hit on her either, which had always surprised Sagan. Talk around the office seemed to be that the guys looked at her like a little sister. Except that this little sister carried a Glock and was a force to be reckoned with, in and out of the field.

Sagan nodded. "Yeah, we've been calling him the Polaroid Killer for so long now, I'm surprised we didn't think of it before."

Cindy hopped up on the desk beside him, crossing her legs at the ankles. "Umm, think of what, exactly?"

"That he might be a photographer. We've been so focused on the carving, I kind of forgot about the pictures, you know."

"Wow. Yeah. I always thought they were his way of toying with us. Letting us know there were others…keeping us on edge, unsure whether we'd found them all."

"Exactly. Like each one is a puzzle piece, and we need to find out how they all fit together."

Cindy asked, "You know, the media has started calling him the 'Sleepytime Killer'?"

"How did that get started?"

"The crime scene photo we provided to the media, on the Ana Sofia case, featured a box of Sleepytime tea. Since the girls were all drugged into unconsciousness, well, some journalist thought it fit, and apparently others agreed."

Sagan looked back at the pictures. "These are Polaroids. Polaroids...dammit. Did you ever have one?"

Cindy responded, "A Polaroid camera? Yeah. The quality was nothing I'd ever write home about."

"But look at these. Look at the photo composition. Look at the lighting. There is no overexposure, no blurriness. Normally, I wouldn't take instant pictures seriously. You wouldn't think a professional photographer would use one, would you?"

Cindy looked at the photo that had been haunting her since they had found it. It was the back of a woman's leg, the white, lacy hem of a dress visible above a dark birthmark. There was a Celtic-looking pattern surrounding the birthmark. At a glance, you would assume it was a tattoo, or a pattern of light and shadow spotlighted on the skin. In both cases, you would be wrong. It was a pattern made from skin cut away and skin left. If you didn't know the woman in the picture was dead, you might think it was beautiful, both the pattern and the photograph.

John was right. Professionals didn't typically use Polaroid cameras. "But maybe this professional does." Cindy was nodding, rolling it over in her mind. "He has to photograph them. And maybe he has to use a Polaroid camera. It's a compulsion and it's an important one."

"Exactly." They both stared at the photos, silent, each lost in their own thoughts.

From behind them, Jakob snidely asked, "Am I the only one working today?" He was holding a small notebook in his left hand, shaking it as if the answer to his rhetorical question could be found there. He looked excited.

Sagan raised one eyebrow. "Whatcha got?"

"I've got a witness. A bartender named Jerome, says he saw her three nights ago, a place called Gallery. It seems legit."

Sagan tried not to get too excited. There had been witnesses before, and those interviews had never resulted in a caught killer. But Jakob's enthusiasm was infectious. Cindy was animated beside him, bouncing from one foot to the other. She reminded Sagan of a dog he had once owned, a cute golden retriever who had always pulled full throttle on the leash, regardless of whether she was wearing a choke collar or not.

"Alright, team. Why don't you two go ahead and interview this guy. I'll go check on the autopsy and the lab work."

Cindy let out a girly squeal and rushed towards the door, pulling Jakob behind her. Sagan shook his head. It almost felt like Christmas…except that it had been a long time since Christmas had felt like Christmas.

He was lucky Cindy and Jakob put up with his shit; he knew he wasn't an easy guy to get along with. He would lock himself in an office for days, living off coffee and junk food from the snack machine, and ignore everyone. They would always knock on the door; offer him food; call him; email him…but when he was in the zone, no one else existed. It was just how he was. He knew it and they knew it, and everybody knew it would never change.

The phone started ringing and he decided to ignore it. If it was important, they would call back. Or leave a message that he would never hear. He put on his Stetson and headed for the door. He had shit to do, and it wasn't going to do itself.

Chapter 3

June 16th, 1996
New Orleans, Louisiana

"Alex! Alex, wake up!" Kathryn was frantic. Alex had not been asleep long, but the fear and anguish in his wife's voice dragged him quickly out of unconsciousness. He immediately got out of bed as she continued. "She's not here! She's not here, Alex, what are we going to do?"

"Hold on, now, honey. It's probably nothing."

"No, it's not nothing! I've looked everywhere! Alex, please. Please. She's gone!" Kathryn sank to the ground, a complete mess, robe falling off her shoulders, tears streaking down her face. Alex noticed that she had mud and leaves on her feet. "I've looked everywhere. I went in to say I was sorry. Sorry for yelling at her, sorry for grounding her, and she wasn't there. I thought that maybe she would be in the kitchen. Or the bathroom. Or the basement. Alex, I even checked the shed. Where is she? WHERE IS SHE!"

Alex hugged his wife and crushed her against his chest. He whispered soothingly and told her that everything would be okay. "We'll find her. Come on, we'll find her. How about we put on some coffee and start calling her friends?"

"O...kay. Okay."

He led her to the kitchen and pulled out a chair at the small, round table. She sat and folded her hands together, looking at the place to her left, devoid of the usual cereal bowl and spilt milk. She looked up at him and her bottom lip trembled, her eyes welling up again.

"What if she's not okay? What if...?" She couldn't finish, but he knew that her mind was quick to imagine the worst possible outcome.

"Look, hon. Let's not jump to any conclusions just yet, okay?" He grabbed a box of Kleenex from the pantry and quietly set it on the table. She pulled one from the box and used it to dab at the corner of her eyes and wipe her nose. Then the tissue disappeared into her wringing hands; he knew it wouldn't be the last one she used today. He poured them each a mug of coffee and brought their phones to the table.

"I'll be right back, okay? I'm going to go grab the phone list from the school and a notebook. It's going to be okay."

She had wanted to scream at him then. Scream at him to stop saying that everything was going to be okay; scream at him to prove it. "Where's your evidence?" she wanted to ask him. Their daughter, Sybil, was missing. Everything was most definitely not okay.

None of her friends had seen her, and as the day wore on, Kathryn and Alex became increasingly concerned. The police were called, an official missing person's report was filed, and their lives were turned upside down. Both parents were investigated, friends and parents of friends were repeatedly questioned, and even though a friend had pointed out a secret relationship that Sybil had admitted to having with an older man, the police had been unable to find a single trace of her.

They hired a private investigator, and after two years of no progress, they hired a cheaper one. They put up billboards; went on TV; offered rewards. Digital age-progression images were created and hung up at rest stops along the interstate: 'have you seen this girl?'. But regardless of how much money they threw at the problem, nothing changed; their daughter had simply vanished into thin air.

Kathryn often thought about how their expenditure had changed over the years. At first, the amount of money they spent directly correlated with their hope of finding their daughter alive. But days became years. The realisation that they would never get to hold their baby girl's hand again; see her smile at her dad's jokes again; yell at her for being late again…that realisation just ate away at their sanity.

One day, Kathryn woke up and realised that the money they were paying to find their daughter was not being spent on locating a living, breathing, feeling girl, aged sixteen plus one year, or two years, or three years. Their money was being spent on finding a corpse; finding a rotten shell that once housed the greatest thing they had ever had a hand in making. On that day, grief washed over Kathryn all over again, a different kind of grief, one with no hope. Because there was no hope of finding her daughter anymore. No mother hopes to find an empty shell. No mother hopes to identify a child from bones or tattered clothes. Or dental records. For a time, they stopped paying; they still had money in the bank, but they were no longer dealing in the currency of the living. Their only currency now was regret, and it was not a currency they were prepared to deal in. Not yet.

Years later, Alex would receive a call from the cops, to be told that his snub-nosed .38 had been used in a robbery in New York. Alex would contact a private detective to find out how in the world his gun had managed to find its way there. What the private eye learnt would lead them to move from Louisiana to New York. It would lead them to adopt a reserved and scarred child, and it would lead them to discover that their only daughter, their only child, had killed herself years before.

They would discover rumours of a sex-ring, and that their daughter had most likely been kidnapped and forced to work in such an environment. They were given a suicide note left by their daughter, addressed to her son. She described his father as a rich but scary man, and outlined how she had managed to escape. Alexander and Kathryn would search for the man who had ripped their daughter from them for years. They would never find him.

January 27th, 2014
Manhattan, New York

Julia was back in Dr Dixon's office. She looked around the room, feeling comforted by the space. The office was not large, but that added to its charm. The right wall was exposed brick, and the hardwood floors were covered in thick, ornate rugs, in red and orange hues. There was a floor-to-ceiling window, letting in a glow of natural light, and a high ceiling.

Nia spoke. "Are you ready to talk about it?" She had started most of their past sessions with the same question, and it had become a running joke. Julia was sitting up straight, in a red leather chair this time, her right ankle on her left knee; her hands clasped in her lap; her thumbs tapping nervously against each other. She sucked in a deep breath and let it out slowly.

"I've been seeing someone." She let the statement hang in the air before moving on. She hadn't told anyone. Not even Bella, her best friend in Michigan.

"And? How's it going?"

"I don't know. Sometimes it's great. Sometimes it's not. I met him through a work connection. He's a photographer. I work for the foundation, as you know, but I also freelance for different people in the art world. Especially in the city. He started off as a crime scene photographer. Sort of." Julia was doing that thing again, where she said a bunch of words as quickly as she could to build up the courage to say the words that mattered. To say the words that would make her admit she had a problem.

"Okay. Sounds like you both have some things in common. That's a good start. What's the problem?"

"Well, I decided a long time ago that I didn't want to be in a serious relationship...like...ever. You know? I have goals and desires, but none of those involve having a man in my life. Or kids. But, well, this guy…he has me thinking that maybe it's possible. He talks about how important family is. But is it?" Julia stood up and started pacing. She was filled with a nervous energy that could not be released through merely tapping her thumbs together. "Do we need to fulfil a desire for a nuclear family to feel that we have purpose? He's just so intense sometimes. I'm scared of letting him down. Of not being…of not being the person he thinks I am. I don't know how to change."

Nia let a few heartbeats tick by, just to make sure Julia was done talking. "What's a map?" Nia asked.

"A map?" Julia looked at Nia and saw the woman nod. "Well, I guess it's a physical representation of a particular place."

"Are they accurate?"

"Usually. I mean, I guess a mapmaker's goal is to make the most accurate map possible."

"Okay. So, we're in Manhattan. I imagine that the first time you visited my office, you used an online mapping service to find me?"

"Yeah."

"Could you have found me if you had tried to use a map of Manhattan from, say, a hundred years ago?"

"No. Definitely not."

"Exactly. Maps change, Julia. You may have thought you had your life all mapped out in front of you. But the map that *was* right for you, maybe even yesterday, might not be the map that's right for you today. People can change. It's not against the rules. Just think about it. Leave yourself open to the possibility that change might be good. Okay?"

"I hear what you're saying. Yeah, I can do that." She meant the words, but they sounded hollow to her ears.

They went on to discuss the exhibition that Julia was working on with the children rescued from the sex-ring. While Julia was thankful that they were no longer a part of that life, most of them had been placed into the foster care system, or into group homes, and she knew how difficult that path could be as well. Some of them had been taken so young; they no longer recalled their own names or the names of their parents.

Julia felt satisfied in her job, felt needed and appreciated, but she was struggling with her responsibility to Kathryn. She was hoping to discuss the possibility of a partnership with the foundation she worked with, so that she could get some help with her plans. She didn't want to try and open up a children's centre on her own and then fail. She needed to stop procrastinating. Nia made some concrete suggestions for Julia to start moving on that front.

It was an excellent session, and Nia felt like Julia was making some real progress. She had spent several months getting to know Julia, and Nia was excited to see how things would turn out for her. "Julia? Eventually, we're going to have to talk about what happened to you in Miami. I know you think that as long as you ignore it, it's not a stumbling block in your life. But…"

"But it is. I know."

"I know you know." Nia walked Julia to the

door. "Right now, focus on your action steps for the group home. I'll see you next time."

Julia stepped out onto the sidewalk of West Twenty-fifth Street and headed towards the Starbucks on the corner. After she had settled in with a venti Iced White Chocolate Latte, she pulled out her cell phone and placed a call to The New York Mountains Foundation.

It was a Monday, so she knew that everyone would be busy. The Foundation owned several buildings, each suited for different things: there was the Holliday Cinema & Museum, named after actress Judy Holliday, a relative of one of the founding members; the NY Mountains Fine Art Gallery; the NY Mountains Centre for Creative Arts, the building Julia spent most of her time in; the NY Mountains Performance Theatre, and a separate building with office space for the board members and advertising department.

It was this last building that she directed her call to. It was answered on the first ring by Trevante, an efficient receptionist who could handle their twelve-line system with ease.

"Good afternoon, Trevante, this is Julia. Julia Rodriguez. I was wondering if you could patch me through to David Washington, please?"

Without acknowledging her identity or asking any questions, Trevante deftly replied, "Putting you through to his secretary. Please hold."

After a momentary silence, a ringing began on the other end. This time, there were eight rings before someone answered. "Mr Washington's office."

"Hi. This is assistant curator Julia Rodriguez. I was wondering if I could speak with Mr Washington?"

"Concerning?" The voice on the other end sounded bored. Julia could picture her filing her nails and popping bubble gum.

"Oh, well, it's kind of personal, I guess?"

"I see. Well, Mr Washington is pretty busy today. He's not in the office at the moment. I can pencil you in for a phone appointment or give him a message to call you during his free time. Which would you prefer?"

"I can leave a message. Thank you."

Julia was relieved she hadn't actually had to talk to the man yet. She had been able to accomplish one of her action steps and she couldn't be accused of procrastinating. It wasn't her fault he was such a busy man.

She was startled when the phone started buzzing in her hand and spat some of her latte out onto the table. She hastily wiped up the spill while answering the phone and tucking it under her chin.

"Hello?"

"Julia, this is David Washington, returning your call."

It hadn't even been five minutes yet. "Oh. Hi! Yes, sir, umm…I have a weird situation and I guess I'd like some advice. And maybe some help?"

He gave her time to continue but she was silent. "Is this something you would prefer to discuss in person?"

He had given her a way out. Procrastination for

the win! Yes, it would mean she would have to meet with a powerful man in person, but that was later. Later was always better. "Now that you mention it, that would be a great idea."

"Wonderful. Where are you right now?"

"Right now? Oh, well, I'm all the way in Manhattan. I'm here checking out some art galleries and meeting with some artists. Well, I will be. Right now, I'm at Starbucks, apparently spilling more coffee than I'm drinking." She was talking very quickly, her words coming out in a rush. "So, we couldn't possibly meet today."

"Hmm. Well, I'm actually in Manhattan. Which Starbucks?"

Shit. "The one on the corner of West Twenty-fifth and Eighth Avenue."

"Perfect. I'll see you soon." He had hung up in time to miss her attempted protest.

Fifteen minutes later, a tall, light-skinned black man walked into the coffee shop, making his way towards her. David Washington. She recognised him from his picture, and although she had seen him at staff meetings, they had never spoken. It almost seemed as if the man had been avoiding her. She was determined that Patrick must have been mistaken. There was no reason why this man would have helped her get the job.

He appeared to be in his late fifties or early sixties, and wore a blue and grey chequered oxford, matching tie, and form-fitting navy suit. His shoes looked like they cost more than she had ever made in a month.

She stood up to greet him and he smiled warmly at her, taking her right hand in both of his.

"Julia. Fortune has shined on us today. What a coincidence! I have been meaning to introduce myself for so long, and fate has decided that today should be the day." He motioned back towards her seat. "Come. Have a seat. I'm going to grab a coffee. And maybe a pastry. Anything for you?"

"Oh, umm. One of those sugar cookies would be great."

"Coming right up."

While he waited in line to make his purchase, Julia tried to form a coherent introduction to her problem. By the time he returned, she was ready.

"Okay, well, as you know, I applied for this position last year. I had been looking for a position in this area since 2012, because I knew I would soon be moving to Hunter. An old…associate…friend, really…well, she left a huge house to me. With the stipulation that I utilize it in some way for women. It was a dream of hers to use it as a centre for battered women. I was going to help her. Work with her. Work with the women there. But Kathryn died before she could see her dream come to fruition. She willed the house to me. She knew that my vision might differ from her own, so she left some wiggle room in the instructions, allowing me to use the house for another purpose, as long as it benefited women in some way." Julia chanced a look up. David's dark brown eyes were on her face.

"Okay. What kind of advice are you looking for?"

"Well, in my last position, I worked with young women who had aged out of the foster system. And I have recently been working with trafficked teenage girls…"

"Fine work, by the way. Those girls are really blossoming."

Julia knew she should say thank you, she just had trouble acknowledging compliments. So, as usual, she ignored it. "And, well, I lost my parents when I was young and…" She trailed off, taking a sip of her latte which now consisted mostly of melted ice.

"Julia, I have to be honest with you…"

Julia was prepared for the usual, heartfelt sympathies. The exclamations of 'oh my god, I'm so sorry'. She was not prepared to hear anything else.

"…I knew your mother."

Julia wasn't sure what she looked like with her mouth hanging open, but she was sure surprise did not look attractive on her. "Whoa…wait…what?"

"I'm sorry. I should have prepared you for that. I just wasn't sure how."

So that was why this man had helped her get the position. He had been a friend of her mother's. "How did you know her?"

"Oksana and I went to UGA together; we were in the Criminal Justice program there. We actually dated for a time. But then my father discovered he had cancer and I moved back here. Finished my education at PACE." He smiled at her. "We kept in touch on and off over the years. I knew she was happily married, but I'm ashamed to say that I had often wished she wasn't." He laughed at this. "She was an amazing woman. My first love."

Julia didn't know what to think. Her mother had spoken fondly of her college years, but Julia had always assumed it was because she had met her father there. It was surreal to think of her mother in this way. When Oksana had become pregnant, she had quit school to stay at home with her daughter. Her father had been on the path to becoming a well-paid accountant, but the decision had still been a hard one to make. It had been a hard life for a couple of years, scraping by on not a lot of money, but they had always agreed it had been worth it.

"I'm sorry to spring this on you now, Julia. We were talking about the house?"

"Yes. Well, I'd like to turn it into a group home for girls. I was wondering whether you might know who I should talk to about getting the correct legal permissions to do that? And I was wondering whether The Foundation might want to get involved? Sort of a joint venture?"

They didn't speak for much longer, but David promised to look into the legalities of her plan. "We'll wait on bringing it to the attention of the other board members until we have a decent proposal. Any ideas for a name?"

"Yeah. I was thinking about the Beaumont Home for Girls? That was Kathryn's last name."

"Kathryn Beaumont? You were friends with her?" He started shaking his head while he crossed his legs, brushing imaginary dirt off his trouser leg. "Such a tragedy. Is that the house where it happened?"

"Yes."

"Hmm. I'm not sure if that complicates things or not. It might make things easier. We'll have to see."

"I'm sorry, David. Mr Washington."

"No, no, David, by all means."

Julia smiled at him. "David. Thanks. I really must be going. I have an appointment in thirty minutes. I'm not sure I'll make it actually."

David pointed down at the table. "Just bring them that cookie. That will more than make up for it."

Julia had completely forgotten about the cookie. "Good idea! Thanks!"

They got up from the table and David embraced her. "If you need anything…anything at all. Please call me. So great to have finally met with you."

Chapter 4

January 28th, 2014
Youngstown, Ohio

He tried calling the hotline, interested to hear the voice of the man who was looking for him. To his surprise, no one answered. There was a recorded message.

"Thank you for calling the BCI tip line. We are sorry, but all available agents are busy now. Please leave your name and number, and someone will return your call as soon as possible."

He then heard a beep and almost hung up. Instead, he started reminiscing into the burner phone, excited to open this dialog. "Isn't the mind an interesting oddity? Things happen to you. But as time goes by, you forget just what those things were. You forget the details, but they never forget you. They sink into you, memories twisting like vines through the grey matter of your brain. I've often wondered: at what point did I become a killer? Was I born at the precipice? Could I ever have been something else?" He laughed to himself. "Did I choose the thug life, or did it choose me? You always hear people say that psychopaths can't feel. If they can't feel, then where does the urge to kill come from? Well, I can feel, officers. Does that mean I'm not a psychopath? Only time will tell, perhaps. I just wanted to put your minds at ease. Those pictures that I left for you…all those whores are dead. There is no one waiting for a knight in shining armour." It was then that he heard the beep which ended his call. He contemplated calling back. Instead, he dialled a different number.

"Youngstown State University, how may I help you?" The woman who answered had a deep, smoky voice that cracked with age.

"Hi there, I'm trying to reach Professor Bass."

"Carolyn or Robert?"

"Carolyn. With the art department?"

"Yes, yes. One moment please." The woman heaved a deep sigh, as if she had spent her lifetime connecting calls to people more important than herself. She offered no form of farewell, and there was a long silence, before a ringing line indicated that the connection had not been lost.

"Carolyn Bass speaking."

He could hear the smile in her voice. "Hello, Carolyn, this is…" He was cut off abruptly when the professor started talking over him.

"Oh, hello! The students are very excited for your workshop this evening. Is there something you need?"

He wasn't fond of being interrupted, but he did appreciate the enthusiasm. "Well, I know that last time we worked exclusively in the darkroom, but this time I'd really like to do some shooting with them outdoors.

I found an awesome location a few weeks ago. You know the old Thomas mansion? There is a spectacularly overgrown family cemetery, about a quarter of a mile behind the place. I stopped by there this morning to see if I could still find it, and it's even better than I remembered. Half the stones are submerged in this boggy, frozen, marsh water, and there are winterberry shrubs in full bloom, covered in snow. I think it would be a great place for a class. Do you think your students can manage to get there, at such short notice?"

"Are you kidding? Those kids would meet you anywhere. Same time?"

"Let's make it an hour later. Please suggest that they wear slip-resistant, high boots. And some warm clothes, of course."

Jakob, Cindy, and Sagan were all back at their current base of operations in Youngstown, worn out from the day's activities. Sagan was wearing a black and white, polyester, plaid western shirt, and his customary boots. He has his feet up on his desk, Stetson covering his face, hands together in his lap. One might think he was asleep.

Jakob was dressed in his usual navy suit and white, starched shirt. He was wearing brown leather brogues, but he had skipped the tie: it was a casual day. He was sitting comfortably with his left ankle resting on his right knee, his hands tracing the dimpled pattern on his shoe, when he asked the question they had contemplated a hundred times already. "Why is he killing them?"

Cindy was dressed in pink sweats, leaning back

in an office swivel chair, her legs crossed, her feet resting on Jakob's desk. Her hands were tented, an elbow on each chair arm. "He's not."

Jakob looked over at her, incredulous. "Come again?"

"Well, they die, sure. But he doesn't care if they live or not. Look at the causes of death. Either they bleed out, or they starve to death, or they have bad reactions to the drugs he gives them..."

"There was also that one that died from drowning in her own blood, after he cut out her tongue," Sagan added.

Jakob was nodding.

Cindy continued. "He's never cut a main artery or delivered any kind of death blow. It's not about the killing. It's about the rape. The torture. The suffering."

"And the scarification."

Cindy looked over at Jakob and agreed. "Yeah, and the scarification."

Sagan shook his head in consternation, his voice muffled under the hat. "If he's so into the torture and suffering, why does he knock them out first? Why give them a drug that renders them unconscious?"

"I don't know. Maybe it's a matter of control. He needs to be able to tie them up, and it's easier to do while they're incapacitated?"

Sagan nodded. "That makes sense. So maybe he's a small guy?"

"Maybe. Or maybe, just maybe, it has something to do with the rape itself. We've been looking at the rape aspect as a secondary thing, right? But what if we consider the killing as secondary...that it's the raping that's important to him. What if his ritual started during a date rape? He finds a girl unconscious and it just...does something for him?" Cindy looked at them both expectantly, hoping to get some support for her theory.

Jakob said, "Well, that just opened up our suspect pool to include half the college boys in the U.S., if not more."

Cindy tutted at him. "Don't be so pessimistic. Surely it's not that bad."

Sagan removed his hat from his face and looked uneasily at Jakob. "Maybe not anymore. And maybe not everywhere. But..."

Jakob finished his sentence, "But there's a reason people talk about rape culture."

Sagan cleared his throat and sat up, moving his hat to the desk in front of him. "So, tell me about the interview from yesterday."

Jakob drove as Cindy navigated, and they eventually arrived at a dilapidated house on Cornell Street.

"I think this is it," Cindy said. The mailbox lay on its side and there were no numbers on the house.

"I hope you're right. This doesn't look like the kind of place to be wrong about."

The house was old, but seemed to be in better condition than many of the others along the street, and was covered in white siding, with a quaint, red brick front porch. Cement steps led up to the porch, with a sturdy looking handrail, newly painted white, on either side. There was a blacktop driveway, full of cracks, with no garage and no car in sight.

Jakob tried the bell and then crossed his hands in front of him, looking back towards their car and scanning the neighbourhood uneasily.

Cindy suggested, "Maybe the bell's broken," and knocked on the door.

They heard a woman's voice, coming from deep inside the house. "I'm a comin, I'm a comin!" she said, and a few minutes later, the wooden floor on the other side of the door creaked. They heard her mutter hastily from the other side of the door, "Who is it?"

Jakob cleared his throat. "Good afternoon, ma'am. We're here to see Jerome."

"Jerome?"

"Yes ma'am, he asked us to come by." There was a long silence. But as Jakob was about to continue, the mystery woman unlocked several locks on the other side of the door and held the door open for them, one feeble hand propped on the handle, the other holding a cell phone.

"Sorry about that, I'm sure you're good people. Look at you, all dressed to the nines. Come in, come in, hurry it up now."

The old woman motioned them into a small sitting room, while she went about securing the locks on the front door. Jakob counted six. After all the locks were turned, the woman shoved a security bar under the handle and made sure it was wedged snugly against the floor.

"Sit, now. Them couches clean. Sit, sit. Let me get y'all some pie. I just finished a lemon pie, and I got some fresh coffee brewin." The woman had a raised lump on her upper back, and she wore a housecoat with pockets, her hair tightly wrapped around some pink curlers. As she walked into the kitchen, she continued her banter, but it was unclear whether she was speaking to herself or her company. "I don't know why I always get visitors when my hair is in curlers. Every god damned time."

Jakob and Cindy looked around the room. There were dark curtains in front of the main windows, making the interior gloomy, and two couches placed in an 'L' shape, a sofa and a loveseat. A little wooden table stood between the couches, bearing a single lamp, and a white, crocheted cover had been thrown over the lampshade, which Cindy was certain must be a fire hazard.

"Ladies first," Jakob said, motioning over to the couch, which was covered in a sickly, green cloth. It did not look appealing, but appeared to be structurally sound, with arms carved from dark walnut.

After getting settled, Jakob yelled towards the kitchen, "Is there anything I can help you with?"

A cackle was the response. "Men always asking me if I need help. Here, granny, let me get this. Here, granny, let me get that. Sit down, granny, let me carry those. Mother fuckers, always trying to tell me I can't do shit I was born doing." She drew out the word 'shit', making it sound more like 'sheet'. Then the old woman walked into the sitting room, carrying a large, oval-shaped, wooden tray; stains and scratches marred the tray's surface. She walked slowly and heavily, coffee sloshing out over the cups, eventually setting the tray down on the coffee table and moving backwards, towards a cushioned rocker. Jakob moved to get up and help her, but she shooed him away. "Boy, I done told you to sit! Now sit!"

Jakob tried to hide a grin as the old woman grabbed a cup of coffee and settled back into her rocker.

"Help yourselves, now, don't be shy."

Cindy immediately grabbed a cup of coffee, adding a couple of tablespoons of sugar and a huge dollop of cream, before bringing it to her mouth and drinking the entire contents in one gulp. She hated coffee. Best to get it over with in one go. Jakob had a theory that morning people, like Cindy, hated coffee because they didn't need it.

The old lady found the whole thing very amusing and choked on her coffee, holding the back of her hand up to her mouth to cover a coughing fit. In her right hand, she held her cup tightly; not a drop was spilt during the whole ordeal.

"Sorry to keep you nice folks waiting. Jerome done gone to the doctor to get me my prescription. I ran out this morning, you see. He such a good boy, such a good boy. He been taking care of me since his mamma passed. I got diabetes, you know. And heart disease, and…well…y'all didn't come out here to listen to me go on about how I'm dying. We all dying, but we keep on living as long as we can, God willing. Jerome said y'all gonna be talking to him about that dead white girl? I swear to you, he couldn't a done it. He was with me as soon as he got off work. He's a good boy, my Jerome."

Cindy was busying herself with pie, so Jakob

spoke up. "Don't you worry, ma'am, we're not here to talk about anything like that. We're hoping Jerome might be able to tell us about her night at the bar…who she was there with, who she spoke with, if she left with anyone, if he knew where she went after leaving…those kinds of things."

Speaking around a piece of pie, Cindy said, "Ma'am, this is the best pie I've had since I was a child. Mm mmm, so good. Jakob, you really need to try some. I'm sorry, what's your name? I'm Cindy. This is Jakob. Maybe you know already, but we're with the BCI, the Bureau of Criminal Identification and Investigation."

"Oh, forgive me, where's my manners? I'm Dorothy Joan Wallace, Jerome's gran'mamma. He's the last one I got left. All my other chil'ren and gran'babies done up and moved. Or died. Ain't no work around here no more. It's sad to see how things been a'changing around here, you know. People don't raise 'em right no more. Dem kids. Used to be they knew what was wrong and right. Nowadays, they just be running around doing whatever they want." Dorothy took a sip of her coffee and shook her head. "Jerome should be back any time now. He's a good boy, he ain't gonna keep you waiting."

Jakob was glad they were not taking shots every time Dorothy said 'he's a good boy'… if they had been, he would bet good money that the old woman could have drunk him under the table. He glanced over at Cindy, who had finished her piece of pie and was looking longingly at Jakob's untouched slice.

Just then, a loud car pulled up outside, and as

Dorothy drew back the curtain, they caught sight of a purple and white, 1970 Dodge Challenger parked in the driveway.

"Speak of the devil," Dorothy chuckled, as she struggled out of her seat and headed to the front door.

Cindy silently asked Jakob if he was going to eat his pie and he shook his head, his face taking on an expression that screamed, 'duh! You know I'm trying to watch my girlish figure'. Cindy's eyes lit up. Keeping one eye on Dorothy, she picked up the second piece of pie and shoved half of it into her mouth. She put the plate down in front of Jakob but didn't let go, trying to time her eating so that she could manage at least half of what was left before the old woman turned back to look at them.

By the time Dorothy had unlocked the door and hugged her grandson, Cindy had managed to eat the rest of 'Jakob's' slice of pie.

Both investigators stood up and waited patiently to greet the man who had just entered.

"Granny, I wasn't gone but twenty minutes now, come on." Dorothy still had her arms wrapped around the boy...man, really, and he patted her tenderly on the back. She finally let him go and he turned his attention to the two visitors by the couch. "Sorry for the wait, I was hoping I'd make it back before you got here."

Cindy responded energetically. "No problem, it's been real nice talking with Dorothy and getting a chance to have some pie. Great pie! So good." She extended her hand and Jerome shook it, repeating the greeting with Jakob.

They all took a seat and Jakob began their questioning. "What I'd like you to do is describe your night, from the time you got to work until the time you left, with as many details as possible. I'm going to tape this interview, if that's alright with you, and then jot down some notes and questions while you are talking to us. If you could start by telling us the date, that would be great, saves me dating the interview later. Does that all sound okay to you?" Jerome nodded his assent, and Jakob started recording on his iPhone.

"It was Wednesday night, the twenty-second, I believe, and I had just arrived at work, around seven o'clock. I had the late shift and worked until closing at two. Candace walked in around eight thirty, and she seemed a bit awkward, you know? I noticed her entrance because her dress caught my attention. This beautiful green number, well, it did have this awful bow, but besides that, it was stunning. She walked a little uneasily in the high heels she had on, so I assumed she hadn't worn any in quite some time. And she was...well...she was flaunting her...stuff...if you know what I mean. I assumed, and rightfully so, that she was there to meet someone. Not someone specific, you know, but someone...someone who might enjoy staring at her goods.

There were a few men who offered to buy her a drink, and for some of them, she accepted, but she didn't really seem interested. Most of them were with friends, and she'd accept a drink and some conversation and then say something like, 'it's been nice talking with you...what was your name again...uh huh, but I'm waiting on a friend and your friends look a little lonely without you. Have a good night'.

To tell you the truth, I didn't think she'd be so good at letting the men down, but she did pretty well. For most of the night she stayed really close to the bar, and we chatted a bit when I had time. We didn't talk 'bout nothing that was important. Just our exes, mostly. Boring shit. Oh, sorry."

Jerome looked uneasily at Jakob after letting the cuss word slip. Damn he was fine, that young officer.

Jakob didn't smile, he just said, "No problem. You were saying?"

"Yeah. Umm, stuff about her ex leaving her for his secretary. And stuff about my exes being no good. It's hard to find good men in these parts, you know." Jerome kept his eyes on Jakob's face for any hint of discomfort. Or interest. But found neither. He sighed deeply. "I know you ain't from these parts."

Dorothy feigned shock and said, "Jerome, don't be flirting with this man up in my house. He don't want nothing to do with your ass. Sorry about that, officer, he a good boy but he can be a little dumb sometimes."

"Granny, come on now."

"It's okay, ma'am. Jerome, you were saying?"

Cindy looked over at Jakob and then at Jerome, trying to contain her laughter. "Jerome, I think Jakob's a lost cause. I'd be saying the same thing if you were a woman. He's married to the job."

Jakob made no acknowledgment of the discussion taking place around him, waiting patiently for

Jerome to continue.

"Alright, sorry, man. Where was I? Oh yeah. So, she was mostly around the bar, but at some point, she left to use the restroom, and then we got really busy. Maybe around twelve? I didn't see her for a long time. I figured she had left, but then I saw her sitting down with someone, getting real chummy. The man's back was turned away from me, but he was well dressed, wearing a form-fitting suit jacket. Good looking and fairly fit, from what I could see. I wish I could help you with a better description. It was dark in the corner booth where they were sitting. I wanna say he was bald…either bald, or just wearing a close-cropped do. I had an impression that maybe he was mixed, but might have been wishful thinking on my part. Candace seemed very drunk, and very happy. Falling all over the guy. They were literally making out at the table. I was happy for her. Pretty sure they left together, I think I saw him escorting her out the door, but we were packed, and I was busy. I couldn't swear to it in court, you know?"

Sagan sighed deeply. "So, maybe mixed. Maybe bald. But definitely 'damn fine'." Sagan attempted to mimic what he imagined a gay man might sound like, and his hand fluttered around his face as if he were hot. His attempts at humour usually backfired, and now was no different.

Jakob and Cindy simultaneously shook their heads, Jakob saying, "Boss. No. No. Just, no."

Sagan ignored them, moving swiftly on. "I don't suppose there's any video footage?"

Cindy shook her head. "Just the alleyway in the back. We took a look, but nothing really stood out. A busboy taking out the trash. Some homeless guy going through a couple hours later. That's it."

Sagan stood up and started pacing. "What about credit card receipts? How were her drinks paid for?"

Cindy responded, "Jerome said he closed out her tab before she went to the bathroom. He thought she had been planning to leave then."

Sagan was thinking aloud, thoughts tumbling out in a stream of consciousness. It was part of his process and Cindy and Jakob were used to it. "It's not the husband. He has an alibi. But it is often the husband. Someone close to the family. Someone who knows what's going on. But nothing, nothing on this asshole. Family. Divorced. Broken up." Sagan walked over to the murder wall they had meticulously recreated here in Youngstown. He started pointing to each victim and naming them. "Sadie. Parents divorced. Amy. Parents divorced. Maria. Divorced. Ana Sofia. Divorced."

Jakob and Cindy joined him at the wall and Cindy picked up the list, her voice almost a whisper, "Alise. Divorced. Nadine. Divorced. Molly. Divorced. Jessica. Divorced."

Jakob finished the list. "Anaya. Divorced. Caitlin. Divorced. Candace. Divorced."

Sagan continued. "So, he seems to be targeting people from broken homes, from divorced families. All but his first two victims were women whose marriages had failed."

Cindy sighed, "The victims we know about, at

165

least."

Sagan nodded and started pulling on his chin repeatedly, as if he had a goatee there. "Why not target the moms in those early cases?"

Jakob added, "Or the dads?"

Sagan continued his pacing. "Maybe he blames his victims for creating their broken homes. Sadie came out as a transwoman. That caused her parents to split up. He feels sympathy for the father, maybe viewing such a transformation as wrong. The mother was always against her daughter's choice. The killer decided that Sadie was the reason for the divorce."

Cindy rolled up the sleeves on her sweatshirt and hopped up onto a desk. "And Amy was a drug addict who played her parents against each other. He probably blamed her as well."

"Okay, okay, sure," Jakob interjected. "So, he has something against broken families and appears to blame the women in most cases. Even if that is true, it doesn't help us figure out who the fuck this guy is. And it doesn't help us to narrow down potential victims. Maybe his parents were divorced, and he blames his mom? What are we supposed to do, check out fifty percent of the families in the US? People are more likely to come from a broken home than not these days."

Sagan sat down and ran his fingers through his hair, letting out an exasperated sigh. "I don't know. Goddammit. I don't know! Let's just call it a day, shall we? I think we could all use a break."

Sagan was drunk when he made it back to his hotel room

several hours later. He thought about calling Joan but knew it would be a mistake. After his wife, his daughter, and their dog Rosie had left him, Sagan had started making comparisons between his life now and his life before their exodus. It used to be that days could be counted by the number of dishwasher cycles. One day meant one load washed. Now, he could count his months by them. And dog walks? Those could be counted by the number of fucks he had left to give about keeping food in the house or keeping it clean.

The girls had left when he was out of town. His wife had tried, over the course of several months, to tell him they needed to talk. She had called him one night, about two years ago now, and he had picked up the phone saying, "Joan, I'm really beat. I just laid down. Call you back in four hours or so?" There had been a deep silence on the other end of the line. How many times had he told her that he would call her back? How many times had he followed through with his promise? "Joan?"

"I...I just wanted to let you know...to know that...I'm taking the girls to my mom's."

"Alright, darling. A trip to Long Island sounds like a great idea. I'll call you soon." He added, "I love you," but she had already hung up.

Over the course of the next few weeks, he had realised that she hadn't tried to call, and every attempt he had made to contact her had ended with a voicemail. At first, he had chalked it up to technical issues. Something had to be wrong with her phone. He had left her a few messages and explained that he was worried, asked her to call him back. But no matter how many times he had asked, she never did.

Arriving back home, he had found most of the furniture gone, a letter, and divorce papers lacking his signature. Her initials were on every page, her signature witnessed by a lawyer. There were instructions written on a Post-it note: call the lawyer. Sign the papers. You know it's the right thing to do. This isn't a marriage anymore."

He had opened the fridge. His beer was left untouched, along with a neat stack of leftovers. Each box had 'John' written on it, and a date. He counted thirty-two. Thirty-two times when dinners had been made without him. Thirty-two times when his girls had filled the empty kitchen with laughter. Light. Love.

He had taken out the leftover containers and put them on the bar, along with his twelve-pack of Blue Moon. He had found a black trash bag and taken a seat, opening his first beer, using the magnetic opener that had been on the fridge. It was in the shape of a beer bottle, with 'San Antonio' written on it, an image of the state of Texas, and other souvenir-worthy Texas-inspired symbols. He had bought it on their first date.

He had developed a rhythm: trying to guess what was inside each container and taking a giant swig of beer every time he was wrong. If he couldn't identify the contents at all, well, that meant another swig of beer. After opening each one, he would bring the plastic box up to his nose and inhale deeply. It was a penance for missing…everything. Every whiff made him sick, made him gag. He breathed in the stench of a ruined life and then threw it into the trash bag. He had run out of beer long before he ran out of food, but he had kept going; guessing; opening; smelling; dry heaving and tossing. By the time he had opened the last box, he had realised he was crying. He had swiped his arm across the bar, empty beer bottles crashing to the floor, and then vomited into the trash bag on top of the putrid food. He had fallen while trying to get out of his seat and had not found a reason to get back up, drifting into a restless sleep, dreams full of empty houses and memories.

As Sagan lay alone in the cramped hotel room, he thought about his failed marriage. When had it all gone wrong? He thought about the last Christmas they had spent together. He had bought a trip to Puerto Vallarta, Mexico, and Joan was thrilled. They hadn't been on a real vacation since their honeymoon, six years before. Their daughter, Angela, was three at the time. He remembered sitting with her on the beach while she built sandcastles...well, sand piles, really. He remembered her joyous laugh every time she poured water over the structure or mashed her hands through a 'wall'. He remembered closing his eyes, the sounds of the other beachgoers becoming distant, and then bringing his face to her head and breathing in her innocence and potential. The smell of his baby girl, and the beach. Joan had caught him enjoying the moment and reached out her hand to grip his. "I love you, cowboy."

"And I love you, darling."

It seemed like another life.

Chapter 5

January 29th, 2014
Manhattan, New York

It was almost six o'clock in the evening, and Ronald had just dropped him off at his apartment.

"I probably won't need you for a few days if you want to go back to the house and check on my mom. And use the facilities. You know you're always welcome. I'll give you a call when I need you."

"Thanks, CJ, I appreciate it. I just might do that."

CJ watched the Cadillac drive away, then rushed inside, turned on the radio and tuned in to the local college station. He felt giddy and chided himself for his excitement. It was only a stupid little interview. But he longed to hear his own voice being sent out in the form of radio waves; he wondered who else might be listening…he hoped Julia might be.

"Good evening, New York! We have a very special guest here with us this evening, a prominent local artist who has donated numerous works to the school. These pieces will, hopefully, be sold at our upcoming auction for the Young Women's Initiative. The auction will be…"

Jesus, how long was this guy going to blather on? CJ considered the pieces he had donated to the school. Two of them featured places on campus where rape or sexual intimidation had taken place. So far, no one had mentioned it, and he felt fairly safe in assuming that no one would put two and two together. If they did? Well, hell, he was just a creative type, trying to alert audiences to current societal issues…why did so few women come forward? Because no one listens to them. No one believes them. Everyone forgets. That, or rape and assault have become so commonplace that no one bats an eye anymore. Society has become numb to the suffering of women. That is what he would say.

His attention was brought back to the radio program. The interviewer had just asked him about the meaning of his work.

"Spring," he heard himself answer.

"Spring?" the young man asked, surprised.

He remembered the little smile on that kids face…god, how he had wanted to rip those lips off with a pair of pliers. He had imagined pulling them slowly away from his face, blood gushing onto those pretty teeth his parents had no doubt paid for.

Instead, he had smiled back and answered, "Everyone thinks Spring is so goddamned wonderful. Their little hearts flutter over blossoming trees and fragrant flowers. They ignore the death lurking just beneath. They ignore the dried leaves, hidden under piles of snow for months. They ignore the wrinkled berries on the vine, the ones not even good enough for the birds to eat. They only see what they want to see. That is what my new series is about...people surrounding themselves with beauty and luxury, ignoring the sins of the world. Ignoring their own sins. They are going through life asleep. They are Sleeping Beauties."

"Interesting. The way you juxtapose luxury against a backdrop of tragedy...well, you just have an eye, I guess. What brought you to Colombia? We're not exactly a place that screams degradation."

"And that right there is one of the points I'm trying to make. You lie to yourself. You surround yourself with this perfect little life and you feel protected. Safe. Like no one can get to you. And you ignore the things you don't want to see. One of the pieces I donated, 'Sleeping through Church', was taken on a Sunday morning, maybe around four a.m., right beside the steps of the Low Memorial Library. The photograph features a homeless man, sleeping on the steps of this pillar of knowledge, surrounded by empty beer cans. And a few steps above him, one of my Sleeping Beauties. She is covered from head to foot in warm finery and wears a hooded, fur-lined robe. She lies in a winterized sleeping bag, the top half turned away from her as if she doesn't need it. She wears a smile in her sleep and tucked in beside her is an empty bottle of thirty-year-old Glenfiddich, a very expensive whiskey. The man's nose is encrusted with frozen snot, his beard is matted with frozen mud. His dark skin is marred with deep wrinkles, his skin gaunt, his eyes sunken in. He looks dead."

"I assume the woman's placement above him on

the steps is a nod to the class differences between them?"

"Absolutely. Another thing we have a tendency to ignore."

The kid had looked uncomfortable giving this interview. He had not known what he was getting himself into.

"And why is it called 'Sleeping through Church'?"

"Here, let me show you a snapshot of the photograph." CJ had dug into his coat pocket and retrieved a small black-and-white of the print. "Why do you think I called it that?"

The young man stared at the photograph for a couple of minutes. Finally, he said, "The man has what looks like a very heavy and expensive crucifix on. And you took it on a Sunday morning?"

"Both of those things. And if you look very closely, you'll see that there is a crumpled-up envelope in his right hand, an offering envelope for Corpus Christi Catholic Church. The title just seemed fitting, don't you agree?"

"Yeah. I see what you mean." The interviewer handed back the photo and asked, "Is it true that you started off as a crime scene photographer?"

"Not exactly. I was never a cop. But my brother was. And there was a point where they got into trouble because none of their personnel was particularly good with a camera. So, my brother suggested I come in and work as an instructor, teaching a class now and again. It turned into a weekly gig and I actually visited crime scenes to give on-the-job instruction in lighting and such."

"And you used some of those photos in your work?"

"Yes. Before then, I had never shown here in the city. I was a freelance photographer and was known by a few people around the world…but I wasn't part of the art scene here in the city. Not until my 'Criminal Lives' series. It really got me noticed. I had to get permission from all parties involved to use the photos, of course, but once I had, I was able to make some amazing artwork. And half of the proceeds were donated to the families of victims featured in the photos."

"And the photos were just straight-up crime scene photos?"

"No. What I did was make a note of the location for each crime scene. Then I returned to each crime scene and photographed happy things that were taking place there. I then superimposed the crime scene photos onto the happy images. They were a hit."

"Hmm. So, presenting things that are hidden is kind of your thing, I guess."

"Absolutely. I want my viewers to feel uncomfortable. I want them to start thinking about all the places they visit in their day and wonder 'what tragedy happened here?'. I want them to start looking at the person beside them and ask themselves 'could they be a murderer? Could they be a rapist? Could I?'."

The interviewer laughed for his audience and innocently asked, "Could he be a serial killer?"

CJ flashed him a winning smile and joined in on the laughter. "Exactly!"

"You also had a moving series connected to the 9/11 disaster, correct?"

"That's right."

"Can you tell us about that?"

CJ's winning smile had disappeared. It was replaced by a sombre, pained expression. His next words came out stifled, yet fierce. He choked back a sob. "I'm sorry. It's still very raw. I'm not sure that we will ever heal. A lot of us didn't make it through that day."

"You were here? In New York?"

"Yes. I was just a teenager, maybe fifteen? I was here on a field trip with my school. I was taking photographs of Saint Peter's Church; there was a couple having a sunrise wedding there."

"Not a lot of teenagers are willing to get out of bed before sunrise."

"Well, I wasn't a normal teenager."

"I guess not." The interviewer tried to find a solemn tone and asked, "So, you were still there when the first plane hit?"

"Yes. The couple had decided on a sunrise wedding because the husband had to leave later that day for Iraq. They had originally planned to get married when he got back from his tour. But they just couldn't wait. Ironically, he would die that morning. Wreckage from flight one hundred and seventy-five. I got photographs of it all. People jumping from the high-rises, firemen covered in ash. The anger. The horror."

"And when did you view these photographs?"

"I used 18 rolls of film that day. And I didn't process them until 2011. I knew some people involved in the dedication ceremony, held at the memorial. The ceremony marked the tenth anniversary, and my photographs were utilized as part of that dedication ceremony."

"But no one knew you were the photographer?"

"Well, a few people knew, but I asked that they be shared anonymously. I didn't want to have any acknowledgment or payment for those photos."

"Were any prints sold?"

"Absolutely. There have been several. And my name is attached to them now. But all proceeds go towards the September eleventh fund."

"You seem to have a very generous nature."

"Well, my mom always taught me that if you do well in life, you should build a longer table. Not a higher wall. It's all about sharing."

"Well, we certainly appreciate your donation. When will your complete series, Sleeping Beauties, be on display?"

"The exhibit will have its grand opening on Thursday, March twentieth. The first day of spring."

January 29th, 2014
Youngstown, Ohio

It was after midnight, and Jakob and Cindy had just walked into their second bar. The entryway was slippery as they walked inside, the flimsy mat doing nothing to combat the snow being brought in by patrons, and the two of them quickly hung their coats, happy to see that there were few others at the bar that night. They had made a deal at the beginning of the evening not to talk about the case. Any case. So far, they had managed to steer clear of touchy subjects.

Jakob ordered a bottle of local craft beer called 'Buckeye', and Cindy surprised Jakob by ordering a White Russian.

"You know there's no whiskey in that, don't you?"

Cindy gasped in feigned horror. "Shit, you're right." She yelled after the bartender who had just left. "Rob, I'll also take a Pappy Van Winkle Rocks with a water back, if you don't mind." The bartender gave her a thumbs up and proceeded to prepare their drinks.

"What the fuck was that?"

"A whiskey and a glass of water."

Jakob shook his head. "You're going to be floating out of here tonight." There was a comfortable silence between them. Then, Jakob asked, "You still seeing that steak guy?"

Cindy laughed. "His name is Angus, thank you very much. And yes, we still see each other. We recently agreed to be exclusive, so no more one-night stands for me." She gave him a pointed look, secretly begging for him not to bring it up.

The bartender dropped off their drinks and quickly left, reading his customers well. They wanted privacy, not chit-chat with a stranger.

"Does that include work husbands?" He looked at her innocently, brown eyes lingering a little too long on her lips.

"You just had to go there." She drained her

whiskey in one go.

"Aren't you supposed to savour whiskey or something?"

"Oh, I savoured it." She looked over at him. "It was one time, Jakob."

"Hence the name, one-night stand. But if only one-night stands are off, what about two-night stands? Asking for a friend."

Cindy grunted. "You are incorrigible."

Jakob relented. "Hey, I'm sorry. I'm happy for you. From what little you've told me about him, well, he sounds like a great guy. And I bet he can make a mean hamburger." Jakob finished off his beer and motioned for another. He asked, "Did Sagan tell you he's got a date next week?"

A gasp of genuine shock escaped Cindy's lips. "No way! How did that happen?"

"The M.E. in town set it up. Apparently, the lucky lady is a friend of hers, some kind of professor at the local university."

"Wow. Do you think he's ready?"

"For a date? It's way past time."

"What about you? You hiding somebody in your basement?" She smiled at him and laughed, trying to diffuse the tension between them. Again, she regretted the night they had spent together. Not that it hadn't been great, far from it. It had been amazing. Jakob was such a patient and giving lover, every touch intense. Every caress a thank you for finding his mom's shooter. Unfortunately, he wanted more than she could give him. Surely, Jakob couldn't think he was in love with her.

They barely knew each other, and she just couldn't feel that for him. She couldn't be with someone that held her up on a pedestal as he did. It was too much pressure.

Jakob looked at her for a long time before answering. "I don't know, Cin. I guess there's nobody. Maybe one day, right?"

They were both quiet for some time then Jakob said, "I've been meaning to ask you something. Well, two things I guess."

Cindy took a deep breath and prepared herself mentally. She didn't think this was going to be about them. It wasn't going to be about the possibility of something developing between them in the future. No, this was going to be about something she *really* didn't want to talk about. "You remember we agreed not to talk about the job, right?"

Jakob nodded and took another swig of his beer. "Don't worry, it's not about a case. I've just been wondering what brought you to law enforcement."

Cindy was quiet for a moment. "Well, that's not really a question." She winked at him. "What do you want to know?"

"Well, when I first heard of you, you'd been working on a task force tracking down gun nuts. But when I finally called you, you were working with Sagan on this serial killer case. Why?"

Cindy had silently ordered another whiskey while Jakob had been talking, and she quickly knocked it back. Jakob waited her out. She didn't look at him when she started speaking again. "In 1999, I was living in Columbine, Colorado."

Jakob was taken aback. This was heavy. "Shit."

"Yep. That Columbine." She took a sip of her White Russian and smiled. "This is pretty good, actually." After a few minutes, she continued. "My daddy was a cop. His daddy was a cop. And my parents never had another child." She shrugged. "So, I just knew I was going to be a cop all along. Daddy took me hunting and I've always been a damn good shot. I could just about outshoot him at age twelve, I was born to it. I grew up around guns, they were just a part of life. I always thought that it made sense. America was born through violence, through the use of guns. It was part of our heritage. Part of who we were as a country. I used to think that every American had the right, the God-given right, to defend their property with a weapon. Defend their family. Now, I'm not so sure."

She stirred her drink with the little black plastic straw that stuck out of her glass, brooding. Eventually, she continued. "After all these years, I guess I'm still trying to decide which side of the line I'm on." She paused, then began again. "Columbine. Columbine came along and changed things for me." She sighed deeply before continuing, afraid of being psychoanalyzed by her partner. She hated looking weak. "I was a senior that year. But after the shooting, I was more than just a senior. I was a survivor. Every breath I've ever taken since April twentieth of that year, well, I've had a moral duty, right? To make every single day…minute…second count." She motioned for another whiskey and it didn't even hit the bar. It went directly from Rob's hand to her own and she held up a finger, the universal sign for 'wait just a minute', as she emptied the shot glass and handed it back to him.

"Another?" he asked.

She shook her head and asked for more water instead. "I'd had a crush on one of them for a couple of years, you know?" Cindy had a pained expression on her face, and she shook it off with a cynical laugh.

"One of the shooters?"

"Yeah." Cindy waited for the obvious question, 'the blond one?', but it didn't come. He didn't know her well enough yet, and she probably hadn't told him that Angus had blond hair. "I guess I don't have the best taste in men."

"Please, high school crushes don't count." He looked over at her. "It's only the crushes you get in your thirties that count." Cindy rolled her eyes at him and snorted. He continued, "So, what happened after that?"

"Well...life." She laughed again. It was a dark thing, a laugh born out of blood; of fear; of constant self-criticism. "The clocks kept ticking. We graduated the following month. Graduation day felt surreal. It was bright and sunny, and it just felt so wrong." She looked over at Jakob. He was peeling the label off his empty bottle. "I used it. Used the experience as a catalyst. I was always going to be a cop, but after that, I decided I was going to be a super cop." She laughed bitterly. "I started attending Community College of Aurora straight out of high school. They had an AA transfer option for Criminal Justice. After that, transferred to the University of Northern Colorado."

They were dangerously near to closing time and

Rob had just announced last orders while turning up the lights. The brightness stung Cindy's eyes and she looked around. The floor was scattered with typical bar debris...barely used napkins, peanuts, crushed cigarettes, unidentified fluids, broken beer bottles, and sticky footprints.

"To cut a long story short, Jakob, I became obsessed with gun violence. I became fanatical about gun safety education and fought for common-sense gun control." She finished her White Russian. "Then there was Sandy Hook." Rob had started shooing customers out of the door.

Jakob nodded. "Yeah. It's hard to believe it was only, what, a year ago?"

"A little more than that. Anyway, I couldn't do it anymore." They stood up and started walking towards the front door. "I think I've told you before that my dad knows Sagan. They met at a convention for crime enthusiasts or some shit. I'd done a few favours for Sagan in the past, liked the guy, and I thought, why not? Asked him if I could be part of the team, and he immediately said yes. So...here I am."

"Why'd you invite me to join the team?"

As they stepped outside, a vicious wind pummelled them with an apocalyptic quantity of snow. It felt like they had barely survived the blizzard from a few weeks ago, and now this? Cindy motioned towards their nearby hotel. She knew any attempt at speech in this shit was pointless. She imagined the homeless out in this weather. The drunks. It would be so easy to take a seat on the ground and let mother nature take over. So easy to give up.

Since surviving the shooting, it was ironic the number of times she had thought about killing herself. Was her fear of being seen as a coward the only reason she was still alive? She didn't know, but she was done with the self-hate for the evening. She began jogging towards the hotel, her head down to avoid the piercing darts of snow.

They entered the hotel at a near run, faces bright red and stinging, ripping their coats off at the door. The receptionist gave them a nervous nod. It was the nod of a citizen whose instinct was to call the cops whenever anything out of the ordinary seemed to be happening. Cindy began to laugh, and Jakob joined in. When you were running on no sleep and half a bar of alcohol, well, you didn't need to hear the joke to know it was funny.

"What are we laughing about, Cin?"

"I...I was just..." She tried to catch her breath, but another laughing fit pursued. "Can you call the cops...on the cops?" She had thrown her coat over a drying rack near the fireplace, kicked off her shoes, and sunk down into the comfy couch in front of the hearth. She had managed to get a handle on her laughter and patted the empty place beside her.

"When we met in November, I was in a dark place. I was close to leaving law enforcement. This thing with Sagan felt like a losing battle. Felt like we were just spinning our wheels, and I needed a win. I needed something to believe in again."

"So, Sandy Hook had been pretty recent. You were feeling disenfranchised..."

"Yeah. I was feeling pretty useless, like nothing I'd ever done had mattered one fucking bit."

"And then I came along and gave you a white saviour complex."

Cindy laughed. "It wasn't that." She reached out her hand and patted his arm. Left it there.

He put his hand over hers. It was so damn warm.

"You made me realise that, despite the violence, despite the shootings, despite the…" She choked back a sob, continuing when she was able. "Despite the broken bodies of dead children, maybe I had done some good. And maybe the world would have been a worse place without me in it."

Cindy dropped her head down onto his shoulder. "And besides, you were a good lay. Figured I might need to keep you around."

She could feel his laughter before she could hear it. Damn, she was a bitch. Typical of her to try and lighten the mood with the exact thing she was trying to avoid letting happen again. Had she just encouraged him to keep on carrying that flame when she had no intention of lighting her own?

She started to drift off and Jakob murmured, "Thanks for bringing me on."

She mumbled something incomprehensible and began to snore, snuggling into the man she would never allow herself to love. The two of them fell into a comfortable sleep, unaware of the receptionist who would spend the night tending the fire to keep them warm. Unaware of the manager who would come and put a blanket over them. Unaware of the skinhead who would shake his head as he passed, angry at seeing a white woman in the arms of a black man. Unaware, too, of the small child who would walk up to them and reach out a tiny finger to poke at Jakob's face. It was a blissful, dreamless sleep, that would in no way whatsoever prepare them for the hangover to come.

February 7th, 2014
Hunter, New York

"I hear things are going well with your project. Would you tell us a little more about that?" David Washington smiled warmly.

Julia was seated at the oval conference table with her immediate boss, several board members, and various other co-workers, for their monthly meeting. Patrick gave her a thumbs up and she nodded in his direction.

She cleared her throat. "As most of you know already, we started working with a group of girls who were saved from a sex-trafficking ring about a year ago. They are producing some amazing work and many of them have voiced an interest in sharing that work. I would like to collect and display some of these pieces in an exhibition, called 'Exploitation and Exposure'. It will feature drawings, paintings, sound recordings, videos, photographs, sculptures, poems, mixed media...you name it. I have not limited the girls in their expression. All the senses will be engaged; I want people to experience the horror of what these girls went through. The ticket sales will be retained by the foundation, but all art sales will be split between the girls. They have already agreed to these terms."

"That sounds like a daring exhibition. When would you like to run it?"

"I think the topic would fit perfectly with the autumn show, and the new exhibition room will be completed by then. It's a chilling topic, so it needs an appropriate season. Autumn tends to make one introspective and full of melancholy."

"Sounds great. I look forward to seeing it." David dismissed her with a nod.

"Actually, one more thing?"

"Certainly, please go on."

"I also have a well-known photographer involved in the venture; he's been taking shots of the girls for the past few months. His works will be available for sale, and any proceeds from his photographs will go to the girls' fund."

"Oh! Now, that's a nice twist. Who's the photographer?"

"Charles Ivanov." There were murmurs of pleasure and surprise from around the table.

"Splendid! That will bring quite a few people to our little neck of the woods. We will no doubt have some bigwigs from the city grace us with their presence. Nice job, Julia!"

Julia was a little red in the face when she sat down; she wasn't fond of being the centre of attention. Patrick smiled and winked at her as she settled back into her seat.

"Alright, I'd like to close the meeting with a reminder to check your emails for information about positions and roles during the spring production of Footloose, as we've made a few minor changes. Right, gang, I guess that's all for today. Until next time!"

Julia rose from her seat with the others, the board members staying behind, as usual, for their own monthly board meeting.

Chapter 6

January 25th, 2011
Ephratah, New York

It feels great to be home. I have gutted the place, and not much remains from my childhood. The renovation project was years in the making, but now, a new project begins: filling the house with personal mementos and naming each room. Renovators located a hidden room several months ago, and it is just perfect. I'm not sure if I should name that one 'Kathryn' or 'Emily'. Maybe I should just go with both. The Emily-Kathryn room. Yes, that has a nice ring to it. I am still waiting to decorate that room; still looking for the right…shall we say…décor?

The Ana Sofia room is one of the most recently completed. It's the library, of course. Ana loved her books. The room has two levels, bookshelves on both, with a spiral staircase, leading up to a wraparound balcony overlooking the bottom floor. There are three kinds of wood utilized in the library: ebony, mahogany, and cherry. All very art nouveau. And there is a huge fireplace, possibly my favourite feature in the whole house. It is made of ebony, tree trunks carved into the columns, with a serpent winding around each one. The frieze is graced with delicate wisteria vines, the blooms reminding me of those that grew outside her bedroom window.

Above the fireplace hangs a portrait. A sleeping Ana, on a chaise lounge, propped up against some pillows with her arms raised above her head. Her lips are parted, and her nightgown is open, exposing her breasts. The portrait is in the style of a classic baroque painting; the edges of the portrait are dark while Ana is bathed in light. The cherry frame of the portrait bleeds into the fireplace, the tendrils reaching up from the mantle to embrace the frame. The whole room is a testament to the blending of two styles: baroque and art nouveau. It is opulent, and I spared no expense. Only the best for my girls.

This is the room where my mother spends most of her time. Currently, she is seated by the window, eyes looking out over the restored garden. The early morning light is bathing her face and she seems content. I go over and press my lips to her forehead. "Good morning, mother. You're looking well." Unfortunately, she is unable to respond. A stroke took her voice, and most other things, away from her. She is seated in a wheelchair, next to my most coveted chair, the 'Proust Armchair', in black. You don't want to know how much it cost.

"Mind if I join you?" My mother blinks at me. You know, they say the eyes are the window to the soul, but I'm not really sure what they mean by that. I've stared for hours into the eyes of my mother and I have yet to see a soul.

"I've been reading about serial killers lately. What makes them tick. How they get caught. But also, more primal stuff. You know? Like why does murder exist? Is there an evolutionary advantage to killing? Spoiler alert, duh!" I can't help but yell this last part. I'm always trying to get a rise out of mamma. But there's nothing from her and I can't help but laugh. "Primates are murderous. And the last time I checked, we are still primates."

I spin around and dance a little jig before taking a seat. "I'm so lucky to have you. The nurse did a great job dressing you today. I've always loved that dress. It looked so good on Ana." There is a flicker of pain across her face, but I'm not sure if it is real, or just my imagination.

"Let me tell you a story. Once upon a time, there was a little boy. The little boy fell in love with a princess. But the princess didn't love him. The princess feared him, so she moved far away. The little boy cried and cried, his house filling up with water. The water pushed him up the stairs and into the highest room of the house. Eventually, the pressure caused the window to burst open, and he was pushed out of the house on a giant wave. A giant bird saw him and swooped down and lifted him up. She brought him to a nest high in the mountaintops, where he learnt how to be a bird. He learnt how to fly. And how to hunt. And as time went on, he would forget boyish things. He would forget human things.

One night, several years later, he was out

hunting. He heard crying far in the distance and he followed the sound across the mountains and through the valleys until finally, he came across the princess. As he gazed upon her face, his memories stirred. She was tied to the trunk of a giant tree, tears streaming down her face. He landed in front of her and she didn't recognise him, for he was no longer a little boy. She called out to him, 'help me! Please, oh great bird, how beautiful you are! Use your sharp beak to free me from my bonds'. And although the little boy had once been scorned by the princess, his heart still burned for her. He released her from her bonds and was rewarded with a gentle caress, the princess running her fingers through his feathers. 'Come' she had said. 'Take me back to my kingdom, my mother will reward you.'

And so, the princess climbed upon the back of the bird-boy, and he flew her home. The distance was so great he could no longer recall the way back, but even if he had remembered, there was no way he could ever get back. Feathers had begun falling from his body, one by one, and by the time they reached the home of the princess, he was no longer a bird, but a handsome man.

The princess did not have time to introduce him to the queen, for as soon as they landed, several guards had taken the boy-man into custody and brought him to the dungeon.

The man was executed at dawn, his body erupting into flames as his neck was severed from his body. The flames created the image of a bird in flight and everyone said that it was a sign that the kingdom was now cursed.

The queen realised her mistake too late. She had thought the man had kidnapped her daughter, but she had been wrong. As she slept that night, her windows thrown open, a breeze had pushed a flame into her room and her bed was engulfed in minutes. The queen awoke to find that she could not move, could not escape, and she died, a scream on her lips."

February 7th, 2014
Youngstown, Ohio

She asked, "What makes someone capable of murder?"

Sagan took a deep sigh and then laughed a little, shaking his head. He was seated across from a beautiful woman with auburn hair. She was composed but friendly, wearing a simple red dress that clung to her figure. Her face showed laugh lines; she had the start of some slackening of the skin in her upper arms, and a bit of a belly, but these were things she seemed proud of. He couldn't stop looking at her.

"People want to think that you can separate individuals into categories like good or bad." He was trying to think of how to continue. He removed his Stetson and held it in front of him while sitting in the chair, his fingers running nervously around the brim, spinning it around and around, his eyes downcast toward his hands. He usually tried to avoid dates like this. Well, any dates, really.

He looked up at her. "You ever seen that artsy short film 'The Way Things Go'?" He looked expectantly at her and she shook her head. "Well, these two guys, the artists, I guess, set up a bunch of random things in a row. Like tyres, tables, garbage bags filled with heavy things…and lots of other stuff. But they set them up like dominoes, set the whole thing in motion with a twirling garbage bag; that bag pushed a tyre, which then rolled to knock over a table and…well…you get the idea. Every little piece included in the set-up had a job to do. The whole thing was a testament to cause and effect. I've always thought of murder in the same way. The end result is murder, yes, but there are usually numerous, often seemingly inconsequential, steps which have occurred and ultimately prompted that end result. It just seems to build up in some people. But…and maybe you won't want to see me after this…I honestly think anyone is capable of murder. Murders require motive, and people come up with motives all the time. You figure out the motive, and you've got your guy. Or girl." He glanced up and saw that she was still listening.

She said, "Most people don't go around murdering other people."

He smiled at her. "You're right about that. But nine times out of ten they sure have thought about it. There's always people in your life who you would rather live without."

She cocked an eyebrow slyly. "Oh yeah? Well, who's yours then? Who would you murder?"

"Aaron Henderson."

She laughed. "Whoa, you answered that pretty quickly. Who's Aaron?"

"The kid who bullied me as a child. He punched me in the nose when I was ten. Broke it. I've been ugly ever since."

She laughed easily, a gentle warm sound. "Ugly, huh?" She gave him a suggestive look and bent down to sip from her straw.

Sagan's voice cracked when he asked, "What about you?" Damn, this woman made him feel like a bumbling teenager again. His crotch had begun to feel tight.

A darkness crept over Ann's face. "Who would I kill?"

Sagan realised they had gone to a dark place here, but he answered anyway. "Yes."

"My uncle. But…he's already dead." She shook off the bad memories. "Don't ask how. I don't want to have to kill again."

They both laughed at that, and spent the rest of the evening exchanging stories about their lives and chatting, the conversation drifting from questions as banal as 'how often do you change your bedsheets?' to intense discussions about whether humanity would ever meet alien life, among other things. They were the last customers in the tiny Italian restaurant, staying until every other table had been immaculately cleaned. When they got up from the table, Sagan realised the only thing left on it was the tablecloth. He could not even remember the waiter picking up their dishes. Good work there, detective. Nice to know you are aware of your surroundings. He shook his head as they walked towards the door. Ann was behind him.

"What?" she asked, as they stepped outside into the cool evening air.

He turned to look at her, taking her hand in his. "It's been a long time since I was able to forget that I'm an agent. Thanks for that. Thanks for the lovely evening."

"Aww. Cowboy, you're going to make me blush." She looked up at this awkward man, full of idiosyncrasies. "You're not what I expected, John."

"Is that a good thing or a bad thing?"

She dodged the question. "Walk me to my car?" They started walking along the street, hand in hand, a comfortable silence between them, before she answered. "You might not have figured it out yet, but I'm a cynic. I was kind of expecting you to be the same. I didn't think I was going to like you. I mean, really like you. I thought we would have a nice dinner, laugh and flirt, then make our way back to some corner or bed and…you know."

Sagan looked calm beside her. But his pulse had quickened, and he had slowed his walking, dreading reaching her car. Dreading the end of this walk.

"But you're not a cynic. Despite your history, despite your job, despite being ugly…"

He laughed out loud beside her, taken aback by this insert of humour, his fingers squeezing her hand.

"Despite all that, you're a romantic. You've got layers, John. And I have to say, you intrigue me. I want to peel back all those layers. I want to get to the heart of you. I'm sorry if this all sounds a little intense for a first date, it's just been a while since…"

He cut her off by stopping their walk and turning to face her, looking intensely into her eyes.

"Can I kiss you?" she whispered, reaching her

right hand up to his face as he nodded. She cupped his jaw, running her thumb over his bottom lip. "It's been a while since...since I've been scared to kiss someone." She had to stand on her tippy toes to reach his mouth, but she brushed her lips against his, closing her eyes and breathing in his scent. He made a soft moaning sound and leaned into her, his arms wrapping around her in a hug, one hand at the back of her neck, the other at her waist.

As they broke apart from each other, Ann's phone began to ring. "It's the babysitter. I need to take this, I'm sorry."

She stepped away from him and he looked around. They were two cars away from her Toyota Camry. It had been a wonderful night, but he feared the future. He had fucked up every relationship he had ever been in. Could he bring himself to subject another woman to his neuroses?

"I've got to go. My son has woken up from a nightmare and he won't calm down and go back to sleep. I've promised him I'll be right there."

"Hey, don't worry about it. I know how it is." He pointed to her car. "Do I still get to walk you to your car?"

She grasped his offered arm with both hands. "Of course. Shall we?"

He led her towards the back of the car and brought her around to the driver's side. She opened the door and turned to face him, the door between them. "I know it's hard, John. But can we see where this goes? I don't want to play games. I want to see you again."

His response was simple. "I'd love to see you again, but I'm not sure exactly how long I'll be in town…" He let the statement hang in the air.

"London isn't so far away. A three-hour drive. I already checked. And, I know, I know, you won't always be in London, Ohio. This job takes you everywhere. I get it. I do. If a single mother who is also a humanities professor can find the time, so can you." She gave him a quick peck on the cheek, smiled, and sunk down into the driver's seat.

He closed her door and waved goodbye, stepping away from the car and moving back towards the sidewalk. He watched her drive away and stood there for a great many minutes after, a solitary figure in the dark. He whispered to himself, "A romantic, huh?" Shaking his head, he walked back in the opposite direction, a grin on his face.

Chapter 7

June 19th, 2014
Hunter, New York

Today is my birthday and you didn't make me a cake. Big surprise there. You did, however, leave me alone for the whole weekend. I overheard you talking to Bella about it. A weekend with this guy, CJ. You've been spending an awful lot of time with him lately. And while I've made good use of the Wi-Fi and satellite service (thank god for porn, am I right?), I have to say, I'm feeling more lonely than usual. I miss you.

It's been a while since I've received any presents. But the last time I got birthday gifts, they were really good. Insanely good, actually. I got an Apple MacBook Air, a Canon EOS 5D Mark II, a universal tripod, Adobe Photoshop with Elements 7 and Exposure 2, and a 60GB iPod. My grandparents were trying to make up for so much.

I also got a bunch of blank journals. And a printer. Thank god for the neighbour's Wi-Fi. I've been using it for years. It's probably the only thing that's kept me from going insane. Well, that and my newly acquired courage to leave this humble abode.

One more year. One more year and I'll be out of here. Maybe I'll look you up. Ha! Give you all these journals I've written to you. Maybe not. There's some stuff in here you probably wouldn't enjoy reading. I guess they're not really for you, anyway. They're my 'Wilson', I guess. Have you ever seen Castaway? Damn good movie.

I've been planning for my freedom. What am I going to do when I get out of here? Well, I'm going to tell you a secret. Have you ever heard of the dark web? It's as scary as it sounds. I've been down there in the depths. Not because I'm a sicko, mind you. But because I'm looking for a sicko. I'm looking for a murderer.

I know what you would say: that I'm wasting my time; that I need to move on with my life. Let the past remain in the past. But I can't. There is a chance I'm wasting my time. Perhaps the man I'm looking for doesn't exist on the dark web. Perhaps he's never told anyone about his sin.

But in a year…just one year, I'll find out for sure. No matter what.

June 26th, 2014
Manhattan, New York

He was cooking her dinner. A man who could cook, how did she get so lucky? She could smell a delicate blend of fish, basil, and lemon, and underneath it all the aroma of earthy spice. It reminded her of the spice cake her mom used to make. Just thinking about that delicious cream cheese frosting made her heart melt. She looked over at him from the couch, seated comfortably with a wine glass in her hand. Feeling her gaze, he looked up.

His eyes looked hungry, and not for the food that he was preparing. His gaze stared at her bare legs and travelled up to the hem of her dress, a white number with delicate pink flowers. It was tucked neatly under her legs, her knees tightly together, obscuring any chance glimpse of what might be hiding beneath. His gaze moved up to her eyes and only then did he smile. God, that smile got her every time. She smiled back at him and imagined opening her legs and letting her hand trail down to her thighs. Imagined lifting her dress so that he could see her naked beneath. Imagined touching herself, eyes locked on his face, while her lips parted, and her breath quickened. Her pulse was already rising and all he'd done was look at her.

She had been uncomfortable with sex for a long time, cringing whenever anyone touched her breasts or tried to incite her passions. It had taken many of her adult years before she had felt comfortable enough to have a romantic relationship, let alone a sexual one. But here she was, flirting.

He gave a sultry chuckle. "You look hungry."

Her eyes moved up from his strong hands to his eyes and her face reddened. She laughed and brazenly said, "As great as that cod smells, I'm really looking forward to dessert."

He seemed to consider her words. "I haven't decided if you're getting dessert."

They both started laughing. Was she so obvious? Did he realise how powerless she was to his charms? A timer went off and he turned to open the oven door. He removed a tin of cupcakes and set them on the counter.

"Alright, time to eat! I'll let the cupcakes cool for a bit." He carried two plates over to the table, both perfectly arranged with large cod fillets nestled upon beds of wild rice and mushrooms, with a basil and tomato white wine sauce poured over each.

She sat down as he pulled out a chair for her. "This looks amazing, Charlie."

He kissed the top of her head, and sat down across from her. "I hope it tastes as good as it looks."

She pictured his tongue tasting her and blushed again. She looked down at her plate and closed her eyes, taking a deep breath. She imagined the aromas as a love spell. Could it be? Was she falling in love with this man? She opened her eyes to find Charlie pouring her some more wine. "Thank you." She picked up her knife and fork and took a delicate bite. "Mmm, this is delicious! Where did you learn how to cook?"

His face darkened briefly, but he shook it off almost immediately. "Oh, here and there. I really enjoy it."

They spent the meal talking about Julia's job and his upcoming show, and as the evening progressed, the wine caused Julia to let down her guard. She told Charlie things she had never told another human being. She told him about her childhood. How her parents had gone to Cuba to visit family and never returned. How she had been moved from Athens, Georgia to Miami, Florida, to live with a distant Hispanic relative. How she had never wanted to marry. "Not until now." She tried to pull away, excusing her comment with, "I am so drunk, I'm sorry!" But he put his arms around her and turned her to face him. He looked sober and more serious than she had ever seen him.

"I've never wanted to marry anyone either. Not until now." His hand held her face, his thumb on her chin. He brought her closer and dipped his head down to kiss her. It was a slow thing, but not gentle. It felt as if he were marking her, as if he were claiming her soul. She had never wanted to be possessed; had always felt proud of her strength and ability to exist alone. But this man made her feel things she had never felt.

As they broke away from the kiss, she whispered, "Will you be mine?" The moment felt tense, like the whole world was waiting for his response. In her drunkenness, she felt the need to lighten the mood. She asked, "Will you be my Valentine?"

It wasn't hilarious, in and of itself, but the couple had an inside joke about Valentine's Day. Julia had always shunned the stupid holiday, but Charlie had not been aware of this little detail. He had been enamoured with Julia since the day he first met her, and unbeknownst to her, had made plans for Valentine's Day. The day had happened to fall on her Friday off, and he had asked Lori to send her a box of chocolates, a large card in the shape of a heart, and a dozen red roses. His instructions had indicated she should tell the florist to say that the gifts were from 'a secret admirer'.

When he had come into the gallery the next week, he had overheard Julia telling one of the clients about her surprise delivery. She had said the flowers had gone directly into her composting bin and that the card had been chucked in the fireplace.

"But I had to eat the chocolates, I just couldn't bring myself to ditch them. I hate Valentine's Day, but I love chocolate more. I have no idea who they were from, but they were good."

He had stood, shocked, glued to the floor, his mouth agape. The female client had noticed him first.

"There's the photographer, now."

"Hey, Charlie! Are you okay?" Julia had looked confused.

"You...you hate Valentine's Day?"

The realisation had dawned on her then. Charlie must have been the one to send her the oh-so-typical red roses. "Oh. It was you. Wow. Okay. Umm...sorry?"

He had laughed then, truly tickled with the woman standing before him. She was so different from the others, of course she hated things that 'normal' women loved.

"Hey, no big deal. How about you let me take you out to dinner to make up for it?"

Now it was her turn to laugh. "How dare you send me flowers...and red roses at that!" She scoffed and shook her head as if she were scolding a child. And that is how they had really started.

"I should have known, you know. After you sent me 'Saying Goodbye'." Julia snuggled into him, her head on his chest. The delivery of the art piece had really surprised her.

"I've always been your Valentine," he said. "I do have one little request."

"Name it, Romeo."

"If we have a girl, we're naming her Talia."

Part 3: Talia

"He married Talia to wife; and she enjoyed a long life with her husband and her children, thus experiencing the truth of the proverb:

'Those whom fortune favours find good luck even in their sleep'."

— Sun, Moon, and Talia, Giambattista Basile

Chapter 1

July 1st, 2014
Manhattan, New York

"He wants kids." Julia paced around the small space, hands clasped behind her as she walked. Her hair was loosely tied into a haphazard knot on top of her head, accidental tendrils framing her face. "He even has a name picked out!"

"And you don't want kids. Does he know that?"

"I've told him. I've told him that there are too many unwanted children in the world. That I can't bring life into this world when there are so many in need. We argue about it, cool off for a couple of days, and then we meet for coffee or dinner and everything feels like it's back to normal. And then he tries again. Makes some off-handed comment, like, how he can't wait to read books to my pregnant belly. And I can either lose it and live without him or stay quiet and enjoy having him in my life."

"Hmm. You know, I do offer couple's therapy."

Julia laughed at that. "You do not want to hear about his views on therapists. There's no way he would be caught dead here. He thinks it's a waste of time that I see you. He says that I don't need it."

"And what do you think?"

"I think that if I don't need you anymore, it's because you've helped me get to a point where I don't."

The women shared a smile at the compliment.

"I appreciate that, Julia. But I was merely the conduit. You're the one who put in the work. You're the one who has changed her own life."

Julia sat down on the couch with a huff. "You haven't asked me."

Nia laughed. "Are you ready to talk about it?"

"Yes."

"Alright. Close your eyes. I want you to think about the people around you. The people in your life. All those people were once children. Growing up brings with it many failures. Memories that are painful. Childhoods are often filled with loss and heartache. You feel as if you failed your parents; that if you had done something differently, they would still be here. Picture that time as it was when you were a child. What happened?"

"I was twelve. We were in Miami at my father's cousin's house. Enrique. Enrique's house. There were a lot of kids there and I was having so much fun. We had spent two weeks in Miami, and it was almost time for us to travel to Cuba. But I didn't want to go. I had heard that Cuba was scary, and I was having so much fun. So, I begged my parents to let me stay. We argued for two days. I was a mess, crying and carrying on so much that I made myself throw up. Enrique offered to let me stay.

He told my parents that it would be his anniversary gift to them. They would be celebrating fifteen years during the Cuba trip. He told them to look at it as a second honeymoon. And they relented. They left me in his care. And I never saw them again."

"Imagine this happening to another person. Imagine hearing this story from one of the children you've helped. You hear her blame herself for the disappearance of her parents. What do you feel for her?"

"Sadness. Pain. Empathy."

"Imagine yourself as you are now. Imagine stepping towards the child. Imagine wrapping her up in your arms. Let the empathy flow out of you. Wrap that little girl in it."

Julia was silently crying. Nia had put on some acoustic guitar, low and gentle in the background. Julia rode the music in waves, telling the little girl that it wasn't her fault. Telling her that mistakes happen. Telling her that it would be okay.

"Okay, Julia. That's good. But there's more, isn't there?"

Julia whispered, "Yes." Her voice sounded like that of a child.

"When you're ready, tell me what happened next. Tell me what happened to that little girl."

Several minutes passed. Julia let the music lull her into a semblance of peace. "Several weeks after my parents left, some cops showed up at Enrique's door. We were told that my parents had been lost at sea. It was decided that Enrique would become my guardian. For a couple of months, I was allowed to grieve. No one touched me. But on my thirteenth birthday, my father's cousin came to my bedroom in the middle of the night. He brought his sons. I awoke to a hand over my mouth. Hands on my pyjamas. Hands on my breasts. Hands in my underwear. Hands everywhere. I tried to fight back. I thought they were intruders. I bit into the flesh over my mouth and tried to scream out for Enrique. That's when he turned on the bedside lamp and I realised it was him. Then he yelled at me. Cussed at me in Spanish and punched me in the face. Between the four of them, there was always someone in my bed. Every night. Every night I let them take me. Let them touch me. Kiss me. Fuck me." Julia wrapped her arms around herself.

Tears freely ran from Nia's eyes as she listened to the pain exhibited by her patient. "You're not that little girl anymore, Julia. You've grown. You've grown so much. Imagine the strength you have now. You are so much stronger. Emotionally. Physically. I want you to imagine yourself there now, as an adult. I want you to take control of the situation. I want you to change the outcome. What do you do, Julia?"

Julia's jaw clenched and she brought her arms down to her sides, her hands tightly balled into fists. She screamed, "No! Stop! Stop!" She jumped up from the couch. "I push them off me. I'm bigger than them. I fight them off. I pick up the lamp and break it across Enrique's head. I shove the hot lightbulb down his throat. I choke them. I destroy them." Julia dropped to her knees, head raised, eyes focused on the ceiling.

"Grab that little girl by her hand, Julia. Take her out of there. Save her. Love her. Tell her all the things you should have been told. Tell her she's safe. Be kind to her. Comfort her."

Nia watched Julia for a few minutes and to her amazement, a satisfied grin appeared on Julia's face. Julia looked her way and then stood up.

"Well, Doc, was it as good for you as it was for me?"

Nia started to laugh and stood up. "Come here, woman."

Julia entered her embrace and the women rocked gently back and forth together.

"I hope you realise how amazing you are. You are not that scared little girl anymore, Julia. You are a fierce woman. Capable of making her own way in this life. No matter how much you love this man, don't let him control you. You will never forgive him. Or yourself."

"You're right, Nia."

"Nia, is it?"

Julia laughed. "Sorry, I mean, Doc."

After Julia left her therapist's office, she immediately called Charlie.

"Hey there, beautiful." His voice was warm and melodic, and it drew her in. It came close to melting her resolve, but she launched ahead anyway.

"Hey, Charlie. Can we meet? Right now?"

"You forgot, didn't you?"

Shit. He was out of town on assignment, following some up-and-coming alternative rock band, getting shots for their album.

"I did. I'm sorry."

"Hey, no biggie. Listen. I was thinking of going out to my mom's place this weekend. It's July fourth, and I don't want her to be alone. She's always loved fireworks. So, I was thinking we could go out there together. I could grill us some hamburgers and hotdogs and we can do the whole patriotic thing. It would be a great time to introduce you. What do you think?"

"Sure. Sounds great, Charlie. But we need to talk."

"I know, sweetheart. Just give me this weekend, okay?" He always seemed to know what was on her mind. "If, at the end of this weekend, you still don't want to have kids with me, well, I'll never bring it up again."

She closed her eyes on the other end of the line and quietly asked, "Promise?"

"Scout's honour."

July 2nd, 2014
Hunter, New York

Julia walked up to the receptionist's desk and stood for at least thirty seconds before she was acknowledged.

"Hold on a second, Rodney. There's someone at my desk." The receptionist held the phone to her shoulder and looked at Julia. "Yes?"

Wow. Julia couldn't believe this unprofessional twat was David's receptionist. She tried her best to remain cordial. "Hi. I have an appointment with Mr Washington."

The young girl rolled her eyes and offhandedly said, "Sure. Go on in," her attention immediately back on the office phone. Julia stepped towards the door and heard the receptionist cuss behind her.

"Shit! Just great, the fucker hung up."

Julia looked back over her shoulder and the receptionist gave her an arched eyebrow and sighed. "Hold on a second, let me buzz him."

As the receptionist dialled a code on the phone to reach David, his office door flung open and he started to stride out. Julia was still at the door and the two collided in the doorway. David, who was quick on his feet, grabbed Julia by the shoulders and held her upright.

The receptionist started saying, "Uncle, I was just about ready to…" whilst Julia and David were apologising to each other over the mishap.

Motioning Julia towards his office, David gave his attention to his niece. "Thank you, Tonya. That's fine, now, thank you." Once the door was closed, David apologised.

"Sorry for my niece, she and her mamma are going through a rough patch right now. This is her first job. I know she's not doing too well at it, but she'll get better. Here, take a seat."

For the next hour, Julia and David sat at a small, round table, poring over licensing documents, only managing to fill out one: a Not-for-Profit Certificate of Incorporation for the soon-to-be Beaumont Home for Girls. They still had to file for an employee identification number, apply for a sales tax exemption certificate, and a mountain of other licenses. Once the home was established as a non-profit, the most important thing would be to get a Foster Care Operating Certificate from New York.

The task was daunting but accepting David's help had been the catalyst that Julia needed to move forward with hers and Kathryn's shared venture.

"Thank you so much for your help with this."

"Not at all. I'll be sorry to see you leave the foundation, but I look forward to organising joint ventures together in the future."

"Oh, I hadn't thought about that." Somehow, she had imagined being able to still work for the foundation while running the girl's home. But David was right, this was going to be more than a job. This would be a twenty-four hours a day, seven days a week commitment. "I'm going to need to hire some help."

"Undoubtedly. It will be a challenge to get everything set up within the timeframe your contract stipulates, but I've spoken with the lawyers and as long as you have put in a substantial effort towards moving the project forward by the due date, they won't revoke your residence."

"Thank you, David. I could not have done this without you."

Chapter 2

July 4th, 2014
London, Ohio

Sagan, Jakob, and Cindy had returned to their home base despondent, and once again, empty-handed. Another murder. Another lead. Another failure. Their detective work had led to nothing. They had researched the photography angle, talking to photography shops all over the state. They had spoken with photography teachers at each murder location, investigated a few. They had chased down every tip that had come in on the tip line.

Sagan was alone in the office. He had given Jakob and Cindy the weekend off, admonishing them to, "Take it easy this weekend. Lick your wounds, and we'll reconvene on Monday."

He was usually pretty good at handing out advice. Not so good at following it though. He was planning to spend Saturday and Sunday with Ann, but tonight he was going to look over the old case files, just in case. The phone on his desk rang and he was so startled by it he jumped a little. When had he invested in a desk phone? He was sure the thing had never rung before.

"Hello? Sagan here."

"Hey there. It's John, isn't it? John Sagan?"

Sagan rolled his eyes. "Yes."

"Hi, this is Agent Parker, with the Youngstown branch."

"Calling me on the fourth? This must be serious." Sagan sat up in his chair and held the phone closer to his ear. The man on the other end had his complete attention.

"Well, sir, we had big plans for the weekend, and I wanted to make sure the tip line would have enough tape in it to last until Tuesday."

"Tape?"

"Yes sir. I'm afraid we have some very old technology around here. Well, I'm not sure it's considered technology at this point."

The young man laughed to himself, but Sagan was losing patience.

"We have five answering machines—"

Sagan cut him off. "Good god, agent, we've been on the phone for five fucking minutes already. What the bloody hell do you want? I don't need the encyclopaedia version."

The young man stuttered. "So...sorry sir...yes sir...we...we have his voice. On tape. We think."

Sagan stood up. "Whose voice?"

"The killer's, sir. The Polaroid Killer, sir."

Sagan was beyond ready to be on his way. "Agent?"

"Yes, sir?"

"Stay there. I'll see you in two hours."

To an empty line, the young man said, "But it's a three-hour drive, sir."

July 4th, 2014
Youngstown, Ohio

Ann was on campus with a group of professors and students, all gathered together to enjoy the night. The college had provided a decent amount of funding for the event and there was a stage with local music; grills stocked with a never-ending supply of hamburgers and hotdogs, and a firework show planned for later in the evening.

Ann's son was with his father, so she had the whole weekend to herself. Tomorrow, she would be heading to London, to spend the weekend with John. She had invited him to the night's festivities, but he had said he needed to pay penance before he could enjoy his time with her.

She closed her eyes and listened to the scattered conversations and laughter around her. This was living. She really felt tied to the community here. She couldn't imagine leaving this place. She considered her budding relationship with John. Was she really willing to put in all the time and effort necessary to handle being with someone who had such a Type-A personality?

"Ann! Hi there!" Ann opened her eyes to see Carolyn Bass standing in front of her. The other woman was dressed in khaki capris and a red, white, and blue tie-dyed tank top.

"Hey there, stranger. Get in here." Ann had

stood up and put her arms out, inviting an embrace from the other woman. "Sit, sit. How have you been?"

"Doing pretty well, actually. I just picked up a writing contract. I'm going to be the co-author of a new book, 'Women of Woodstock: The Art of a Generation'."

"Wow! Exciting! Congratulations."

"Thanks. What about you? I hear you've had a few dates."

"Oh, they sure do like to talk around here, don't they?"

"They sure do." The women shared a laugh before Ann continued.

"Well, I've been seeing an investigator. His name is John Sagan, he works…"

"John Sagan? I was supposed to call him back. He left messages for me a while ago, when I was out of town for that photography retreat with the kids."

"Really? It must have been about the case he's working on."

Carolyn's curiosity was piqued. "What case is that?"

Ann seemed reluctant to discuss it. "Well, I guess I can talk about it since it's in the news and everything. But you know that murder that happened back in January? I think her name was Candace…something…?" Carolyn nodded. "Well, John thinks that her death is related to a serial killer case that he's been working on for the past three or four years. He's been following a photography connection. Looking for a photographer who might travel across the states frequently."

Carolyn had begun to feel a sinking sensation in the pit of her stomach.

The worry must have been showing on her face because Ann asked, "What? What's wrong?"

"Do you have John's number? I think I may need to speak with him."

Charlie had given Julia directions to his mom's estate, telling her to be sure to follow them to the letter.

"The cell reception out here is shit, so you won't be able to call if you get turned around. The one main thing to look out for is starting down the wrong driveway. There's one that leads out to old man Henderson's place, and trust me...you do not want to go onto his property."

"How will I know if it's the right driveway?"

"Once you hit Freedom Dairy Farm on the left, just start counting. Once you've counted the fifth driveway on the right, go ahead and turn in. If you've gone a mile in on a shitty dirt road and you still haven't seen a house...you're on the right one. We own a bunch of properties out there. The Henderson place is the only one that comes close to being near us, but even though our driveways are located in about the same area, their house is still miles and miles away from ours. You might as well be alone in the world when you're out here."

"Are you sure you can't come pick me up?"

He laughed. "Baby, it'll be fine. I promise. Besides, I'm trying to get things ready here. I want everything to be perfect."

"Alright. But if you don't hear from me by

dinner time, send out a rescue team." Her laughter sounded hollow to her ears. She could fucking do this, right? It was just a huge house in the middle of nowhere.

His tone was serious on the other end of the line. "I could find you anywhere, babe."

She believed him.

Julia made the drive without incident, only getting nervous when she had driven for ten minutes along what she was sure was the right driveway without seeing a house. But not long after, the maple and poplar woods thinned out and she was stunned by the hundred yards of wildflowers growing on either side of the path. The dirt road became a gravel one and trees were once again visible, this time purposely planted black tupelo trees.

Charlie had previously told her that his family had money, and that he had made plenty himself, but he had always downplayed it. He had never come across as someone who had come from money, not that she knew how to identify someone who had, but she had not been expecting anything like this.

The place was a mansion. She brought the car to a halt several hundred yards away, just to take in the immensity of the structure. The house was built from multi-coloured stones, with gradients of grey, tan, and white. It looked like five houses had been cobbled together, the main entrance graced with columns. Julia counted at least ten pointed gables and two rounded towers. She had thought Kathryn's place was huge. It was nothing compared to this. What had she gotten herself into? How could a man this rich need anything from her? She came close to turning around, close to ending it all. Then she remembered his pledge. He had said he was willing to give up having children for her. He had promised.

She put her red Camry into drive and continued up the road, her awe only growing the closer she moved towards the building. To the right of the main house, she could see a tennis court. She had never been a tennis player, but seeing it made her excited. Was it possible there was a pool here? She hadn't brought a suit, but she would swim in underwear if she had to. God, she didn't recognise herself. Was she really getting excited over this flagrant display of wealth? Yes. Yes, she was. She felt almost giddy.

There were three other cars in the driveway. She spotted Charlie's blue Mazda Miata, but didn't recognise the other two vehicles, a huge brown Ford truck, and a small white hatchback of some sort. Charlie stepped out of the massive front door, at least twice his height, and waved as she parked. He was wearing a collared, button-down blue shirt with casual khaki pants, and looked as if he belonged here. She looked down at the blue and white striped romper she had thrown on, and suddenly felt self-conscious. She smiled through the window and stepped out, hoping his family was as down to earth as he was.

Charlie met her in the driveway, looked over her appreciatively and gave her a big hug. "I'm so glad you made it. Did you have any trouble finding the place?"

"No! The directions were great." She spun around with her arms out wide, looking at the massive house around her. "Charlieee…"

"What?"

"You gotta tell a girl if you're stupid fucking rich, you know."

"What? This old place?"

She lightly punched him in the arm. "I'm nervous about meeting your folks. Your family. Is your brother coming? Who will be there?"

Charlie laughed. "Hey, slow down. Do you want to keep asking questions or do you want me to start answering?"

"Hmm." Julia, stroked her chin with her fingers, doing her best to look inquisitive.

"Oh, stop you." He looped his arm through hers and bumped his hip against her. "You have absolutely nothing to worry about. I haven't seen my dad in years, my brother's working, and my mom can't speak. So even if she hates you, which she won't, she won't be able to tell you that she does."

"I'm still nervous."

"Shush." He tapped her on the tip of her nose with his finger, then followed the gesture with a kiss. "You are absolutely the most perfect woman ever to grace this house."

He always made her feel a little weird with his declarations of perfection. She was far from perfect. No one alive was perfect. Would he leave her when he figured that out? Julia pointed to the other vehicles. "Whose cars are those?"

"Oh, the truck belongs to one of the maintenance guys, and to tell you the truth, I have no idea about the other one. We have a few people milling about. Maybe it belongs to the nurse?"

As they stepped into the foyer, Charlie asked, "How about a tour?"

She had decided there was no way to feign nonchalance. She craved a tour. "Yes! Absolutely!" She tugged on his arm. "Like, right now?"

He laughed and pulled her in for a kiss. "Right now."

The tour took a couple of hours and Julia was constantly in awe of the artistry that had been put into creating the mansion. Even with a lengthy tour, she still hadn't seen all of the bedrooms, the pool, or had a stroll through the gardens.

"There are fifteen bedrooms, but one has been renovated for my mother's care. And as you've seen so far, a lot of bathrooms. I'm not sure how many there are, actually. Maybe we can find out this weekend."

The floors of the huge house mainly consisted of parquet designs of inlaid wood, forming different patterns from room to room. One of Julia's favourite spaces was the ballroom on the third floor, a circular space with a one-hundred-and-eighty-degree view of the gardens in the back and the lake in the distance. To the left, she could see a pool. Curved sliding glass doors allowed access to an outdoor balcony, which spanned the entire backside of the house.

Julia stepped outside, plopped down onto a thickly padded sun lounger, and sighed contentedly, raising her arms up and placing her hands behind her head. "I could be happy just staying here, right here, for the rest of the weekend."

Charlie perched on the edge of the lounger opposite hers, looking not at all relaxed.

"What's up, babe?"

"I'm just worried about my mom. She hasn't been doing too well lately. Normally, I don't see it. I don't see her. I get daily updates from the nurses, of course. But they always try to sound positive." He shook his head and nervously pulled at his ear. "I lie to myself every day. Tell myself she's doing well. Tell myself she's going to be around forever. But she's not. And she won't."

Julia reached out a hand and he took it, intertwining their fingers.

"Well, screw this tour, babe. Let's go meet your mom."

"Yeah?"

"Of course. I'm sure you want to spend as much time as you can with her." Charlie's face split into a wide grin and he kissed her.

They headed back down to the main floor, walking towards a closed door. They had skipped this room earlier, and Julia had been curious about it. Charlie knocked before entering.

"Hey, mom, I'd like you to meet Julia." The woman was in a lavish library, seated in a wheelchair and dressed in a red, white, and blue blouse and blue silk pants. Julia stepped up to her and smiled, trying to hide the horror she felt for the fate of this poor woman, immobilized.

"Nice to meet you, Mrs Ivanov." Julia patted the old woman on her hand. The woman made a sound deep in her throat and appeared to be agitated.

"Mom, should I call for the nurse? Should we send you to bed?" Charlie moved to the woman's side, his face a mask of concern. He whispered to the woman, but Julia had stepped away and couldn't hear his words.

"Alright, now. Everything's okay. Let's have a seat, shall we?"

Charlie wheeled his mother into the sitting area, parking her across from a loveseat where he sat with Julia. They would spend the next hour listening to Charlie regale them with stories from his youth, how he learnt how to cook at his mother's side and how his mother had provided him with the tools to feed his creativity. He told of their fourth of July parties from when he was young, his dad standing in front of the grill for hours, and how proud he had always been of the ribs that ended up burnt more often than not.

"So, we'd eat his burnt ribs because we knew he'd make up for it with the fireworks. My dad always spent hundreds of dollars on fireworks. I'm not sure they were actually legal here then, but my dad wouldn't have cared one way or another."

"Speaking of grilling, I'm getting pretty hungry, Charlie."

"Wow, you're right. Look at the time. I'll go get started right away. Would you like to help me?"

"No. You go ahead. I'll wait here with your mom. Bore her with the story of how we met."

"Well, I wouldn't say it's a boring story." He

planted a kiss on her forehead, then walked over to his mother and repeated the gesture. "You ladies behave yourselves now."

Shortly after Charlie had left the room, the nurse came in to attend to Mrs Ivanov, explaining that the elderly woman would rest until the fireworks display. Julia felt guilty, but she was relieved to have the debilitated woman out of her sight. She had spoken to her for a few minutes, sharing dating stories, but while the woman often stared in her direction, she wasn't sure how much she understood of the one-sided conversation.

Free of the poor woman, Julia wandered to the back door and out onto the deck. She stood watching Charlie in front of the grill. He had a beer in his left hand and was wearing an apron which read, 'Grill King'. He felt her staring and turned to look at her.

"Hey there, beautiful. Almost done here. There are some of those hard lemonade things you like in the fridge. Why don't you grab one?"

Julia returned to the deck and sat down at the picnic table, hard lemonade in hand. Charlie was just pulling the last of the burgers off the grill. As he laid out the tray of meat, he said, "I'll be right back. Just gotta grab the toppings."

He brought back an enormous spread: a tray lined with soft Boston lettuce leaves, thinly sliced ripe tomatoes, sandwich-sliced pickles, fresh jalapeño slices, sweet relish, and probably twelve different types of condiments. There was hot chili, strips of crispy bacon, sauerkraut, grilled mushrooms with peppers, diced white onions, and rings of red onion, with gourmet sesame-seed buns and potato hot dog buns ready for filling.

"Holy shit, Charlie. You've really outdone yourself. When did you do all this?"

He sat down next to her and then leaned in for a kiss. "Only the best for my baby."

The next couple of hours were taken up with the couple building burgers and hotdogs, each trying to outdo the other with the most outrageous mix of toppings. But it wasn't until Charlie brought out the Patrón that the competition really kicked off, with both of them commencing a frantic search of the kitchen in order to find the most unorthodox ingredients.

"Okay, okay! Charlie, look, here's a timer. This is what we're going to do. I'm going to set the timer for three minutes. We meet back at the picnic table when the timer goes off."

Charlie was drunk. He felt good. "And what are we going to do at the table? Oh, we're racing to the table?"

"No, no, Charlie, listen! We have three minutes, okay? Three minutes to make a burger masterpiece. Then we meet back at the table and present them okay? Okay? Go!"

Three minutes later, the couple, breathing heavily, met back at the table.

Julia introduced hers first. "May I present to you, the greatest burger in the world, the s'mores burger! It has chocolate syrup, bacon, and marshmallow cream all presented on graham crackers!"

"Ooh. That's good! But may I present to you,

the garden special, a flower lover's favourite! It starts off with a one hundred percent pure beef patty, topped with petals from five different flowers, some freshly picked mushrooms, and for added fibre, freshly cut grass!" So that's why he had rushed out of the backdoor.

"Eww." Julia shook her head from side to side, a sickened expression on her face.

"Okay, who wins?"

"Hmm. Whoever finishes their burger first?"

"You never said we were going to have to eat it." She shrugged her shoulders at him. "Alright, dig in then!"

After two bites, Julia's stomach started to churn. "Ugh. I don't feel so good."

Charlie handed her an empty flowerpot to throw up in and continued eating his burger. While she proceeded to hurl into the offered container, he deftly finished his burger and proceeded to dance around the deck, celebrating his win. "The burger-eating champion, Charles Jerard Ivanov, steps to the centre of the ring to accept his award." In his drunken stupor, he finally realised that Julia was sitting on the steps of the deck, wiping spittle from her face. He staggered over and dropped heavily beside her.

"Hey, Charlie."

"Hey, babe." Charlie leaned his head over to rest it on her shoulder and breathed in a big whiff of her vomit, causing him to release the contents of his own stomach, barely missing their shoes.

Relieved of their nausea, they collapsed back onto the deck, laughing together. Charlie reached out his hand to catch hers.

"I love you, Julia."

"I love you, Charlie."

"I know. I know that you don't want to have kids. I know that terrible things happened to you when you were a child and you're scared of the commitment. You're scared of fucking up some kid. You don't think it's right for us to have a child when there are so many out there…who are unwanted. Unloved. I love you, Julia. And if you really don't want to have kids, we won't. But I think about my mother, how little time she has left. She always wanted grandkids, and I know that she can't be the grandmother she'd like to be. But she's in there, Julia. Even if we can't communicate. She's in there, and I'd love to give her a grandchild before she dies. She makes me think of my own future. Who will take care of me when I get old? I'm thankful that she has us, myself and my brother. And now you. I have so much love to give, Julia. And I want to share that love with a child. I know that you would make a good mom. That we could make a perfect family." Julia looked over at him and he tried to reach his right arm over to touch her face. "I can't. I can't move my arm."

They both erupted into laughter.

"I think you're drunk, CJ."

"And I think you're right. What time is it?"

"Hold on." Julia struggled to raise her left arm and it took at least five minutes for her to get her watch into focus, reading its face with one eye closed. "Wow, it's only four thirty."

"Yippee! That means we have four hours until

fireworks!"

"Charlie, we are not in any condition to be setting off fireworks."

"Oh, we won't be doing it ourselves, I've got a man for that."

"A man?"

"Yeah, like a personal assistant guy. You've met him before. Ronald?"

"Oh yeah. He doesn't work at the gallery?"

"No. He's mine. He works for me. He's my slave." Another laughing fit ensued.

"But I thought I was your slave."

"You're just my sex slave." Charlie managed to get to his feet. "Speaking of, let's go to bed, little miss sex slave." Charlie offered Julia a hand and she took it.

"Yes, sir, right away, sir. But I think I'm going to need a shower first."

"You? Naked in a shower big enough for ten people? I think we can have that arranged."

Charlie had not been joking. Julia had never seen such a luxurious bathroom. In the centre of the bathroom stood a circular bathtub, tiled in red marble, a crystal chandelier hanging above it. Located behind the bathtub was a walk-in shower, with five separate showerheads. In the very centre of the shower was a square rainfall showerhead, large enough for two people to stand beneath. The shower included floor-to-ceiling windows, with the lake and woods visible beyond. A large bench stood between the two windows. Opposite the shower-lined wall was a red marble fireplace, a giant, flat-screen television above it.

"Wow. It's almost too much."

"You won't be saying that in a few minutes."

Julia stood on a lush mat in the entryway to the bathroom, watching as Charlie went and turned on the rain shower. He stripped off his clothes as he walked back towards her. God, he was a gorgeous man. He had light chestnut skin, closely cropped dark hair, two-day-old black stubble, and the most startling blue eyes she had ever seen. He was completely naked by the time he reached her. She stood motionless while he undressed her, caressing every inch of skin as it became available to him. He unhooked her bra, tracing her nipples with small, circular movements of his fingers. He slid down to his knees, catching her breasts with his mouth on the way. Julia sucked in a breath and closed her eyes, her hands reaching for him.

His mouth moved to her panties and he pulled them down with his teeth, looking up at her face. Julia held on to his shoulders as he lifted first one leg of hers, and then the other, removing the last piece of clothing that had covered her. He picked her up and carried her to the shower, placing her on the bench and stepping away after a kiss. He stood over her, merely looking, the soft water falling against her.

"You're beautiful. And you're all mine."

He fell before her, grasping her legs and spreading them wide, moving his face between her legs. Tasting the woman that would bear his children.

After their shower, Julia and Charlie napped in the spacious four-poster located in the master bedroom. Julia felt content and safe, snuggling into the feather-topped mattress, and pulling Charlie's arm around her.

"How long do we have?"

"Two hours. I've set an alarm. If you feel like napping, go ahead. Just relax, darling."

"I'm still feeling a bit drunk."

"Really? I'm pretty sure you threw up all the alcohol in your body."

"Ugh. I hate tequila. I can still taste it. Never again, babe. Promise me."

He kissed her on the ear and whispered, "Never again."

Julia grunted an acknowledgment and started to drift off.

"Julia?"

"Hmm?"

"I was thinking that perhaps you'd like to spend part of your summer vacation here. With me?" Julia was silent for a bit and Charlie was sure she had nodded off, until her soft voice surprised him.

"You know this group home I'm working on?"

"Group home? What?"

Julia laughed and elbowed him in the ribs.

"Oh, you mean that project that you can't stop talking about, ever?" He smiled at her.

"Yeah, that one. Well, it's more than a project really. It's a commitment. It's going to take up a lot of my time. And I had planned to spend my vacation going through the house and getting things in order."

"Julia. I've been trying to stay out of it. You know, give you your space." He turned her face towards him and looked her in the eyes. "I know you feel some loyalty to this woman."

"Kathryn. Her name was Kathryn."

"Okay. You feel some loyalty to Kathryn. But you don't have to do this. In fact, you don't need to do any of it. Let me take care of you. You could be my manager or something."

Julia closed her eyes and fought back tears. It would be so easy to lose herself in this relationship. So easy to lose control. To be taken in by his sultry eyes, his tender lips, the warmth of his voice against her naked skin.

"Just think about it. That's all I'm asking." He planted kisses all over her face until she smiled. "But not right now. Right now, you're supposed to be relaxing!"

She moved her hand down the length of his body to find his cock erect. "How am I supposed to relax with this in the bed?"

"Hmm. Good point. I love it when you touch me. Usually..." he gasped.

"Usually, what?"

He growled, low and deep in his throat, rolling over to pin Julia beneath his body. He entered her roughly and found that she was already wet.

"Usually, I prefer to be in control."

A few hours later, Julia and Charlie, who was pushing his mom, made their way down the path to the lake. At the end of the dock was a huge floating platform, decorated with lush plants and complete with furniture. There was even a hammock. A spread of light hors d'oeuvres, fruit, and desserts had been placed on the table, and Julia was again blown away.

"Charlie, I knew you were rich. But I didn't know you were this rich."

"Well, the money for this place came from my mom's family. Some uncle of mine, or something. And you don't see them, but there's a lot of staff here. Nurses for my mom, a couple of gardeners, a chef, and Ronald, of course."

They stood looking out over the lake. The sun was setting, and the fireworks would start soon.

"How much land do you have here?"

"I'm not sure. A lot. It has to be at least a hundred acres."

"Wow." He could see the wheels turning; her expression was complicated, more than just awe.

"Penny for your thoughts."

"I was just thinking about the girl's home, Charlie." He nodded and smiled at her. "I know you've been giving me space with this project. And I appreciate that."

"Okay, but...?"

"Well, you've suggested I drop it. Drop everything. What if instead...what if it became *our* project?"

Charlie looked out across the water. "Come on, let's sit." Charlie led her to a rattan sofa bedecked with white cushions.

As they sat, Julia said, "I know you haven't even seen the house yet. And I know you usually space out when I'm talking to you about all the details..."

Charlie feigned shock and looked aggrieved. "Who, me? Never."

Julia hit him good-naturedly on his upper arm. "But...but I think it would be good for us. It could be a kind of...you know...family, for us."

Charlie was silent.

She continued. "You don't have to answer now. But...will you think about it?"

"You know what? I don't have to think about it. I think it's a great idea."

Julia was surprised. "Really?"

"Really."

Julia gave an excited yelp and kissed him on the lips. And that's when the fireworks started. Way out in the middle of the lake, Julia could see a boat briefly illuminated in the glare. The fireworks were almost constant, sparks of coloured light filling the night sky. She stood, pulling Charlie up beside her, then clasped her hands in delight. She was a child, seeing fireworks for the first time.

"God, it's beautiful."

Charlie was looking at her, her face aglow with wonder, fireworks reflected in her eyes. "You're beautiful." He reached down and took her hand in his.

Fifteen minutes after the fireworks had started, the finale sequence began. A rainbow of hanging colour was created, a red firework bursting up first, quickly followed by orange, yellow, green, blue, indigo, and purple. Then, the sequence was repeated, a second rainbow forming, followed by bursting flowers behind.

"This must have cost a fortune, Charlie."

The fireworks came to an abrupt stop, and dim lighting was turned on around them, coming from behind the plants along the deck and some lamps that Julia had failed to notice before. Charlie's hand was still in hers and as she turned towards him, he began to kneel.

Julia was confused. "Charlie...what..." but she was unable to finish the question, because before her eyes, the man she loved was reaching into the pocket of his thin blazer to pull out a ring box.

"Oh my God, Charlie..."

"Julia Rose Rodriguez, you make me smile and laugh. You make me want things I never thought possible. You make me a better man. You're unlike any woman I've ever known: brave, kind, loyal, and so full of hope and love. Somehow, you snuck under all my defences and found me. I love you. And I don't ever want to let you go. Will you marry me?"

Julia stood silently, tears sliding out from under her eyelashes.

"I'm broken goods, Charlie." He stood up and embraced her, the ring still in his hand.

"You're no such thing. You're perfect."

"I'm not."

He stepped back slightly so that he could look her in the eyes. "You don't have to answer now. You can think about it." He smiled mischievously, parroting back her own words to her.

She smiled. "I don't have to think about it. I love you. Of course, I'll marry you."

"Well, then, let's get this ring on your finger."

She laughed as he returned to the ground,

kneeling before her in supplication, his hand outstretched. She placed her left hand in his and he slid the ring delicately over her knuckle. It was a vintage style ring, set in rose gold, the main gemstone a radiant-cut blue sapphire. Two halos of diamonds surrounded the sapphire. Julia was rendered speechless.

"Charlie, I didn't need all this."

"And that's one of the many things I love about you. But I needed this. I needed to show you how much you mean to me."

Charlie looked over at his mother, whose eyes were wet. "Look at that! Mom is so happy, she's crying. Come on, old lady, let's get you back up to the house."

As they strolled back to the mansion, Julia's arm looped through Charlie's, she thought her life couldn't possibly get any better. She contemplated the past few years of hiding from this. From love. From feeling. She didn't blame herself. She just hadn't been ready and there was nothing wrong with that.

Chapter 3

July 4th, 2014
Youngstown, Ohio

Sagan had made it to the Youngstown office in record time, and he tore into the empty parking lot, siren blaring. He parked across two handicapped spots and slammed the door as he got out, his anticipation driving him to enter the building. Before he reached the entrance, a young agent stepped out.

"Agent Parker, I presume?"

"Yes, sir."

"Just bring me to the recording, then you're more than welcome to join whatever festivities you are currently missing."

"Yes, sir, thank you, sir."

Sagan took a seat and spent the next few minutes playing the recording over and over again, his eyes closed as he listened to the jeering tone of the psycho on the tape. "Oh, I'm coming for you, motherfucker."

His phone began vibrating in his front jacket pocket and he pulled it out, almost ignoring it once he saw the caller was Ann. As it rang for the fourth time, Sagan picked it up.

"Hi there, Ann. I'm really looking forward to tomorrow." God, he was doing it again, already pushing the woman away.

"Hi, John, what? Oh. Yes, absolutely! But I'm calling because I have someone here who needs to speak with you. Carolyn Bass, she's an art professor at Youngstown. She has a lead for you. Hold on, I'm handing her the phone."

"Oh. Okay, great."

"Hi, officer. I'm sorry I haven't gotten back to you until now, but I just completely forgot about it. So sorry about that. I'm hoping I'm wrong, but there's a man who comes here once or twice a year, a photographer named Charles Ivanov. I can give you his number, if you'd like?"

Sagan scribbled down the number and asked the woman several questions. The guy sounded like he could definitely fit the profile. From what he could understand from the professor, Mr Ivanov was often on the road, driving across the US, getting involved with photography classes at universities and colleges or finding locations to shoot. He had spent a lot of time in the state, working on a book called 'Untamed Ohio', but he was typically based in and around New York. It might be a long shot.

According to Carolyn, the guy was extremely kind and generous, but Sagan knew that all sorts of people committed murders. And serial killers often hid their true identity well. After thanking Carolyn, he waited for her to hand the phone back to Ann.

"Alright, thanks, Ann. I appreciate the tip."

"Sure thing, cowboy. See you tomorrow?"

"I hope so. Have a good night now."

Sagan stared down at the scrawled number and thought of how he should proceed. If he were able to reach the man, he would surely know if it was the same man who had left the message. The killer's voice was burned into his mind. But he didn't want to tip the guy off. If he was the murderer, and he got a call from an officer, it was almost guaranteed that the man would flee. Sagan opened an app on his phone that would allow him to record the conversation and slowly dialled in the number, hoping that if the guy actually picked up, his instincts wouldn't fail him.

On the third ring, a man answered the phone and Sagan started. "Hi there, I'm looking for Charles Ivanov."

There was a brief delay before the other man said, "Speaking."

"Wonderful. My name is Daniel…Daniel Wood, and I'm with the Criminal Convention." Shit. Yeah, bring up crime. That won't scare him at all. "Umm…Have you heard of us, sir?"

"I can't say that I have."

"Well, we've been around for a few years and we're currently in the process of planning for our event next year. I got your number from a friend. We're looking for a photographer for the event."

"Oh, well…"

"Could you tell me a little bit about your work?

Would I have seen it anywhere?"

Sagan listened intently to the man's voice while he droned on about how he would be a perfect addition to the convention.

"I could not only take photographs during the event, but I could easily run a lecture on crime scene photography. I could give one every day of the event, even. I also have a series, 'Criminal Lives', that I could discuss as a workshop. How many days will it be?"

Sagan was convinced this wasn't the man who had called the tip line and decided to cut this call as short as possible. He interrupted the litany of suggestions by the overenthusiastic photographer.

"Excuse me. I'm sorry, I have a very important call coming in that I really need to take. I'll send you some information in the mail. Thank you for your time."

Another dead end. But at least they had the guy's voice now. If they could find a suspect, they would be able to match up a voice to the recording.

July 1st, 2010
Carbondale, Illinois

Tonight is the night. I've been watching her for weeks. Following her around campus, listening in to her conversations. There's a big sorority party tonight, and I know that she'll be there.

The first time I saw her, she had just finished a tennis match. She was wearing these tiny little black gym shorts and a maroon-coloured tank, with the college acronym, SIU, in big letters across her chest.

"Hey, man, you know what SIU stands for?"

I had been caught staring by some jock on his way to the gym.

"Of course. Southern Illinois University."

The jock had laughed. "Nah, man. What it really stands for. Slut. It. Up." He had erupted into a fit of snorting laughter, as if what he had said was the funniest thing ever, in the history of humanity.

I had smiled at him, giving a half-hearted response. "Yeah, that's funny."

"Don't bother with that one, though, I hear she's married."

I hadn't seen a wedding ring on her finger.

"Well, that's a waste."

"Yeah, man, you're telling me. Well, anyway, I gotta get to the gym. See you around."

"Later." I knew it wasn't a good idea to follow her after being seen admiring her. But I couldn't help it. There was just something about her dark features that drew me in.

There she was now, fresh out of the showers, speaking to a friend with her speakerphone engaged.

"My phone is fucked up; it only works on speakerphone right now."

"Dude, that sucks."

"Yeah."

"How are you holding up? What a piece of shit." She wasn't even paying attention to me. I probably could have walked right next to her all the way across campus and she would never have noticed.

"He just couldn't handle it. I mean, I don't blame him. It's a lot to ask. He's young. He doesn't want to be tied down to a wife with an invalid for a mother. He did try. For a few months. It was terrible."

"Well, he kind of promised he would help you when he said his vows."

"I don't know if that's fair."

"For better or for worse, Ana Sofia."

"Well, he said he'd help pay for her to be in a home, but I couldn't do that. She's my mom, you know. She's the woman who taught me…everything."

Her friend said, "It's going to be really hard taking care of her alone."

"I have a nurse coming by. And it's nice being out in the country."

"And how are you going to pay for it?"

"Well, mom's house is paid off and I'm driving her car, so I don't need to save for that anymore. And I still have plenty of money left in savings from dad's life insurance. And I just got my tennis scholarship extended for another year."

"That's great, congrats!"

"Thanks. I'm going to have a party this weekend to celebrate."

"I don't know if that's generous of you. Or stupid."

"Well, you know what my mom always used to say."

They chorused together, "If you're doing well, you build a longer table, not a higher fence."

"I'm not sure there'll be many people up to a

party this weekend. So many people already have plans for the fourth."

"Shit! I forgot about that. Mom loves the fourth. She used to make my sisters and I wear matching outfits when we were little. Then she'd do stupid shit with our hair. We always looked like someone had puked red, white, and blue all over us." Ana Sofia sighed. "I guess this weekend is a no-go. That's okay. I could go for a chill weekend with mom. Are you heading to the big party tonight?"

"No, I'm on my way to see my parents. I don't have any more classes this week. So, I'm just going to call it 'Freedom Week' and get the hell out of here."

"Freedom Week, huh? Sounds good. I guess I'll start my week off at this kick-ass party without you, bitch."

"Yeah. You have fun throwing up. I'm going to let my mom take me shopping. Later, bitch. Be safe."

When Ana Sofia left the party, there was a handsome man in a uniform standing outside by a taxicab. He was wearing a white shirt, black tie, black pants, and even had on one of those driving caps. He was smoking a cigarette. Perfect.

"Wow, a chauffeur. I didn't know you guys really existed. Think I could bum a smoke?" The driver shook a camel out of his pack and then lit it for her. "Who are you here to pick up?"

"Someone named Hugh Jass. But he called quite some time ago and hasn't shown up yet, so if you need a ride, I'll be happy to take you."

Ana Sofia started laughing. "You said, you said…huge ASS! Someone got you big time." She stumbled towards him, wobbly on her feet, laughing hysterically.

"You look a little sick, ma'am. Would you like to sit down?"

"I think…I think that's probably a good idea."

"Here, have a seat and I'll get you home." The chauffeur opened the back door to the car, and she climbed in. She was wearing her black gym shorts again. "I've got some cold water here, drink this."

After sitting down, Ana reached for the bottle and drained it in one, long gulp. "That was so good." She closed her eyes and then leaned down, until her head met the seat. "I'm just going to close my eyes a minute."

"Yes, ma'am. Of course, ma'am." He took the dangling cigarette out of her hand and stamped it out on the sidewalk. Then he quietly closed her door and looked around. There were a lot of college kids milling about, but no one seemed to be paying them any attention. He opened the driver's side door and slid in behind the wheel. No comment came from the backseat. He waited until he heard gentle snoring from the girl, then pulled out into the road, intent on bringing her home. They were going to have a very good week.

The drive from the university out to the house in Murphysboro only took fifteen minutes. The house was on a huge lot, far away from any roads. He knew Ana Sofia's habits. Knew that she would come out looking for a smoke. Knew that she normally called a cab. Knew that she'd be close to knock-out drunk. Knew that she wouldn't be able to detect the flunitrazepam in the water.

He knew too that the nurse would be gone, and Ana Sofia's mother would be in her hospital bed. He had already spoken to the woman on several occasions, entering the house at night and then finding her in bed. The first night, she had been asleep, but the second night, she hadn't been. He had told her that he would be coming for her daughter one night. He imagined she didn't sleep well after that.

"She's my first REAL one, so I plan on taking my time. And maybe, if you're lucky, I'll let you watch. I am quite the artist."

She couldn't speak, but she could grunt. She had very little control over her facial movements, but he had become quite fond of guessing what she was feeling or thinking.

"Now, just blink your right eye if I'm right. You're thinking that you wish your daughter was still married." He looked over at the motionless face. "It was your fault, you know. You and your daughter. She could have put you in a home for invalids. Then she would still be married, and you wouldn't be in this position right now."

The woman was crying silently.

"You know, it's actually quite enjoyable talking with you. You are such a good listener!" The man started to laugh and then became very quiet, silently pulling out a knife. He showed it to the woman in the bed, watching her eyes trace its movements as he moved it from side to side in the air close to her face. She started to get very restless, her eyes flitting everywhere, animal noises surging from her mouth.

"Shh, now. I don't want to have to hurt you. Physically, I mean. But I will if it's necessary. Do you understand what I'm saying?" The woman quieted down and blinked her eyes. "I'm going to assume that's a yes."

He could not wait to go striding into the mother's bedroom, her daughter in his arms.

Chapter 4

July 17th, 2014
London, Ohio

"One doesn't have to look very hard to find racism in this country. The ones saying that it's not here, they're lying. I don't know if they're lying to themselves, or lying to me, but either way, the hate keeps on keeping on. I get harassed by the police sometimes. But I ain't been killed yet. I reckon maybe my white skin is good for something." The old man had crooked teeth, half of which were missing, and he appeared to be homeless. He cackled. "Nope, ain't been hanged yet." He was standing in front of a huge group of black people, chanting and holding signs which read 'I can't breathe'. None of them had been asked to contribute comments to the news broadcast.

Jakob was at Jim's Bar, eyes glued to the tiny television behind the counter, just like everyone else in the place. What they were watching was video footage of Eric Garner being forced to the ground in a chokehold. After the video clip was shown, the newscaster announced that the black man had been declared dead about an hour after being taken to the hospital. Jakob was surrounded by mostly white cops, and he had never felt so conflicted. He stepped away from the bar and went over to an unoccupied table, bringing his pint and shot with him.

He had just managed to get comfortable on the booth seat when Sagan walked in and headed his way. The cowboy looked over at the commotion by the bar and asked Jakob, "What's going on?"

"Black man choked to death in New York. By a cop."

"Holy shit."

"Yeah."

Sagan watched the screen for a little while, enough to have seen the raw cell phone footage at least twice. "I know I'm going to sound like a real asshole for asking this, but..."

"Oh shit, Sagan, are you about to make one of those 'I'm not racist but here's a thing I'm going to say that shows I'm a racist' comments?"

"No. At least, I don't think so."

Jakob liked Sagan. He didn't tiptoe around the race thing. Jakob made sure he was always the first person to bring it up in any of his relationships with white people. He had hoped that addressing the elephant in the room would make people more comfortable to talk about it, but usually white people were too scared of saying the wrong thing. Sagan wasn't like that. Sagan tried to understand people. "Go ahead, man. Say what you gotta say."

"You saw that video there, right? That man was talking about being harassed by the cops. He didn't offer up his arms to be handcuffed. He resisted arrest. There's this contention between cops and black people. You know, there's this stereotype where blacks don't call the cops, cops are the enemy, that kind of thing. Where does that come from?"

"You mean, besides from cops killing unarmed black men?"

Sagan looked Jakob in the eye and nodded. "Yeah, besides that."

"Sagan, you gotta pick the worst times for these questions of yours. You're not going to like what I'm gonna say. I promise you."

"Just give it to me straight, Jakob."

Jakob nodded. "I guess white people just forgot their history. They've forgotten what it's like to tie a noose around a black man's throat and watch him hang. They've forgotten what it's like to hear a black woman screaming for help, knowing no cop is gonna come running, no matter how loud she cries, knowing they could just show up and get a piece of that screaming ass for themselves. Maybe they forgot because they're too busy complaining about their Starbucks latte not having enough milk in it. Or maybe they're too busy bringing stuff back to Walmart without a receipt and walking out with cash. Or maybe they're too busy asking a man if he's selling loose cigarettes. Black people remember, Sagan. They remember walking with Ruby Bridges to the all-white school on her first day. They remember refusing to give up their seats with Rosa Parks. They remember sitting at the lunch counter reserved for whites. Drinking out of the water fountain marked

'Whites Only'. They remember a man named Martin Luther King Jr. They remember what happened two hundred years ago, and they'll remember what happened today."

They were both silent for a moment.

Jakob continued. "After slavery was abolished, they hired more cops. You see, the white folks figured out they could hire criminals to do manual labour. They didn't have to take care of criminals. Didn't have to feed 'em or clothe 'em. A bunch of laws targeting black people got added to the books. You know it was illegal for a black man to preach to a black congregation without getting the permission of a white sheriff first?"

"Shit. Really?"

Jakob nodded his head. "Yep. Our criminal justice system was built on racial inequality. Built on criminalising people with black skin." Jakob motioned towards the bartender for two more beers. "After emancipation, the sugar industry started going under. Until the system of leasing convicts began. They had these hulking machines that the workers would add the sugarcane to, with these grinding teeth on 'em, and workers would get themselves all torn up sometimes, you know? They were working for hours on end, with little food, and maybe they weren't so careful. It was so bad for the continued production that the owners would assign a man with a sword to stand at the machine all day. Somebody got stuck? Just cut off their arm and keep on working. Sad shit."

Sagan was quiet for a while, then asked, "Mind if I have that shot?"

"Help yourself."

Sagan tipped back the Jack Daniels and looked at Jakob. "I can't pretend to know what it's like to be a black man. But I know we can't go on like this. You think there's anything we can do?"

"You mean, can we somehow end racial discrimination by individuals and within the system?" Jakob was shaking his head. "You one crazy white man."

"Seriously, Jakob. What do you think it would take?"

"A lot of fucking training, that's for damn sure." Jakob finished off his beer. "If we're talking seriously, then cops would have to live in these neighbourhoods. Not just going there to 'protect and serve,' but going in to talk to people. Going in to help. Mowing grass, taking out the trash, beautifying places. Talking to the kids. Talking to the parents. It's about building relationships. I don't know, man. I don't have the answers. But I sure as hell know that cops killing black men won't help."

Brittany walked over and delivered a Blue Moon to Sagan, and two more beers to Jakob.

"Thanks, Britt. Can you bring me something a little stronger? Some Jack? And make it a double."

Jakob took a swig of his new beer. "Did I ever tell you about getting shot?"

"No, you didn't."

"I was off duty and on my way to visit a friend. I hadn't even left my neighbourhood yet when my tyre blew out. I realised my jack was back in my garage, so I locked my car and started walking home. About five minutes later, a cruiser rolls up beside me and the guy

252

flips on his siren just to get my attention. I turn towards him and he rolls down his window. I start walking towards the car and he yells at me to stop where I'm at. I start to tell him I'm a cop and he tells me to shut up. At the same time, he's throwing the car into park and calling in for backup. I roll my eyes and start shaking my head, hands on my hips. I try talking to him again and he cuts me off. I had my badge in my back pocket and started reaching for it when he shouted at me to drop to the ground. Then he shot me."

Sagan was shaking his head in disbelief. "He fucking shot you?"

"Yeah. In the back. Missed my heart by an inch. The doctors said I was a lucky bastard."

Sagan took a deep inhalation of breath, then let it out slowly. "Even as bad as it is, I'm starting to think that solving racial tensions between cops and black communities would be easier than catching this god damn serial killer."

Jakob could hear the frustration in the older man's voice. "We've got his voice. You don't want to go public with that?"

Sagan responded, "We might have to, eventually. But I'm not sure we have the resources to follow a thousand bad tips from people who swear they recognise it."

August 10th, 2014
Hunter, New York

Julia had spent the better part of her vacation with

Charlie and his mother at their family home. Now, she only had one day before she was due back at work. She was cursing herself for not coming home sooner, but the time spent with CJ had been a much-needed break.

After Kathryn and Alexander were brutally murdered, their assets had been tied up in the courts while legal matters were attended to. The house had been left just the way it was. Julia was now faced with the task of going through Kathryn's office and moving the contents to a storage facility. The door to the office was made of dark wood, suggesting an entrance to a stuffy space where men might separate themselves from the 'women folk' while sipping brandy and smoking cigars.

She opened the sliding wooden door and stepped inside. It was the first time she had entered the room since she had moved in. The expectation of finding a solemn study was far removed from the reality of the space and it took Julia by surprise. Unlike the rest of the house, the office was undoubtedly Kathryn's. Every detail in the room had been meticulously and deliberately planned. Julia set the cardboard boxes she had been holding to the side and stood in the entrance, rooted to the spot, for quite some time. She could imagine Kathryn in this room, alive and full of hope.

The room was quite large, with a high ceiling, the opposite wall featuring two arched French doors panelled with white wood and glass. The overall colour scheme for the office was white and gold, with a modern take on French country decor. Through the clear glass, the side patio and an outdoor seating area could be seen.

Positioned in front of the doors was an ivory chaise lounge, a throw pillow decorated with a honeybee placed haphazardly upon it. Kathryn had loved the creatures, having grown up on a honeybee farm in Louisiana. Her parents had always called her the 'honeybee queen' because she had never been stung. She would spend hours covered in the creatures, her eyes closed in silent meditation; she had always said that was where she found God: among the bees. It was hard to imagine the tough-as-nails lawyer that Kathryn had been sitting cross-legged and peaceful, covered in bees. Although she had never repeated the practice as an adult, this room was a testament to how much bees had meant to her.

There were several bee details throughout the room. To the left stood a kidney-shaped table with graceful legs, a honeycomb-patterned bookshelf on the wall behind it. To either side of the honeycomb, long, straight shelves extended, utilized not just for books, but also for the little knickknacks Kathryn had enjoyed collecting. One cubby hole held a wooden square, a bee and daisy masterfully painted on its surface, with the words 'Bee Happy' written on it. Another held a glass figurine of a hive, complete with two little worker bees. Most of the books had been given their own cell and Julia read a few of the titles: an illustrated children's book named *The Beekeeper*, a young adult book entitled *Kissing the Bee*, and the New York Times bestseller *The Secret Life of Bees*.

The honeycomb bookshelf blended perfectly with the hexagonal drawers, gold bees acting as drawer knobs. Julia went over to one and pulled it out. Inside were a whole load of files, neatly organised and labelled with Kathryn's crisp script. Every drawer held the same: files and more files. Mostly they were old case files that Kathryn had worked on during her life, organised by year and client last name. But one drawer only had a single subject tab: Emily. It was the case that had caused Kathryn to fall into a deep depression for a time. Julia didn't know the details of the case, but Kathryn had barely spoken to her in the months that followed. Julia hadn't planned to look through any of the files, unsure if attorney-client privilege still applied, but her curiosity was piqued. Just this one, she told herself. Just this one. She pulled out the first file from the 'Emily' drawer and sat down in the padded armchair by the desk.

Opening the file, she started reading, feeling a bit like a criminal. After a few minutes of arguing with herself and flipping the cover open and closed, she had convinced herself to put it away. But as she started to close the file for what she thought would be the last time, she saw a name she recognised and gasped. There was no going back now. She had to read every file in the drawer. But first, she needed alcohol. Leaving the file on the desk she walked over to the bar service. There were five glass bottles, all unlabelled. She had no idea what any of them contained, but she didn't care. Did liquor go bad? She decided she didn't care about that either. She picked one with an amber-coloured substance and brought it, along with a crystal goblet, back to the desk. She had drunk half the contents of the bottle before she could open the file again.

Julia's head hurt, and it wasn't just because of the alcohol she had consumed last night. She had spent most of the evening reading and crying, completely unsure of her next course of action. The unfamiliar terminology used in the law documents had sent her head spinning, but if she had understood them correctly, Charlie had once been accused of 'Social Acquaintance Rape', or date rape, as it was known to most people.

The rape had occurred in 2005, with Charlie claiming innocence during the whole ordeal. The prosecutor's office hadn't thought there was enough of a case to bring it to trial, so while it had not been brought to the criminal court, the complainant, a woman named Emily Bowman, had filed a suit in civil court. After suffering some kind of mental breakdown during the civil trial, Emily had no longer wished to pursue the case and the defence had moved for charges to be dismissed.

Julia didn't know what to think. Maybe it had all been one big misunderstanding, but it didn't sit right. With her history, she knew that her thoughts might be muddled. Didn't she know that any man could be guilty of such a crime? She quickly sat up in bed and let out a miserable cry while throwing her pillow across the room. The movement brought on a thunderous headache and she was unable to hold back a stream of vomit that ended up all over her unicorn slippers.

Why had she drunk so much? And why hadn't

she hydrated after? She told herself these were rhetorical questions, but her brain answered them anyway. You were a little preoccupied with wondering if your fiancé is a rapist, maybe? She had been working with Nia on changing her inner dialogue, on giving herself the benefit of the doubt. Of treating herself with more kindness. She didn't think the second cynical voice inside her head had been what Nia had in mind. But maybe it was progress.

Fiancé. Julia turned on her bedside lamp and looked down at her left hand to find that she was no longer wearing her engagement ring. Fuck. She had no recollection of taking it off. But she wasn't about to hunt for it. She might never be able to put it back on, but even if that were the case, she hoped she hadn't thrown it away in a drunken rage.

Just then, the alarm on her cell phone started to chime, an annoying siren sound that came from the other side of the room. Forgetting the state of her head, she rushed to her feet, throwing up the contents of some hidden second stomach. How the hell had all that come out of her body? God, she felt miserable.

She made her way slowly to the sitting area, her phone alarm chirping from somewhere within the hidden depths of the sofa. After retrieving the phone, she collapsed onto the cushions. No way was she going to work today. It was too early to call her boss, but an email would suffice. Her laptop was on the coffee table in front of her, but it seemed miles away. Instead of reaching for it, she slipped to the floor, her legs sliding under the glass top.

She didn't normally leave her laptop on and unplugged all night, and she feared the worst. Sending out a silent prayer to the battery gods, she flipped up the screen and was delighted to see it come to life when she pressed the power button. Wonderful, sleep mode had not taken all the juice.

She brought up her Gmail account and sent in an email to the HR department, copying in almost everyone else. She didn't have the mental capacity to figure out with whom she had meetings today, and she was sure some of the people receiving her email wouldn't be affected.

She set up an automatic 'out of office' response and then checked her phone. Charlie had texted her last night, and she had apparently never noticed. He had written 'Thanks for spending the last month with me. It was perfect. I can't wait to start our lives together', finishing off with a heart emoji.

She was about to text back when her computer dinged to let her know she had just received a new email. The subject line was 'Re: Charles Ivanov'. What the hell? She moved the cursor to click on the email. The laptop died.

"Motherfucker!" She slammed down the lid of the laptop and picked up her phone. Fuck this, she was going back to bed. She sent a quick text to Charlie. 'SICK. Taking drugs and going to sleep'.

Surprisingly, he answered back right away. Strange of him to be up so early.

'Should I bring over some soup?'

'You don't even know where I live. And I don't

want to throw up any soup'.

'My assistants know where you live'. He had inserted a winking face. 'Aww. I'm sorry, babe. Get some rest, sleeping beauty. I'll see you on the flip side'.

She didn't text him back, just powered off her phone and threw it across the room. It felt good. She was in the mood to throw things. But not throw up things. She laughed. She knew all the lame dad jokes. A brief pang of grief hit her. She always missed her parents the most when she was sick.

She made herself get up off the floor and retrieve a small pink trash bag from under the sink in the bathroom. She hated the thought of throwing away her favourite slippers, but she reasoned that she would probably just ruin them anyway if she tried to wash them. Thanks to capitalism, there would always be another pair of unicorn slippers, just waiting to be bought. Her cynical voice chimed in with 'that's not the only thing for sale. Ever heard of sex trafficking?'. Ugh, she couldn't wait to pop some Benadryl and go back to bed. She had never known Benadryl to work for her allergies, but it damn well put her to sleep.

After mopping up the mess, Julia headed for the shower. She preferred the bathroom downstairs, the one with the giant garden tub, but she was not in the mood for a lengthy soak. This would be a utilitarian affair to wash the chunks out of her hair and hopefully make herself feel half human again.

She couldn't bear the thought of putting anything into her stomach, but she made herself do it anyway. She took small sips of water in intervals while preparing for bed. After a quick and tepid shower, she brushed her teeth, using the smallest amount of toothpaste she could get away with. Just the whiff of mint as she removed the cap caused her to dry heave.

Walking out of the bathroom, she glanced at her laptop. There was not enough Benadryl in the world to put her to sleep until she'd figured out what was in that email. She was going to have to find her charging cord, and it was probably in her laptop bag by the front door. She silently cursed herself for her hatred of smartphones and walked downstairs to retrieve it.

A few minutes later she was seated on the floor in her bedroom. She logged back into her Gmail account and sat for quite some time with the cursor poised over the email.

"Dammit, Julia. Just open it."

She hadn't been this scared in a while. She had just gotten used to the idea that maybe, just maybe, she could have a real relationship. A real life with someone who cared about her. Was it all a sham? She could delete the email, burn the file, find the ring, and put on a smile. She could become that little girl again, hiding in the shadows, fearing the dark, fearing the world.

No. Enough with the bullshit. She deserved to know the truth, whatever it may be. She had recovered once. She could do it again if she had to. The email 'Re: Charles Ivanov' had been sent to her by BrightEyed_86@gmail.com. She took a deep breath. Then she opened the email.

Dear Julia,

It's taken me several hours to decide to write you back. I'm hoping that you are who you say you are and that this is not a ploy by a journalist to get my story, or something far more sinister. I would appreciate it if we could meet via Skype before I share any personal information.

Please send me your Skype details and I will reach out to you after that.

There was no signature attached to the email. She didn't recall sending an email last night, so she scrolled down to read the text from her original message, hoping she didn't sound drunk.

Dear Emily,

I'm sorry if what I'm about to write brings you any pain. Part of me wants to contact you, but the other part wants me to run as far away from you as possible. As suggested by the subject heading, this email is regarding Charles 'CJ' Ivanov, but also your former lawyer, Kathryn Beaumont.

I'm not sure how long it's been since you were in contact with her, but I'm assuming you know of her death. She and her husband were brutally murdered a few years ago. Kathryn and I were friends, and as crazy as it sounds, she left this giant house for me to finish her work.

And that is what leads me to you. I've recently started cleaning out Kathryn's office and there was an entire drawer about you. About your case. There were files about past rape trials in the US, news clippings following the trial, transcripts, and a journal full of notes that she'd written.

'I knew that this was the case that affected her so much that it led her to quit her practice. So, I took a peek, just to quench my curiosity.

Then I noticed a name I recognised. I'm in a romantic relationship with Charles, so you can imagine how horrified and scared I am right now. Would you be willing to talk to me about all of this? If not, I'll understand, but it would mean a lot to me.

Thanks, Julia

Wow. For someone verging on blackout drunk, she sounded surprisingly coherent. Thankfully, written correspondence was the typical norm and not video. Skype, huh? She hit reply.

Emily,

Thank you so much for writing back. You can find me on Skype at HealingThruArt. I look forward to hearing from you.

Julia

Julia opened her Skype app and looked longingly at her bed. She contemplated unplugging her lamp to connect the laptop instead. That way, she could just go to sleep and let Skype wake her up. But even this small amount of effort seemed too daunting. Instead, she left her laptop open on the coffee table, Skype indicating that she was 'online', and stretched out on the couch. She was asleep within minutes.

Several hours later, an incoming Skype call roused her. From a nearly prone position, she accepted the call. The face looking back at her was not at all what she had expected. Here was a man, with short brown hair, hazel eyes, and a full black beard. She didn't know what to say.

She must have looked shocked, for the person on the screen quickly said, "Hi, Julia. I'm Cayden. I know you were expecting Emily." Here the man paused briefly before continuing. "I am the person who *used* to be Emily, but I no longer identify as a woman."

It took Julia's fogged brain a minute to catch up. "Oh, okay. Nice to meet you." She sat up and grimaced. "Sorry, I had a rough night."

"I can imagine. Mine hasn't been too great either. I've been thinking a lot about what to say to you. I haven't slept a wink since I got your email."

Julia looked over at the man in front of her. The photos she had seen of Emily hadn't been very good, but it was hard to imagine that young woman as the man in front of her. "I really appreciate you taking the time to speak with me."

Cayden took a deep breath, then began. "The memories I have of that night unequivocally have Charlie as the perpetrator of my rape." Julia took in a huge inhalation of breath and Cayden held up a finger to show that he wasn't done. "But I was under the influence of A LOT of alcohol. And I'd taken some pills, I don't know what. I've gone over my memories of that night so many times. Was Charlie in the house when my rape took place? Yes. But when my friend, Kirsten, came in, he was dressed. She said he looked upset, and he was calling 911." Cayden shook his head. "For a long time, I thought that his actions had been an attempt to cover it up. But maybe I was wrong." Cayden looked at Julia. "We were in a relationship. We hadn't had sex yet, but we were close to it. We thought we were in love. Charlie had said we could take our time. He said he wasn't in any hurry to have sex. Brains are a funny thing. Perhaps in my drugged up, dazed state, I projected his image onto my rapist. Either way, there's a rapist who never paid for what he did to me."

"I'm sorry, Cayden." Julia looked away from the screen. Right now, this was the only person in the world she wanted to talk to about this situation. "Do you think we could meet? You know, in person?"

Cayden laughed. "Not unless you feel like coming to San Francisco."

"Wow. That was a move!"

"It was exactly what I needed. I needed to just...get away from everything, you know? I teach at Berkeley. Do some classes on women's studies, and research gender and LGBTQ issues. I'm sure I could bore you with it for hours."

Julia laughed. "Actually, that sounds really interesting. I don't know very much about that...kind of stuff."

Now it was Cayden's turn to laugh. "That kind of stuff, huh?"

Julia was embarrassed. "Yeah, I mean, no offense. I don't judge anyone for any of that. But I guess it does make me kind of uncomfortable. Ugh, I just, I guess I don't know too many…"

"Weird people?"

Julia laughed. "No. You know what I mean. I guess all that stuff gets kind of muddled with sex, and I've always been a little weird about sex."

"Hey, I get it. Some people aren't comfortable with it. That's why I got involved with education, really. I want to build knowledge pathways between people of all backgrounds." Cayden laughed at himself. "Knowledge pathways. That sounds so lame."

Julia shrugged her shoulders and grinned. "I kind of like it."

"I have an extensive online study at the moment, if you'd like me to send you a link. Right now, I'm just gathering data on views about LGTBQ and gender topics."

"Yeah, absolutely. I would be really interested in that."

"Great." They were uncomfortably silent. "How is Charlie?"

"He's doing really well, you know."

Cayden was nodding. He looked uncomfortable. "Are you going to tell him you spoke to me? Or ask him about all of this?"

"I don't know, Cayden. I keep going back and forth about it in my mind. Like, I want to confront him about it, but if I do, it will come from a dark, accusatory place."

"And if he didn't actually do it…"

"Exactly."

"I'm not sure if I want him to know my situation. I think I've talked myself into believing that it wasn't him. But I still have a lot of fear. Not as much as I used to. I had nightmares about him finding me after the trial…finding me, raping me, then killing me. Those nightmares are gone now, but the fear is still there."

Julia could sense the anxiety in him. "How about this, Cayden? If I do talk to him about it, I won't mention you."

"Going to be kind of hard to do that, since it's literally about me." He smiled.

"You know what I mean. And…that was about Emily. You're not her anymore."

Cayden appreciated the gesture. "Thanks, Julia. Oh, and by the way, I was aware of Kathryn's murder. That took a lot of time to heal from. I actually thought Charlie could have been the one to do it. I was sure of it. Called the cops and told them. I called a lot of police, every day, to talk about it. I probably seemed like a crazy person."

Julia must have had a look of doubt on her face because Cayden then said, "I probably seem like a crazy person now. But I was determined that someone look into it, and I wasn't going to stop calling until they took me seriously."

"Did they?"

"Eventually. I received a call from a Detective Rosso. He did look into it. Said that Charlie had an alibi. Some party for most of the evening, and then later, on a job, and then at home with his brother. The detective thought that would be the end of it, but I told him I didn't believe his brother. Is his brother still a cop?"

"Yep. And they still live together. I don't know why. They could afford to live in separate houses every day of the week. Of course, Charlie is out of town a lot."

"From what I could tell, they've always been close."

Julia was nodding her head. "Why did you think he was the one who killed her?"

"I just figured he was mad at her for representing me. I don't know."

"But the death was years after the rape trial, wasn't it?"

"Yeah. Thinking about it now, the connection seems flimsy. But you have to understand the fear I had then. It consumed me for years. I saw Charlie everywhere I went. Not literally. But every man who looked close to being him...I just had this physical response. My heart rate would go up and I would break out in a sweat." Cayden shook his head and looked away before turning back with a smile. "My transformation was a big part of my healing process. It helped me feel like I was in control again." Julia was nodding and offering encouraging sounds while listening to Cayden's account. He tried to change the subject, feeling a little self-absorbed and asked her, "I guess you're an artist?"

"What?" Julia was confused, then recalled her Skype screen name. "Oh, right. HealingThruArt?" Cayden nodded. "Sort of. My official title is Assistant Curator, but I feel more like a social worker on most days. Or not really that, either, because that role seems to be associated with disenfranchised people, tired of helping the poor." She laughed. "Actually, I know some pretty amazing social workers. I don't know what I am. I'm just trying to make the world a better place through art. I've been lucky to work with some great people, trying to do the same."

"Healing through art? That sounds like it would make for an interesting study."

"I guess it would be interesting to see the numbers, see how many people have good outcomes after art therapy. But for me, it's not just about the art. Yes, the art is a way to work through pain, but you're not doing it by yourself. What I do is introduce damaged people to a community. A community where they feel safe enough to discuss their trials and tribulations, a community that appreciates artistic pursuits...I introduce people to family. I guess that's a little cheesy."

"No, not at all. That sounds a little bit like what I'm trying to do in the world. Make us all family."

Julia smiled. "Well, Cayden, it was very nice speaking with you. Great to meet you. But I'm still feeling a bit wrecked. I think I'm going to go back to sleep."

"Sounds like a good idea. Feel free to email me anytime."

Julia disconnected from Skype and looked around for her phone. After a few minutes of searching, she finally remembered that she had thrown it across the room earlier that morning. She struggled to her feet and walked around until she found it, grimacing at the jolt of pain that spread through her head as she bent over.

It was dead, of course, and now her stomach was rumbling. She grabbed her laptop and headed downstairs, plugging in her phone when she reached the kitchen. She was starving, but she didn't quite feel well enough for solid food, so decided on a smoothie, taking out some random ingredients from the fridge: a small pot of peach yogurt, some frozen raspberries, and an overripe banana. She threw in some ice and just a splash of orange juice, blending it all together.

Pouring the concoction into a tall glass, she walked over to the large island in the middle of the kitchen, taking a seat on one of the stools. She flipped up her laptop screen and visited her old pal, Google, typing the name 'Charles Ivanov' into the search engine. She scrolled through the first four pages of results. The most recent results discussed his current series and the photos that would be on sale during the 'Exploitation and Exposure' event. There were mentions of his 9/11 photos and his 'Criminal Lives' series. Forbes had an article on his generous contributions. But there was nothing about the case with Emily. She went back to the search box and added 'rape'.

For the next hour, Julia sipped on her smoothie and read about the trial. She read articles about the rape culture in the US, victim-blaming, and 'women who lie'. Charlie had never brought up this part of his past, but Julia couldn't blame him. Who would want to discuss a previous rape charge with the woman they loved? She decided to talk to him about it, picking up the phone and calling his number. He picked up on the first ring.

"Julia! How are you doing?"

"Hey, Charlie. I'm feeling a lot better. But I need to talk to you about something. Can we meet?" Normally Charlie would add some comic relief to situations that seemed tense. She expected him to do so now. But he surprised her.

"Of course, Julia. Do you want to drive into town, or should I come to you?"

"Can we meet at that bagel shop in between?"

"Perfect. See you in about two hours?"

"Thanks, Charlie. That sounds great."

"Julia?"

She sucked in a breath. She knew what was coming next, and she wasn't prepared for it. "Yes?"

"I love you." There it was. The silence hung between them and she filled it up with tears.

"Julia? Are you okay?"

There was genuine concern in his voice. Genuine love. How could she have ever doubted it? "I love you too, Charlie. I guess I just haven't really had enough sleep."

"We can get together later in the day, if you'd like to rest first."

"No!" She said it too quickly and too forcibly, but it couldn't be helped. She had to confront him with this. Today. As soon as possible, or she would never bring it up. "No, Charlie. I'm going to get ready now, I'll see you soon." He was silent. "Charlie?"

"Yeah?"

"I love you, too."

Chapter 5

August 11th, 2014
Harriman, New York

Almost exactly two hours later, Julia pulled into The Bagel Byte, a bakery and café located in Harriman, New York. They had met here multiple times over the past several months, a cute little island amidst the chaotic seas of their busy lives. She could see Charlie's Miata in the parking lot and there was a free spot right next to him. She pulled in beside his car but found she was not quite ready to face him.

During the journey, she had pondered what to say to him. How should she start? The task was daunting. She had decided to drive back and never see him again at least five times. But she knew she couldn't do that. She had to face him.

She stepped out of the Camry and headed inside. Charlie was sitting in a large booth, a coffee for himself and a hot tea for her already ordered. His was in a paper take-out cup, but hers was in a proper dine-in mug. The right-side wall of the restaurant had a bank of computers, a couple of printers and scanners, and even what looked like a fax machine. To Julia's surprise, two of the computers were actually being used.

Charlie had chosen a table near the bank of computers, but furthest away from any other patrons. He stood up as Julia walked over and pulled out her seat, waiting for her to sit down. He didn't try to touch her, but after she was seated, he stood behind her a moment longer than was needed. Julia had just begun to feel uncomfortable when he came around and sat down.

Julia found she couldn't speak. Every word seemed incapable of leaving the confines of her mouth.

Charlie spoke instead. "Is this about Emily?"

Julia just looked at him. His face was tight with pain, his eyes sorrowful. She gave a slight nod. He looked her in the eyes.

"I'm sorry, Julia. I'm sorry I didn't tell you. I should have told you. I thought about it. I did. But after I learnt about your cousins…I just couldn't do it. I was so scared…I am scared…of losing you." Charlie looked down at his hands. His voice was a whisper. "Emily was my first love. I thought that I had been lucky to find 'the one', you know, so young in life. I had planned on spending the rest of my life with her."

Charlie looked off towards the front door, but Julia didn't think he could see it. He seemed to be looking at something else.

"After her rape, I didn't think I'd ever be able to love again. I didn't think I'd be able to feel so much for someone again. I certainly didn't want to think about the possibility of marriage again. It was a tragedy. What happened to her. And I beat myself up over it. If I had just been with her every second of that night…if we hadn't gone to that party…" Charlie looked over at Julia. "I understand if you can't trust me right now. If you need time. And space. But I promise you, I did not rape her. I loved her. And I love you. And I will do anything…anything…to make this up to you. Just say the word."

Julia was crying. "Oh, Charlie…" She reached a hand across the table and he raised it to his lips, then held her hand against his face while he wept. She got up from her seat and came over to embrace him. "I'm sorry I doubted you."

"What?" He looked surprised. "No. No. Of course you would. I should have told you. I should have told you a long time ago." He looked up at her and smiled. "You and I make a damn good team, you know? When this exhibit is over, I'm going to come over to the house. The group home. And we're going to make it our number one priority, okay? After December, I won't take on any more jobs until we've got everything rolling and under control. Whatever you need, we'll get it done."

Julia was shaking her head. "What about the wedding, Charlie? We haven't done any planning for that."

"I can't think of a better wedding gift than this. This is how we start our lives together."

They spent several hours at the café, just talking, before Julia headed home to get some much-needed sleep.

September 23rd, 2014
Hunter, New York

The opening day for 'Exploitation and Exposure' had finally arrived. Julia was meeting with a journalist from the Catskill Mountain Journal at ten o'clock, for a live podcast about the show. This was the third podcast she had done with Andi, but she was still extremely nervous. Today's podcast would be a little more personal; a question and answer interview about her own personal work, and the journey that had brought her to where she was today. It was something she had never really spoken about to anyone, other than Nia, and she was not sure if she was ready.

They got set up in her office, both seated in chairs across from each other. The women both wore headsets with microphones, and Andi did some audio adjusting before they were ready to begin.

"Good morning, listeners! This is Andi Buchanan, and I'm here in the office of Julia Rodriguez with The New York Mountains Foundation, for our third, and final podcast about the exhibit, 'Exploitation and Exposure'. Good morning, Julia."

"Good morning."

"Before we begin, can you give us a summary of what the exhibition is about, for any listeners who are joining us for the first time?"

"Certainly. Tonight's exhibit, 'Exploitation and Exposure', consists of work from multiple artists, including young female victims of a sex-trafficking ring that was dismantled in January of last year. Charles

Ivanov, a photographer from New York, will also have some pieces for sale. Over the course of the past year, Charles has taken several candid shots of the girls during their creation of the art that will go on sale tonight."

"Thank you. Now, I would like to get a little more personal, Julia. During the course of my coverage, I had the pleasure of meeting some of the brave young artists who will be displaying work this evening. While speaking with them, I learnt that you, personally, were involved in the creation of one of the art pieces for sale this evening. Can you tell us a little about that? Have you, yourself, been involved in a sex-trafficking ring?"

Julia inhaled and let out a deep breath. She imagined Nia listening to her now and that gave her strength. "When I was a child, I was not a part of a sex-trafficking ring, but I did experience multiple rapes at the hands of family members. I escaped that life, only to end up on the streets, where the quickest way to earn money was through the sale of my body."

Andi was shaking her head. "How awful. How old were you?"

"I was fourteen when I ran away from my cousin's house."

"I know this must be difficult for you to share with us. Julia, when I look at you, I see a young, thriving, professional woman. Over the past three months, I have witnessed your compassion for these girls. I have seen your pain and perseverance. I have seen your strength. I look at you and I see an example of someone who has healed. Who has overcome her past, and who has used those terrible experiences to help others. How did you get here?"

"Thank you, Andi. That means a lot." Julia hoped her voice would not waver. She hoped she sounded as strong as Andi seemed to think she was. "When I was fifteen years old, I was beaten by a man who had paid me for sex. He left me to die on a beach in Miami. Another homeless girl found me, Krista. She nursed me back to health. Brought me food and water. And sometimes pills. I'm not sure what the extent of my injuries were, or how long she took care of me. My memories of that time are very hazy."

"Wow."

"Eventually, I was healthy enough to contribute to our living circumstances. Krista was a street artist. She would illustrate people and couples and sell them the work or draw pictures of the beach and sell them to tourists. I was never very good at painting or drawing, but I liked to write. We would sometimes combine our work, my poem, her drawing, that sort of thing."

"And this was in Florida?"

"That's right."

"And how did you come to find yourself way up here?"

Julia's eyes teared up. She hadn't talked about Krista in a long time. "It seems obvious to say, but Krista had become the most important person to me. I had lost my parents, been victimised by family…she was the only one I had. When I first met Krista, she had this dream to go to Detroit. She had met a boy the summer before. He had said his uncle had this non-profit there, The Parker Foundation, helping young, unfortunate artists. He told her that if she made it up there, he would introduce them. When she met me, she had almost saved up the bus fare to get up there. But nursing me back to health had depleted what she had saved up. She asked me to come with her. So, we both started saving. Her dream became our dream."

"Julia, can we take a moment?"

"Of course."

Andi was visibly shaken. "I'm sorry, listeners." There was a waver in her voice, and she took a deep breath. "I've heard it said that you should be kind to everyone because you never know their personal story. That has never meant more to me than it has these past few months in speaking to these young girls who have been affected by such tragedy. And here today, we learn that Julia Rodriguez, a well-respected member of our community, has, herself, had similar experiences." Andi seemed more composed now and asked her next question. "Did you and Krista make it to Detroit?"

Julia smiled. It was a sad smile. "*I* made it to Detroit. I have no idea what happened to Krista. I woke up one morning, and she was gone. She hadn't taken any money from our stash. I waited for a few weeks before I left, every day sure that she would come back. But as time wore on, I feared the worst. I took the money we had earnt and bought a one-way ticket to Detroit. I was there for years, moving here early last year."

Andi was shaking her head in amazement. "Listeners, as you know, I have been meeting with Julia and tonight's artists for the past three months. The bond that has developed between these girls and Julia is amazing to see. It was one of the girls, Ava, who insisted that Julia be included in tonight's exhibition. Julia, I hear you spent a long time protesting but finally agreed after the girls threatened not to show."

Julia laughed warmly. "That's right. They can be a stubborn bunch."

"Can you tell us about your piece?"

"Sure. I wrote a poem, entitled 'Little Girl', that I shared with everyone during one of our speak-and-shares. Ava was moved by it and asked if she could make a painting inspired by my poem. I told her of course. Then, other girls thought that was a cool idea. So, they each decided to make some form of art, inspired by the poem. They came to me with the idea of using all of these 'Little Girl' pieces as one series within the exhibition."

"Including your poem?"

There was a smile in her voice when she answered, nodding. "That's right. With my poem. I finally agreed, with the stipulation that the poem be included as a joint endeavour. We took a large canvas, about a square meter, and Ava primed it and painted on a striped background in the colours of the rainbow. Then we each painted a self-portrait on the canvas, letting it dry between additions. When everyone's portrait was done, Ava painted in the words to the poem in black and white."

"And that piece will be on display this evening?"

"That's right. It will be the centrepiece of the 'Little Girl' series."

"Well, Julia, I bet you can guess what most of

our listeners are thinking right now."

"Oh gosh," Julia laughed nervously.

"Would you read it for us? Or perform it for us? I'm not sure what the correct terminology is."

"I would be honoured, Andi." Julia cleared her throat and then read the poem aloud. For the first two stanzas, she pushed the horror, the hate, the uncertainty, the guilt, the fear, the almost dying, and the unfairness of it all into her voice. She gave herself up, heart bared to the world, exposed and vulnerable. For the last stanza, she offered the listeners hope, empathy, forgiveness, and love.

Little Girl

Glancing back over my shoulder
I see a little girl
With hope and optimism
Roaming free with wind in her hair
A smile on her face
Innocence in her heart
In front of her a twisted line of broken promises
and shattered dreams
A cruel life

Looking back, I see fences forming
Tenuous at first
Fences, unsure of themselves
Chicken wire becomes slatted wood
A white picket fence
And then cement

Towering above her
Blocking the sun
Shadows of barbwire beneath her feet
Vines poke through the cement
The scent of roses
Life finds a way
Even when she feels dead
A cruel life

And optimism exists despite it all
She imagines that one day she may slowly take
down the wall
But we are at a Berlin Wall crossroads
The past the east
The future the west
There is no time for slow
New dreams and desires
A new smile to bring the wall down
Another chance
For that little girl

Andi let the last line of the poem hang in the air, giving
herself and her listeners a moment to digest. Giving Julia
a moment of silence. "Remarkable, Julia. If you could
go back and change it all, change the course of your
life…would you?"

Julia smiled sweetly while shaking her head.
"That's a hard question to answer, you know? If I had a
magic wand, I would make sure that no one on earth
had to experience anything close to what I've
experienced. But I don't have a magic wand and we live

in the real world, where bad things happen to people. I am thankful. Thankful for the fact that I have helped some amazing people get through an incredibly tough period in their lives. I am thankful to be here in this community, in this position, with this foundation. I am thankful to be alive. I don't know who I would have been if I had never experienced those things, but I wouldn't have been able to help these girls in the same way."

"Thank you. Listeners, the exhibit 'Exploitation and Exposure' opens tonight at six. We've been speaking with Julia Rodriguez, one of the organisers of the exhibit. She, Charles Ivanov, and several other artists, will be attending the grand opening this evening. This first night and the last night will be the only days where all the artists will be in attendance. The exhibit will run for three months from now until December twenty-first, finishing just in time for Christmas. Julia, thank you again, so much. See you tonight!"

Andi sighed. "Wow, Julia. That really is the best interview I've ever had. Thank you so much."

"You're welcome, Andi. Thank you so much for the podcasts. I have received so many emails from people in the past couple of months, saying they heard about us and the exhibit through your podcast and the Journal's website. There were a lot of people asking if they could donate some money to the girls. The outpouring of help from this community has been amazing. Largely thanks to you."

Julia and Andi walked towards the closed office

door when there was a knock from the other side. Julia repositioned herself in front of Andi and said, "Excuse me, let me see what this is about."

"Absolutely, go ahead." Andi stepped to the side as Julia opened the door. Her office opened into a huge meeting space, which was currently filled with people. At her entrance, they burst into applause, Ava and the other girls enveloping her in a tight circle of hugs and tears. As they stepped away from her, co-workers came up to offer hugs and well wishes. Julia was overwhelmed, unaware of the tears dripping down her face as she hugged each person, some of them mere acquaintances. The board members were present, handing out champagne glasses, each filled with alcohol-free sparkling cider.

Suddenly, Charlie was beside her, slipping her left hand into his right, casually rubbing her engagement ring with his thumb. She offered him a smile and he kissed her forehead, then enveloped her in a quick bear hug.

He whispered, "I love you," into her ear, squeezing her hand as he did so.

Once everyone was holding a glass, David Washington stepped up onto a table and raised his glass. The entire room fell silent; sniffling was the only thing that could be heard.

"Julia." He held up the glass in her direction, then moved it in a sweeping motion to include the children circled around her. "Girls. I think I speak for everyone here when I say that this exhibit will be the most powerful we've ever had. What you all have endured is unfathomable, but I hope that this exhibit marks the beginning of some amazing careers and lives for all of you." He raised his glass to the sound of 'hear-hears' from throughout the room, and everyone took a drink before returning to their conversations once again.

Chapter 6

October 13th, 2014
Hunter, New York

Julia had just finished the LBGTQ survey Cayden had sent a couple of months before. After completing it, she sent Cayden an apology email, letting him know that she had finally filled it out. Julia had also provided him with a few email addresses of co-workers who had said they would take it as well. It made the apology seem more legitimate somehow.

She was surprised when, a couple of minutes later, she received an email in response.

Julia,

Thanks for taking the survey! We actually have it open until the last day of November, so you had a little more time. And thanks for the email addresses, I've sent your co-workers a link to the study as well. Feel free to share the link I gave you with anyone else who might be interested.

I'm going to be coming back to New York in December. It will be the first time I've been back. You know, since I left. I haven't even seen my parents in person since my transition. It took them a long time, and they've finally accepted it, but I'm not sure things will ever be like they used to be.

We've talked a few times over Skype, and they've invited me to come to stay with them for a couple of weeks around Christmas. So, I've decided I'll do that. Perhaps you and I can meet, after all?

Cayden

Julia immediately replied with an assent. She held onto the hope that, one day, Charles and Cayden might be able to meet and put the past behind them. She knew that such a feat might help to heal the broken pieces both of them still carried around.

She shivered, as the thought of having to meet her dad's cousin and sons flitted through her mind. That was different. That man was guilty. Those boys were guilty.

The boys. She had struggled with blaming them. *Were* they guilty? Hadn't they just been children too? Just as much victims as she was herself? She wasn't sure she would ever be able to decide. Would meeting them help heal her?

Maybe not. Okay. She understood Cayden's reluctance. Cayden may have logically decided that Charles hadn't raped her. But that didn't mean that the thought of meeting him again wasn't traumatic. She was not going to push it. But she was damn sure going to meet Cayden and give her…him, she reminded herself…one of the biggest hugs he had ever been given.

November 22nd, 2014
London, Ohio

When Sagan finally got home that night, the light on his answering machine was blinking red. He was exhausted, but he made his way over to the flashing red button anyway.

"Hey, Dad. It's Angela." His daughter was crying. "It's almost Thanksgiving. And after that comes Christmas." He could hear her sniffling and sighed. "But you know that. Shit. Oops. Sorry. Dad? I just miss you. Christmas?" He listened to the message a half a dozen times before making his way to bed. He made a mental note to call his daughter first thing in the morning.

He had been asleep for about fifteen minutes when his cell phone rang. The call was from Jakob. "Hello?" Jakob was silent, but Sagan could hear the clinking of glasses and what he thought was the raucous noise of drunk cops in the background. "Jakob? Everything okay?"

"Have you seen the news?"

Sagan stretched out a hand and fumbled for the remote, searching every part of the bedspread before finally giving up, getting up, and walking over to the TV to turn it on. He flipped through the stations until he caught sight of a news channel, broadcasting a cell phone video of a black kid waving around a gun.

"Residents here say that Tamir Rice, only twelve years old, had been outside playing with the fake gun for quite some time. Shortly after arriving on the scene, cops shot the young boy, and he has since been taken to MetroHealth. We are unsure of his current condition, but we will keep you posted."

Jakob sounded as if he was crying. "He…he's only twelve years old, man."

"Shit." Sagan pulled on his pants, stumbling as he did so, but managed to stay upright. He pulled on a button-up shirt and stepped into his boots.

"You know that forty thousand Americans die of gunshots every year, man? Shit, man. You know what the number one cause of death for a black man under the age of thirty-five is? Gunshot. Getting shot with a fucking gun. And this boy is up here in the hospital fighting for his fucking life because we gotta have our guns. We gotta play with guns and be all big and tough with our guns. Fucking twelve, man."

Sagan could hear Jakob taking another swig of whatever he was drinking. He had just made it to his car. He started up the engine and hoped Jakob was at Jim's.

"You know what my mama did one time?"

"What did she do?"

"That woman was amazing. We was at this playground, down in Athens, Georgia, okay? Visiting a friend of my mom's. This friend had her a whole mess of kids. Maybe like five or six. And there we were, all of us playing on this playground, and my mama and her friend were just sitting on a bench. Sitting there talking and laughing. You know how women do. And then these hoodlums start walking over to them. There was four of 'em. All of 'em wearing fucking durags, with their pants sagging, grills full of gold. Just looking like they was up to no good. Now, most people, most sane people, they would have steered clear of those boys. They would have gathered up all us children and walked somewhere else.

But not my mama. My mama, she starts unpacking the picnic she's brought for all of us. Then she asks those boys if they can help her start the charcoal for the grill. She says 'I've always been scared of starting up this here charcoal, but I've got some nice ol' dogs and burgers to throw down. Y'all wanna join us? I got some fresh baked cookies in here too. Can one of you start this fire?'. And you know what the hell they did? They got that charcoal going. They cooked us up some food. They sat and ate with us. And my mama sent them off with cookies. Now, had they planned on fucking with my mama? I don't know. But that woman used food as a way to bring people together. And I sure wish she was still around. Sagan? You still there?"

Jakob was at a booth, head laying on his arms which were resting on the table, phone held between his ear and an arm.

"Yeah, man. I'm here."

Jakob was startled to find that the voice had come from his immediate right. He looked up and saw Sagan, minus his hat, with a shirt half-way buttoned up and hanging out of his pants.

"You son of a bitch. Hey there, man."

Jakob tried to get up, but Sagan said, "Whoah, man. Just stay there. Come on, scoot on over, let me in there."

Jakob half scooted along and was half pushed by Sagan, until the large cowboy of a man had made a place to sit. Jakob patted him on the shoulder and laughed. "This ain't no strip club, Sagan. You wanna put some clothes on?"

"What? This is the new style, man."

"If I had walked into this place dressed like that, they would have shot me." Jakob burst into delirious laughter and then choked back a sob. How long would it go on for? How long would cops keep getting away with killing little black boys?

"Come here, man." Sagan wrapped his arms around Jakob and let the man cry for a few minutes.

Eventually, the tears dried up, and Jakob sat upright. Even through the alcohol, he felt embarrassed. He knew that times had changed, that men were supposed to be allowed to cry, but damn. Not in a cop bar. And never as a black man. He tried to laugh it off. "Don't you fucking tell Cindy about this."

"Wouldn't dream of it. You gonna be alright?"

"Yeah, man. How about you?"

Sagan became introspective. "I'm starting to feel like I need to move on, Jakob. This guy is killing all over the country. Nothing ever seems to pan out. This search has put my career in the toilet. And I don't want to keep dragging you guys down too. I once promised I'd never give up on this guy, but I think I'm pretty close to my limit." Sagan thought about the call from his daughter. Thought about his broken life. Thought about the past few months he had spent building a new relationship with Ann. "Maybe, it's just time I admit it's over. Admit I'm an old dog. Maybe it's time to retire."

Jakob looked over at him. "Come on, man.

Don't talk like that. What you need is a vacation."

"A vacation, huh?" Sagan thought it sounded like one hell of an idea. "Yeah, that's a good idea, Jakob. Maybe take some time and go see my girl."

"Yeah. Where's she at again?"

"She and my ex are up there on Long Island. Joan's mother lives up there. A nice big place by the water. Her mom always hated me, but other than that, she's a nice lady." Sagan leaned his shoulder against Jakob. "What about you, Jakob? You need a vacation?"

Jakob started laughing. "Nah, man. Ain't nothing got me down."

The men were surprised when Cindy sat down across from them. "Well howdy there, boys, fancy meeting you here." She looked over at Jakob. "Damn, man. You alright? You look like you've had a few."

"Hey there, Cin. Fine and dandy, girlfriend. Boss and I were just talking about taking a vacation. You game?"

Cindy's eyebrows shot up. "Vacation?"

Jakob saluted with his beer bottle and nodded his head. "Well. Either that or retiring."

"I'm pretty sure I'm going to have to ban both of you from drinking without me. Retiring? Shut the fuck up. Vacation? I'm game. I could use a little downtime with Angus."

"Alright, it's settled then." Sagan brought down his right fist in a definitive thump on the wooden table. "Vacation in December. I'm gonna go see my little girl."

December 19th, 2014
Hunter, New York

Julia sat in Kathryn's old office. It had been stripped of all her old paperwork, but Julia hadn't changed anything else about it. Julia liked being reminded of Kathryn, and she loved the bee theme. She would never have done such decorating herself, but she couldn't bring herself to change it.

She sat at Kathryn's desk, looking over at the family photo on the left side. The frame had a silver honeycomb pattern around the edges, and the four by six photo was framed in black trim. In the photo, Kathryn and Alex each had a hand on the shoulder of a boy with black hair, with a star-shaped birthmark on his face.

Chapman. What had become of him? Julia had never met the kid, but Kathryn had often spoken about the boy. She had always given him the benefit of the doubt, admitting that he was strange and broken, but fiercely insisting that he would never cause harm to another. Had the boy been the one to kill them? Most seemed to think so. And if he hadn't been the one, what had happened to him and who had killed them?

Julia fired up her laptop and sent an email to Cayden to discuss the exhibition, and possible meeting times.

December 20th, 2014
Atlantic City, New Jersey

"Wow! This place is amazing, Dad!"

Sagan watched Angela run over to the window of their hotel room and pull back the curtain.

"Oh my god! There's a balcony! And we can see the ocean!"

Sagan walked over and looked out. "It is definitely a beautiful view." But it would never compare to the view of his daughter, with joy in her eyes. It would never compare to the simple innocence of an eleven-year-old child, *his* eleven-year-old child. God, how he had missed her.

"You said they have a pool here, right? Cause it is way too cold to go swimming at the beach right now. You know that, right?"

"Nah, we could definitely go swimming out there. It's not like the ocean can freeze over."

"Dad. Are you trying to piss mom off?"

Sagan laughed. "I'm not sure I have to try very hard at that."

Angela went quiet and turned away from the window. Sagan was sad the conversation had taken a dark turn. He decided to let her in on a little secret.

"If you think the view's cool, just wait until you see where we're going tomorrow."

She turned to face him, eyes bright. "Ooh, where? Where? Where?" She hopped up on the bed and began jumping up and down.

"Oh, you've probably never heard of it before.

293

It's called The Sugar Factory and they have these giant milkshakes with cheesecake and Oreos and…"

"Dad?"

"Yeah, honey?"

"You totally had me at 'sugar'."

Sagan laughed. "Alright, pumpkin. Let's get our suits on and head down to the pool. Did you bring some sandals?"

"Of course, Dad." She rolled her eyes then went over to her suitcase, pulled it up on the bed, located her swimsuit and sandals in record time and headed for the bathroom to change. Sagan hadn't even unzipped his bag yet. "Last one ready is a rotten egg."

Sagan was looking down at his phone and saw that he had a text. "Oh, of course."

Sagan left his phone in the hotel room and he and his daughter headed down to the pool. He told himself to leave it alone. To forget about it. He told himself he was on vacation. That he was spending time with his daughter. That she deserved for him to be present.

But he couldn't leave it alone. He couldn't forget about it. The text had read: 'Sorry to interrupt your vacation, but I know you'd never forgive me if I didn't. You know that fax you sent out over the summer? The one to hundreds of police precincts, about our guy? Well, we got a hit. A recent development and you'll never guess where'.

Sagan lasted all of two hours at the pool. "How about we go back up to our room and get some room service?"

"Sure!"

When they got back to the hotel room, the first thing Sagan did was text Cindy back: 'Where?'. Then he ordered some room service while his daughter took a shower. He set up a table for them in front of the television, and handed her the remote when she came out, her head wrapped in a pink towel. She was wearing a cotton white nightgown adorned with a rainbow-coloured Pegasus, and unicorn slippers.

"You still have the slippers I got you?"

"Of course, Dad." She rolled her eyes again.

Sagan laughed. "Well, I liked those slippers so much, I had to get myself a pair."

She cast him an incredulous look and sat down at the table. "Sure, you did. What did you order us to eat? And when is it getting here?"

"Some steak and french fries. And two vanilla shakes. Should be here in about ten minutes."

"Sounds good. Can we rent a movie?"

"Maybe. Depends on what it is. Take a look."

Sagan heard his phone chime and he plucked it out of his pocket. The response read: 'Atlantic City'.

"Shit."

"Daddy! Your mouth!"

"Sorry, baby."

A knock at the door announced the arrival of their food and Sagan hurriedly answered it. He handed the guy a twenty and asked him to set the food out on the table in front of his daughter.

"Sweetie, I've got to make a phone call real quick. Give me just a minute, okay?"

"Dad. You're on vacation."

"I know, darling. Just give me a minute."

Sagan stepped out into the hallway and called Cindy. By the time he headed back into the room, Cindy had found him a babysitter, with references, who could stay the night to watch Angela. He walked over to the table and sat down. Angela had eaten all the fries, including his own, sucked down most of both of their milkshakes, and was watching something that involved Nazi zombies.

"What the hell is this, Angela?"

"Dead Snow. I rented the first one and the second one. A zombie marathon."

"Angela, I'm pretty sure that both of those are rated R and your mother would not approve."

"Well, if you don't tell her I watched scary zombie movies, then I won't tell her that you stood in the hallway on our vacation talking to someone about work." She gave him a pointed look.

Shit, this wasn't going to be easy.

"About that, sweetie."

Angela paused the movie and glared at him. "What?" That single word held a lot of grief, and Sagan crushed the girl to his chest in a big bear hug. She was stiff in his arms.

Chapter 7

December 21st, 2014
Hunter, New York

It was the last night of the exhibit, and all the artists had attended, even Bella. She had come all the way from Michigan, had even brought her parents. They had plans to spend their Christmas vacation in the Big Apple and had invited all of their kids to stay at an Airbnb apartment they had reserved for two weeks.

By the end of the night, every single piece had been sold, which had never once happened before during the foundation's existence. Julia was tired. Most of the other participants had gone out after the show ended, but Julia had wanted to go home. Charlie found her standing out front, waiting for a cab.

"Why don't I take you home, Julia?"

"There you are! I've been looking for you. Ronald just left with Bella and a couple of the other girls. I thought maybe you were in the limo with them."

Charlie wrapped her up in a hug. "You know I wouldn't leave you without saying goodbye."

"Well, you were drinking quite a lot tonight. I thought maybe you'd passed out in the limo or something."

"Julia?"

"Yes?"

"You remember my promise?"

"What promise?"

Charlie stepped back a little so that he could look her in the eyes. "We're done. I finished my last job in New Jersey yesterday. I haven't taken any photography jobs for next year. My Ohio book has gone to press. The exhibit is done. It's time."

Julia laughed. "Charlie, I hope you don't expect me to start working on the house with you right this second. I am beat!"

"Hey, a man's gotta keep his promises." He was wearing a wicked grin.

"Alright, fine. Take me home. Come see our joint project. You can start working on it tonight, but I'm going to sleep." She tucked her head under his chin. She belonged there.

"That show was amazing, Julia. What you accomplished tonight...with those girls...that was magical."

"Come on, Charlie. I didn't do anything."

"Don't sell yourself short, love. Those girls would not be where they are today if it hadn't been for you."

She snuggled into his warmth. "It wasn't just me. It was Bella, and this foundation, this community...and you, love. We had so many people coming to see this exhibit, all because your name was attached to it. Thank you, CJ. Seriously."

They were engaged in a kiss when the cab pulled up. Charlie opened the door for Julia and followed her in. She laid her head on his shoulder and drifted during the short ride to the house.

"You feel a little warm, Julia."

"Yeah, I'm really not feeling too well, honestly."

When the cab arrived at the house, Charlie stared in disbelief. "You live here?" He finally put it all together. Kathryn. The woman who had left her the house was Kathryn. *That* Kathryn. This house.

"I know, I know, crazy, right? I still can't believe it. I can't believe this is your first time here."

He made no response. He continued to stare at the house as if he feared it.

Julia opened the door and got out. She leaned back into the cab and tugged on his arm, saying, "Chaarliiee, come on! What's wrong with you? It's just a giant house! Is your manhood threatened or something? Come on, your mom's house is ten times bigger than this."

He looked sad when he glanced up at her from the taxi. It was a look that said goodbye. The look of a lover on his way to a war, gun slung over his shoulder, whose kisses already tasted of loss and death. Julia envisioned him closing the door and driving away, never to be seen again.

The cops didn't know it, but she had been his first kill. The work had been sloppy. It had been passionate and way too fast. But she had been the only person he had ever killed that he knew personally. Everyone else had just been a substitute. A way of trying to get back to that night. Of trying to feel that passion again.

His work now was…exquisite. He took his time with his victims. He savoured their pain. He was careful not to leave DNA at his kill sites, but part of him didn't really care if he got caught. If he ever did get caught, his memories would be enough to sustain him. He had lived for years revelling in the solitary memory of that night. He had been able to give that bitch what she deserved. He had been able to shut her up. But damn if he didn't regret not being able to take his time with her. He had been able to make up for it. With the others. They let him finish slowly what he had completed too quickly then. He thinks back on it now.

He can see her. She has on a tight business suit with the skirt way too short, especially for her age. She gets out of the cab and hands the cabbie some cash. She has a big smile on her face and the cabbie says something funny. She throws her head back and laughs. He is close enough to hear it. It makes him sick.

"It's been a pleasure. Tell your daughter I said good luck with the bar! Here's my card. Tell her to call me if she needs any help." Kathryn hands the cabbie a hundred-dollar bill and her business card. "And keep the change."

"Mrs Beaumont, that's so kind of you. Are you sure about her calling you? She'll probably call you even if she doesn't need help!" The cabbie tucks the bill and business card into the front pocket of his shirt. "Besides, I doubt my Lily would ever admit to needing help."

Kathryn laughs. "She sounds like my kind of

woman. I'm sure, Ralph. Tell her to call me at any time. I mean that."

Ralph beams. "Will do. I'll just wait here until I see that you're safely inside."

Kathryn waves a dismissive hand at the man. "No need. I'm going to have a smoke on the porch before I head inside. I'll be fine. Thanks anyway." Ralph looks at the deserted street and glances sceptically at her. "Really, Ralph, I do it all the time. My husband hates it. Go on. Have a great night!"

Kathryn turns toward her front walkway, and as Ralph drives away, she hears him making a call over his car phone. "Lily, you'll never believe who was just in my cab!"

She smiles to herself and takes off her heels as she looks up at the wraparound porch. It's a warm summer night. She continues standing and staring. For a moment, he thinks that she sees him hiding in the shadows. He thinks that maybe she senses that something is wrong. Maybe she senses that she is going to die tonight. Or maybe she just feels guilty for living in such a decadent home.

Eventually, she climbs the main steps and sets her purse down on the small table outside under the doorbell. She unlocks the front door and throws her shoes inside. They fall near a well-organised shoe rack, looking out of place. As she starts to back out of the foyer, her hand on the doorknob, he rushes her from behind. The impact of his body slams the door open and she falls, face first, onto the wood floor. He quickly shuts the door and straddles her, feeling her tight buttocks beneath him. She smells faintly of vanilla and roses. She is gasping for breath. He grabs a fistful of her dark brown hair and slams her face into the floor until her forehead splits open and blood gushes down her face. God, she is so beautiful.

He picks her unconscious body off the floor and moves her into the living room. He is covered from head to toe in black spandex. After placing her on the couch, he takes off his mask and removes a knife from the pouch at his back. He takes a deep breath and looks down at her, savouring the moment. Her suit jacket is askew, and her silk blouse is stained with blood. Her pink bra peeks out from underneath her pink shirt and he unintentionally stiffens. He does not want to be attracted to this bitch. But fuck, he feels powerful right now.

"Kathryn?"

He hears a voice calling from the stairs. Shit, he had thought the husband and kid were gone. He quickly moves to the wall, hidden from view.

"Oh my god, Kathryn!"

Presumably, the husband has seen the blood in the foyer. He watches the husband rush over to the dark puddle and then comes up from behind him. As he stabs the husband several times in each kidney, he sees a phone fall to the ground.

"911, what is your emergency?"

Shit! There is no time to think. He rushes back to the living room and stabs Kathryn in the chest, between her ribs and into her heart, twisting the knife as he pulls it out. Even though he is in a hurry, once is not enough. He stabs her again. And again. He wipes the knife off on the couch, the blood seeping into the floral fabric. He quickly leaves through the back door, grabs the sweater he has stashed in a hidden backpack at the treeline, and throws it on over his catsuit. He heads back to the party, hoping that no one has noticed his absence.

"Charlie?"

She sounded concerned now. He shook his head and came back to himself. "I'm sorry, Julia. It's just…amazing. I wasn't expecting something so grandiose. And trust me, my manhood is still intact." He gave her a winning smile and hopped out of the cab. Julia was once again at ease, and he watched her run up to the front steps, taking off her heels halfway there. When she reached the top step, she looked back at him. He was standing on the front path, staring at her. Staring at the house.

"Come on, slowpoke! You're going to have to help me to bed before you start working." She was so gorgeous, her blonde hair cascading in curls down her back as she turned from him. There was a run going up the pantyhose on her right leg. He couldn't wait to follow its path with his tongue while she moaned in pleasure.

He had never killed in this state since that night. He had never killed someone he knew in real life since that first kill. But being here, coming back to this house, he realised that the universe had given him a grand opportunity. He was determined not to fuck it up.

He would not fuck up again. He took a deep breath. was it possible that the cops knew who he was by now? Surely, they had to be close. If so, he needed to enjoy what little time he had left. He ran up to the front door with a big grin on his face. He felt like a little kid in a toy store. "I hope you have some champagne because we have a lot of celebrating to do!"

They had finally caught a break. Not only had a woman survived, but they had a witness. They had even come damn close to catching the guy. A sketch artist was working with the witness now, and the victim was in surgery. Sagan shifted back and forth on his feet, full of nervous energy.

Finally, the local sketch artist walked out into the lobby. She had a confused look on her face.

"What's wrong? Is she having a hard time remembering?" Sagan tried to keep the impatience out of his voice. He was like a racehorse, straining at the bit, ready to run. Ready to win.

"No, it's not that. Not that at all. I know this guy. I know who he is."

A big grin spread over Sagan's face. Could it finally be this easy? Could they finally catch this guy? "Brilliant! Where can I find this sick fuck?"

In the next few minutes, Sagan learnt that the face in the drawing belonged to one Charlie Ivanov, a crime scene photographer known to the sketch artist here in Atlantic City. It didn't take him long to have a team ready to go. Within three hours, he and local law enforcement were on their way to a small apartment in the Upper West Side neighbourhood of Manhattan, warrant in hand.

"How can he afford to live in such a posh neighbourhood?" Sagan knew what the typical cop made as a crime photographer. He had asked Carla, the sketch artist, to tag along just in case they needed more input about their perp.

"Well, he's not just a crime photographer, he does a lot of creative work on the side. He usually shows a few times a year and his pieces typically sell for a good amount of money."

"How can he work as a cop and have time to do that?" Sagan asked, shaking his head. Was he annoyed that someone could have a life outside of their work?

"Actually, he's not a cop. His brother is though, and he pulled him in on the job a few years ago when we were short of photographers. It was just supposed to be a temporary gig for him, but brass made an exception, and he's been around ever since. He's always done a phenomenal job." She hated saying it because they both knew it was cliché, but she added, "He's a nice guy. I really hope this is some kind of mistake.

Charlie Ivanov. Ivanov. Where had he heard that name before? It finally dawned on him. Charles. Charles Ivanov was the man he had spoken to over the phone. Shit. Had he fucked up? Sagan looked at Carla but didn't speak. He really hoped there wasn't a mistake. He was ready to get this guy. He was ready for it to be over.

As they approached the apartment building, he could see that a couple of cars were parked against the yellow line and he cursed under his breath. Had no one thought to tow them before they pulled up? He supposed it might have looked suspicious, and they were trying hard not to tip the guy off.

It was three a.m. Sagan prayed that this asshole was home, and that he would be able to personally pull the prick out of his nice, warm bed.

My whole life I've wished I could remove the birthmark on my face. I've always thought of it as a star-shaped stain of shame. I was tormented relentlessly as a child, not only for my birthmark, but for my status as an orphan, an unwanted sin, an unwanted child.

I would make deals with an invisible god, promising him, or her, that I would be the best follower, the best servant they had ever had, if they would just remove this blemish from my face. As a child, you don't wish to find people who will love your faults, you just wish for your faults to be gone.

After years of unanswered prayers, I started making other deals. I started asking 'dear God, whoever you are, if you can't take away this mark, at least take my sight so I can no longer see the stares. Make me deaf, so I can no longer hear the taunts, please…'. But I knew that if I had been struck blind, or deaf, there was only death left to wish for. And there were times. So many times, that I'd wished for death. So many times, that I'd cursed whatever god may exist.

When you walked in tonight, followed by the man who killed my grandparents, I wished away every curse I had ever given the god who allowed me to be born as I am. I have spent years looking for the monster who stabbed and murdered my grandparents in front of my eyes. I have spent years hiding in the depths of this house, living like a rat, scuttling along not only the passages of this house but the passages of the dark and depraved web where only the vilest have been. I have searched long and hard, the dream of vengeance in my heart festering and spreading until my splotched face became a thing loved. On my face, revenge. In my heart, retribution. In my hand...what? I had to find a weapon. And fast.

Charlie popped the champagne and filled up two glasses, handing one to Julia. "Are you feeling okay?"

"I'm feeling pretty sick, actually. Give me just a minute." Julia ran to the bathroom, getting to the toilet just in time. After throwing up, she spent some time dry-heaving, her stomach settling into a rhythmic pulse of clench-and-release. She could hear Charlie on the other side of the door.

"Are you okay?"

"Yeah, but I probably shouldn't drink anymore."

"Sure, I can finish this champagne by myself. Here, I brought you a glass of water."

Julia wiped off her face and flushed the toilet before opening the door and taking the offered glass.

"Thanks, hon."

"You're welcome. Make sure you drink all of it, throwing up can be very dehydrating."

She rolled her eyes. "Yes, Daddy."

He took the empty glass from her. "Why don't you have a shower then lay down to rest? I'll take a self-guided tour of the house."

Julia looked relieved. A quick shower followed

by her bed sounded like just what she needed.

Chapman had snuck into the basement and climbed the stairs. He stood behind the door, hand cupped around his ear and pressed to the wood, listening, to whom he could only presume was the man named Charlie.

He overheard the man say that he intended to take a tour of the house, so Chapman listened until he heard the man walk to the base of the stairs and move up, each stair creaking as he did so. Chapman could hear the shower going in the main floor bathroom, its door wide open. He would have to walk past the open door to head towards the foyer, to find the weapon he needed.

He took a deep breath and steeled himself to the task, first opening the door outward, on hinges oiled most often by himself, then walking toward the front door. He was quiet on tiptoes, controlling a body that had grown used to silencing itself, rebelling against its master only with the tiniest of sneezes once he reached the credenza by the front door.

Chapman stood rooted in place, turning his head to glance up the stairs and down the hallway. No one came running to investigate the small sound. Although the sneeze hadn't seemed loud, Chapman knew that he was treading treacherous waters. He had watched this man destroy the only real family he had ever known; Chapman had no doubt the murderer would make short work of a skinny seventeen-year-old boy.

When no one came pounding down the stairs, when no shouts were heard from the bathroom, Chapman, still looking toward the stairs, slid open the left door of the credenza. He knew that the taser Julia had purchased a few months ago was located on the top of the left-side shelf, all the way in the back corner. He started reaching into the cabinet, eyes still glued to the stairs. His fingers deftly slid past lightbulbs and batteries, passed unopened envelopes and weeks of collected coupons. He longed to feel, what he imagined, was a comforting rubber grip.

Julia turned off the water and stepped out onto the warm plush rug, her wet feet leaving deep indentations on the mat. She dried off and wrapped the towel around herself, still feeling woozy but even more tired than before. As she stepped out into the hallway, she heard a ding from the kitchen, an indication from her laptop that she had received a new email. She turned in the direction of the kitchen, intent on finding some crackers and checking her email.

She walked over to her laptop on the kitchen island and logged in. The email was a response from Cayden to her last email: 'Re: Getting together'. Julia moved to turn off the laptop, then realised she had suggested they meet for an early lunch tomorrow. Well, today, really. In…she looked at the time on the bottom right of the screen…in eight hours. Ugh. She had better respond with a new time. She didn't think she would be in a position to meet anyone in eight hours.

She clicked open the email to see a response in all caps. 'HE DOES NOT HAVE A MOTHER OMG HIS MOTHER IS DEAD! CALL ME! ARE YOU OKAY?!'

What the fuck? What was Cayden talking about? She couldn't remember saying anything about anyone's mom. Julia's mind was foggy, and she was finding it hard to stay awake. She leaned heavily against the counter and scrolled down to her previous email.

Cayden,

Hey! I completely understand it if you don't want to come to the last night of the exhibition. Maybe you can check it out during the day when he's not there? It might give you some ideas for one of your classes or something. Plus, it's just a really powerful exhibition. Of course, it might be a triggering experience. And maybe you don't need that right now.

Anyway, the only time we would be able to meet would be for lunch the day after, or when we get back from Charlie's mom's place. We're going there for Christmas, but we won't be staying long. Just a few days. I feel so badly for her. It must be awful spending all day in a wheelchair, and even worse not being able to communicate. Strokes are scary.

Julia stopped reading there. What the fuck was going on? Julia heard a noise behind her, and she turned, everything spinning in front of her. Blinking back tears, she crumpled to the floor, knocking over one of the barstools as she fell. She was going in and out of consciousness and struggled to crawl away from the man in the doorway. Instead of moving towards her, he started rummaging through the drawers, locating the plastic wrap.

She heard him say, "I think two rolls should be enough."

As he moved towards Julia, a mewling sound erupted from her throat. *He* didn't have a mother. CJ didn't have a mother. Then who was the woman he was taking care of? Had everything she knew about this man been a lie? She tried to speak.

Charlie crouched down beside her and put a finger to her lips. "Shh. Let's get you to bed, shall we?" He lifted Julia and carried her up the stairs. "I don't have my usual kit here, of course. This was quite the surprise. I usually don't like surprises, but what the hell? Did I really think I could pull this off? This whole marriage thing? I do like a challenge. Maybe I could have."

Charlie had stripped Julia's bed of its sheets and comforter. He placed her down on the bare mattress and started whistling as he opened the plastic wrap. He continued talking to her. "I've never used plastic wrap, but I think it should work. I want to thank you, Julia. You have been super fun. God, when you told me about your cousins, I almost couldn't believe my luck. I had plans for you, Julia, plans for us." Charlie stroked her face and began wrapping her right arm to the bedpost with the plastic wrap.

Julia was fighting sleep and trying hard to fight back, but it was useless. She could barely manage to mutter, "No," before drifting off. When she came to, he was working on wrapping her left leg. He was working diagonally. Her left arm and right leg were not secured yet, so she couldn't have been out of it for long.

Charlie moved up to her other arm and looked

311

at her face. "You've never looked so stunning, darling."

She tried to whisper out something.

"What's that?" Charlie moved so that his ear was against her mouth. "Go ahead, darling. What did you say?"

Before she lost again to the drugs circulating through her body, she managed to get out in a strangled whisper, "I'm...pregnant."

Chapman finally wrapped his hand around the stun gun. He wasn't sure that would be enough, so he walked to the kitchen, quickly walking past the bathroom, to find a sharp knife. This man deserved to pay for murdering his grandparents. Murdering his future. Murdering his chance of finally having a family. And tonight? Tonight, he finally would.

Chapman heard the water in the bathroom turn off and quickly sprinted past, looking up at the stairs before heading into the front living room. He crouched down behind the sectional and caught his breath. He was scared shitless. He knew that he was in the right. That killing this man would bring justice. Wouldn't it? The events of that night played through his mind.

He had been in the front living room, on the floor, leaning against the couch. He had been writing a letter to his mom in his journal. A mom he would never meet. He had been fond of writing to her since he was a young child. He would often imagine presenting her with the stack of journals as a gift. 'I've never forgotten you, mom', he would say. He often imagined them sitting together on a couch, him snuggled up in her lap while she read the journals aloud, laughing at all the funny anecdotes about his life that he had written down for her. He had imagined her crying at the sad parts, about the children making fun of him, or the families who had used him as free labour.

He had heard the cabbie pull up in front of the house, and heard his grandmother telling him she was going to stay out for a smoke. 'She must think we're still gone', he had thought. He and Alex were supposed to have left on a camping trip. And they had. But the Jeep had gone crazy, the electrical system had bugged out, and the two of them had been left stranded on the side of the road. Alex had called for a tow truck and had the Jeep brought to his mechanic, while he and Chapman had taken a cab home. Alex had known that Kathryn would be tired when she got home, she always was after big company dinners. She had been a guest speaker at some political dinner, he couldn't remember now what it had been for. But she had been 'networking' as she liked to say. Building relationships with people with money. She could have her networking, Alex had always said. He had his camping.

As Chapman and his grandfather had walked into the house, Alex had said, "Hey buddy, I'm sorry our camping trip didn't work out."

"That's okay." Chapman had given Alex a rare smile. "There's no Wi-Fi out there, you know."

Alex had laughed and tousled his grandson's hair. "That's what makes it so awesome."

Chapman had shaken his head. "Well, the s'mores are pretty good. Usually."

"And the fish. Don't forget the fresh fish."

"Really? You think fresh fish is in the same league as s'mores?" Chapman had shaken his head. "You know what the best part about s'mores are?"

"What?"

"You can buy the ingredients in a grocery store!"

Alex had laughed again. "Your grandma should be home soon. I'm going to go light some candles upstairs and put on some music. Do you think you can entertain yourself for a while?"

"Always."

"After I get things ready upstairs, how about we go into the kitchen and make us up some s'mores? Obviously, they won't be as good, but I can make the sacrifice. Sound good?"

"Yeah!"

Alex had smiled at the boy and then headed upstairs.

Chapman had then turned on one of the lamps in the front living room and made himself comfortable, opening his journal. He had started to get up when he heard his grandmother open the door and he had been about to call up to Alex that it was time for s'mores, when a man came barrelling in, ramming into his grandmother, and falling against her. Chapman had taken a dive behind an armchair and folded himself up into a ball, holding both of his own hands against his mouth to stifle any sound he might make. He had grown used to crying quietly. If you cried in the orphanage, or the group home, well, let's just say things didn't often work out for you. So, he had learnt to hide his emotions, keeping them bottled up in his journal. Keeping his eyes dry until bedtime. He would wait until he could hear the rhythmic breathing or snoring of the other kids, and then he would silently cry himself to sleep.

Chapman had watched the man carry Kathryn into the living room and place her on the couch. He had then straddled her and ripped off his mask. Chapman had seen that he had a knife. He had watched as the man drew it down her face, leaving a small line of blood.

That's when Alex had called from the stairway. "Kathryn? Oh my God, Kathryn!"

Chapman had watched the man jump off his grandmother and run to the corner of the room by the stairway, hiding from sight. He had heard a cough from the couch and looked towards his grandmother, her eyes open, and full of shock. She had mouthed a single word at him. Hide. Over and over again, her lips formed the word. Hide! Hide! Hide! Hide!

Chapman had sprinted to the bookshelf behind the couch, unlatched the hidden door, and quickly hidden inside, pulling the door closed and securing the bolt. He had opened the secret observation panel and watched in horror as the man had stabbed his grandfather and then come back to stab his grandmother. Chapman hadn't watched the knife. He had watched the man's face. He had burned the man's face into his memory.

Chapman had heard his grandfather gasping from the foyer. Heard a 911 operator saying 'help is on the way'. He had heard a horrible squelching sound as the knife plunged into his grandmother's chest. Again. And again. He had heard the sirens as the ambulance and cops had arrived. As he lay on the mattress in the hidden room, he had heard the EMTs announcing Kathryn's death. He had listened to them trying to stabilize Alex. He had heard the officers processing the scene. He had heard the shutter of a camera clicking, the horror being catalogued as evidence.

He had heard someone say, "Wasn't there a kid in the family?"

"Yeah, we haven't found him. Pretty fucked up little guy from what I hear."

"You think he stabbed them and split?"

"That's what we figure. We're canvassing the neighbourhood. He wasn't even old enough to drive. He can't have gone far. We'll get him."

"Well, good luck with that. I'll get back to these pictures and leave you to your work."

"Of course, thanks man. See you later, CJ. You seen Lucas around?"

Chapman had covered his ears then, laying on his side, drifting off into an uncomfortable and fearful sleep that was full of knives and dark red blood.

Sagan led the task force into the apartment building and up the stairway. When they arrived at the correct door, Sagan stood back as two local cops used a battering ram to crush through the door.

Sagan heard an exclamation of, "What the hell?" from inside the apartment and stepped to the side.

He called to the occupant. "Sir, I suggest you get down. This is the police, we're coming in!"

He heard the man say, "I'm down! I'm unarmed!

I'm unarmed!"

Sagan and the locals stood to either side of the door anyway, and the agent used a mirror to look inside the room. There was a man, dressed only in boxers, face down on the floor, hands behind his head.

"Alright, gentlemen. I'm going in. Give me some backup. I'll secure this one. Please give me a sweep."

Sagan stepped into the apartment and walked over to the prone man, snapping his wrists into handcuffs behind his back. He dragged him up to his feet while three other cops secured the rest of the house. Sagan looked the man over. He was a light-skinned, bald black man. He had some similarities to the man in the drawing, but he was far from a dead ringer. "Do you have some ID, sir?"

"Yes, sir. If you check the side table there by the front door, you'll find my driver's license. And my badge."

Sagan didn't even have to look. "You must be Lucas."

"Yes, sir. May I ask what all this is about?"

"Let's have a seat and discuss it." Sagan led Lucas over to the sofa and sat him down. "I'm looking for your brother. Do you happen to know where he's at?"

"What's this about? You don't tear a hole in someone's front door without a damn good reason."

"I'd rather not say at this point, sir. But it's in your best interest not to withhold any information from me right now. I'll ask again." Sagan crouched down and spoke directly into the other man's face. "Do you know where your brother is?"

Lucas clenched his jaw in disgust and moved his nose to the side. "Damn, man. What did you eat for dinner?"

Sagan balled up his right fist and swung it, connecting with the man's cheekbone and nose. Blood went flying across the room and two of the cops grabbed Sagan as Lucas started cursing.

"Fuck, man! He had some art exhibit in upstate New York somewhere. I don't fucking know where he's at now. Have you tried fucking calling him? Damn. You broke my nose, bastard!"

Sagan stormed out of the apartment and immediately got on the phone, his voice heavy and echoing in the narrow hallway. Cindy picked up on the first ring. "We're here, boss. Just landed. Where do you need us?"

"Can you find a spot to login and boot up? I need some intel."

"Sure thing. Give me a minute."

Sagan paced back and forth down the hall, then sprinted down the stairs and walked outside. The police had set up a roadblock on either side, and even at this early hour, there were plenty of curious bystanders. His breath came out in quick puffs, and frosted air filled the space in front of his face. His lungs ached with the cold of it all.

"Alright. We are live. What do you need?"

"Charles Ivanov. His brother said he had some exhibit tonight in upstate New York somewhere." Sagan continued his pacing while Cindy did some digging.

"Hmm. I've got some kind of exhibit in Hunter, New York. At some art foundation, the New York Mountains Foundation."

"Okay. Find me a contact."

"Give me a second, boss."

A couple of minutes later, Cindy gave him the number of a man named David Washington. Sagan placed a three-way call and left, leaving Cindy on the line. The man confirmed that Charles had been at the exhibit hours before but thought he may have either gone out after the event or gone home.

"Should I call his fiancée? Is he in trouble?"

"Sir, can you give us her number and address?" After David had given them the information, Sagan asked him to call Cindy if he found out anything else pertinent, then thanked him for his time.

"What's the plan, boss?" Cindy asked.

"Well, we still don't know where the hell this guy is yet. I'm going to call the authorities up in Hunter. See if someone can run by this Julia's place. I'll meet you at the station here in NYC. We'll see what the guys up in Hunter say and then go from there." They were hours away from being able to get storm in and save the day.

"Boss?"

"Yeah?" There was a long silence between them. Cindy seemed reluctant to say what she said next, but the words felt like a line drawn in the sand. They reminded him of his night of leftovers. And of the long months he'd been ignoring his failed marriage.

"Why don't you go back to your little girl? We can take it from here. We'll let you know if there are any developments."

Sagan sighed. He sounded so damn tired. He was disappointed. He thought he finally had this guy. He had been so close to having the satisfaction of finally, *finally* nailing this fucker. And the bastard had slipped out of his hands again. And for what? Angela had given him her heart again. Had given him her trust again. And he had trampled all over it. "Shit. You're right, Cindy. I hope you guys get him. I'm going to go get my girl. If she'll still have me."

"She'll still have you, boss. I know what it's like to be a daughter. She'll still have you."

"Thanks, Cindy."

Chapman crept up the stairs and heard the man speaking to Julia. He was telling her how he regretted having to do this. How it was really for the best, though, seeing as how he had really fucked up the day before.

"I thought I'd have enough time. That this girl would be my last one...you know...for a while. We would get your group home going, get married, and then I'd go on a 'photography' trip whenever I needed to. I mean, who would suspect a generous, married man who helps run a group home of being a serial murderer?"

The man's laugh made Chapman's stomach turn. What a disgusting piece of shit. Chapman's heart was beating in his chest, a roaring sound filled his ears. He felt alive for the first time in a long time. Silently, he bent down and placed the knife on the floor, then raised the pink taser gun to chest level. The murderer leaned down towards Julia.

Chapman heard Julia say, "I'm pregnant."

That's when he let out a strangled cry, "YOU MURDERER!"

Charlie's head swung round, and Julia's eyes briefly focused on Chapman's face.

Before passing out, Julia mumbled, stunned, "Chapman?"

Charlie lunged towards Chapman as he pressed the trigger of the stun gun, one probe hitting right above Charlie's heart, the other much lower. Charlie began spasming and fell to the floor. Chapman stayed glued to the spot until the electricity had stopped discharging from the weapon. While it had only been seconds, Chapman felt minutes had passed. He dropped the taser gun to the ground and picked up the kitchen knife, circling around the bed, keeping his eyes on the prone figure of Charlie on the ground.

Using the knife, Chapman cut through the plastic wrap keeping Julia secured to the bed, freeing the sides furthest away from Charlie first. After that was done, he looked around for something to tie Charlie up with. Spying a roll of plastic wrap on the ground, Chapman figured he would give it a try. Picking up the plastic wrap, he walked towards the unmoving figure on the ground.

Chapman reached out the tip of one toe and nudged the man's leg with it. When there was no response, he jumped on the man's body, securing himself on his upper thighs and butt. There was still no response. Had he killed the man? Chapman listened for breathing but heard none.

Not trusting that the man was dead, Chapman proceeded to wrap up his arms and legs, using the whole roll. He turned back to Julia, who was still passed out. What should he do? Wait around for her to wake up and thank him for being her knight in shining armour? Wait around for the cops to arrest him? Definitely not. He had other plans. And they didn't include sticking around to answer any questions.

Chapman made his way downstairs and into his hidden room. He packed up some of his meagre belongings, some food, his money, and a few notes from his murder wall. This murder may have been solved, but there were others out there that hadn't been.

He left the bookshelf door open to his hidden room, and scribbled a note for Julia, leaving it on the kitchen table. He was too scared to go back upstairs. Chapman didn't leave by way of the front door, he took his customary route, heading out the cellar door and walking away into the woods. He did not see the parked baby blue Prius with California plates by the back of the house. Did not see the man sitting in the car.

But the man saw him. With his eyes, the man followed Chapman's path into the woods until he could no longer see him. He then slowly drove up alongside the house until he had reached the front lawn. He parked the car and got out, walked to the front door, and finding it open, made his way upstairs.

Sleepytime Killer Found Dead, Longtime Missing
Minor Wanted for Questioning
New York (AP)

The man known as 'The Sleepytime Killer' has been found dead at a Victorian Mansion in Hunter, New York. A woman named Julia Rodriguez was found incapacitated at the scene. It seems that she was to be the killer's next victim, but in a strange turn of events, the *killer* ended up being the one to lose his life. An inside source says the man was incapacitated by a stun gun, which has been found at the scene. The cause of death is yet to be determined.

This isn't the first time this stately Victorian home has been in the news. In 2010, Kathryn and Alexander Beaumont were found stabbed to death in a brutal attack there. Their deaths remain unsolved. The couple were guardians to their grandson, Chapman Beaumont, who disappeared at the time of their murders. Many theories surround the odd disappearance. Some thought that the grandson had been the one to commit the crime, others thought that the killer had kidnapped him, or that the killer had taken his dead body and dumped it elsewhere.

It appears now that the grandson may have been living in the house for the last four years. A source close to the investigation says that a hidden room has been found in the house, stocked with plenty of food and a generator. Police are searching for the boy, now seventeen, and say that finding him is crucial to understanding just what took place.

While 'The Sleepytime Killer' has not been officially identified, an anonymous tip suggests that the killer is famed local artist, Charlie 'CJ' Ivanov, who first came to the attention of the media when he was involved in the date rape case of Emily Bowman at the age of eighteen. He was exonerated of all charges and spent a great deal of time in interviews after the trial. His notoriety provided him with a great deal of publicity, and he was able to harness that attention and point it toward his astonishing, but often melancholic, photography.

Charlie became a sensation, raking in thousands for each piece of art, and donated almost all proceeds from his first year after the trial to women's organisations. In addition to his own projects, Charlie became a casual photography instructor, not only for police departments, but for colleges around the U.S. His first big show, entitled 'Criminal Lives', cemented his position as an up-and-coming artist, and he has been booked in galleries all over New York since its release.

If the deceased is 'The Sleepytime Killer', one can only imagine the value of his artwork now.

Julia,

Umm, hi there. I'm not sure there's a way to make this less creepy than it is, but I'll try. I've lived in this house for years. I used to think of it as my house. Then I started to think of it as *our* house. But now it's yours. I know you'll do amazing things with it. You'll make my grandmother proud. She was a great woman, and I still miss her so much.

I'm going to keep this short. My grandparents were murdered in this house. Right in front of me. And when I realised that the man you brought here tonight had similar plans for you, I could not sit back and watch it happen again.

So, I used your taser. Pink. Good choice. I'm pretty sure it killed him. He doesn't seem to be breathing. But I'm no doctor, so I've tied him up just in case. I'm not quite sure how I feel about it.

I've been searching for the man who killed my grandparents for years. Delving into murder chat rooms and talking with seriously fucked up weirdos online. I never would have thought that...that he would come back here.

I used to dream of killing him. Of stabbing him, just like he'd stabbed my grandparents. I thought about it a lot tonight. But I couldn't do it. I had him tied up, maybe dead, maybe not, and I just couldn't do it. I used to think my only purpose in life was to find him and kill him. Now I realise I have more to offer the world. I've learnt a lot over these last few years. I think it's time for me to put it to use.

Chapman

P.S. You should invest in a security system ASAP. And stop letting creepy guys into your house!

Epilogue

February 17th, 2015
New Orleans

I'm not good at pretending to be normal. I'm not good with people. I never have been. I think back to the night I saw Charlie and Julia together. A violent serial rapist and murderer had been more socially adept than me. How was that even possible? He had been so good at pretending to be normal.

Maybe it was possible for him to be socially accepted in the same way that I am not a serial killer. Looking back at my history, it would have been an understandable path for me. I've been through some things.

I am settled onto the top bunk of a group room at The Quisby in New Orleans. It reminds me of the adoption centre. Except more spacious. And homier. And full of more light. I am staring out of the window, hands folded neatly in my lap. Today is Fat Tuesday. There are throngs of people outside, watching a lively parade of purple, green, and gold. The colours are blurred, and I can't pick out individual floats or costumes. Children stumble and crawl over each other to catch beads and candy. What is this holiday even about? I place my hand against the glass. I can feel the vibrations of music and merriment. People are smiling and oblivious to my staring face. I feel like I am all alone in the building. All alone in the world, perhaps, the outside activities a movie that I can pause with the press of a button.

I have always felt like this. Alone. Unable to make real connections with people, feeling closer to people through observation rather than relationships. When you talk to people, they can lie to you. They can make promises they have no intention of keeping. But when you watch people from the shadows or from behind the lens of a camera, when you observe their actions, you really learn who they are.

I've often tried to imagine what I look like. I wish that I could observe myself from the outside. Figure out who I am. I have so many emotions coursing through me right now. Sadness and loss and pride. Confusion and expectation. What could that possibly look like? Looking in a mirror wouldn't help, though. People act and look differently when they know they're being watched.

I plug in my phone, queue Concrete Blonde's Bloodletting album and sigh deeply. The man who killed my grandparents is dead. And here I am, in a brand-new city. Here I am, ready to chase ghosts. I take a battered envelope out from underneath my pillow, tracing my name with my index finger. How was it possible to miss someone I never even knew?

I pull out the worn letter and start to read it

again. Tears run down my cheeks and I brush them away with the back of my hand. Not for the first time, I make a vow. I will find the bastard. I will find the bastard and destroy him.

Acknowledgments

First and foremost, I would like to thank my mother-in-law, Marianne Lundqvist, for supporting me in this adventure; your enjoyment really inspired me to keep going! And Klas Claywood, thank you so much for letting my characters and words take up so many of our conversations. I appreciate you just going with the flow whenever they popped up in discussions that had absolutely nothing to do with serial killers, police brutality, art, photography, or gun laws and racism in the US. You are such a great person to bounce ideas off. Laura Daniel Robertson, thank you so much for your support over the years. You've always believed in me, and you'll never know how much that means. Susan Tajima, while I feel lucky to have an aunt who is an English teacher, you may not feel as lucky to have a niece who is an author. About my next novel...

Jessica Course, thank you so much for reading my book, your words of encouragement really spurred me on. Erica Williams, thank you so much for reading this novel as quickly as you did. I hope I can have the sequel out for you as soon as possible! Stacy Westly, thank you for the comma discussion. There are a lot in this book! Berenice Edmonds, although this book might not have been your cup of tea, I appreciate your suggestions, nonetheless. And finally, MJ DiLorenzo, thanks for taking time out as a busy mom to read my novel and offer suggestions; when your children's book is completed, I look forward to doing the same!

About the Author

Jennifer Claywood is an expatriate living in cold Sweden with her warm husband and their children, and one very crazy and well-loved dog. While she has written on and off since childhood, most of her time has been spent being a mother, waitress, graphic designer, student, and middle school science teacher.

She's a voracious reader with eclectic tastes, especially loving horror, sci-fi, fantasy, and crime thrillers. Those tastes bleed over into other areas of her life, where she is a recovering World of Warcraft devotee (14 years sober), a fangirl of MOST Quentin Tarantino movies (especially Django Unchained), and a collector of goth paraphernalia you'd most likely find in a teenager's room. She's obsessed with the fusion of concepts, mixing the macabre with the beautiful, science with art.

On a typical day you can find her planning science lessons, cooking dinner, and talking plot points with her kids and husband. On a special day you can find her planning a party while channelling Martha Stewart and Morticia Addams.

Summers are dedicated to a frenzy of writing, and she's currently working on a sequel to While Sleeping, and an epic dark fantasy that blends Ancient Egypt, the 1500s of Wales, and the 1990s of Athens, Georgia.